FUGITIVES FROM JUSTICE

THE SETTLERS
BOOK TWO

REG QUIST

Fugitives from Justice
Paperback Edition
Copyright © 2022 Reg Quist

CKN Christian Publishing
An Imprint of Wolfpack Publishing
9850 S. Maryland Parkway, Suite A-5 #323
Las Vegas, Nevada 89183

cknchristianpublishing.com

Paperback ISBN 978-1-63977-450-0
eBook ISBN 978-1-63977-449-4
LCCN 2022948283

ALSO BY REG QUIST

The Truth Through The Story (Book 3)

The Settlers

Rustlers and Widows (Book 1)
Fugitives from Justice (Book 2)

FUGITIVES FROM JUSTICE

"HELLO, RANCH! LOOK'N FOR SHERIFF JAMISON. WE'RE need'n the sheriff in town. Sheriff! Sheriff, you somewheres here abouts?"

The voice was loud, carrying from the ranch roadway to the house and further, taking in the barn and the neat little cabin that sat between those two structures. The rider, holding his hat from blowing away, was just easing his horse to a slower pace, not sure if he should race on toward the barn or call again at the house or cabin.

Key Wardle had ridden, with obvious excitement, into the yard of the Double J Ranch. His excitement had twin sources. The first and most troubling was the fact that the Double J was home to the very beautiful Jamison sisters. That alone was enough to make a young fellow kick his toe in the dust of the roadway and whip his hat off in deference.

Key was new to town, having arrived just weeks before from a ranch in the mountainous section of Wyoming, off to the northwest of Laramie. He hadn't met either girl, but Dusty Macklin, owner of the Roundup Ranch Supplies Store, had pointed them out.

The second reason for his excitement was that the bank had been robbed, but somehow that seemed like a dull matter compared to the other.

He had just made the decision to carry on to the barn, or perhaps even into the grazing pasture where the men might be working, when, glancing around, he saw two doors open almost simultaneously. The first to open, by barely a second, was the house door. And there, as if she had just floated in from a special, dreamy part of the universe, stood Nancy, the younger of the two girls. He pulled his gelding to such a sudden halt that he jerked forward in the saddle, his face almost touching the animal's neck, a most unhorseman-like action for a ranch-raised man, someone who had been riding since before he could walk.

Neither of the young people spoke, although they both had questions ready. The questions were halted by the opening of the cabin door. Sheriff Jamison stepped out and asked, "What's all the hollering about?"

Pulling his hand away from the hat he was about to lift in admiration of the girl he had been longing to meet, he turned his head toward the sheriff.

"Been a bank robbery, Sheriff. Folks in town are pretty wrought up about it. Dusty Macklin, who I work for down at the Roundup Ranch Supplies, he sent me out. Said to bring you in. So here I am."

"Yes. I can easily see that you're here all right. Tell me more about the robbery. Was Jesse Ambrewster hurt?"

"Banged up pretty bad but not yet dead. Leastwise, not so I know about it. Still alive last I heard. When he refused to open the big safe, those boys thought to beat him till he changed his mind, but he done no such a thing."

"What about his clerk?"

"Robbers took him."

"What do you mean the robbers took him?"

"Seems like pretty clear use of the language, Sheriff. Took. Seems like they were done whopping on the banker. Giv'n 'er up, you might say. One fella, bleeding pretty bad, he was already outside, trying to fit his foot into the stirrup. The other, he hustled the clerk out by a twist of his collar and threw him on a saddled horse that was tied there. Wasn't no way his horse neither. Anyway, they took the clerk and scampered out of town just as fast as their mounts would carry them. One was bleeding pretty bad, like I just said. Shot in the shoulder or arm. There wasn't time to sort all that out. Anyway, there was blood dripping all down his arm and leaving a trail off the ends of his fingers. I seen that much from clear across on the opposite boardwalk. He might have been look'n a bit sickly too. Like I said, there wasn't a lot of time to fit all the details in."

"Who shot him?"

"Him? Why the banker. That's who. Wasn't no one else there, sept'n Ma Gamble and the clerk, and neither one was tot'n a firearm. How he managed to do what he done while they were a'whopp'n on him with fists and feet and the butt of a pistol, I don't know, but that's what Ma Gamble, her from the dining room, said. She was there. Making a deposit of her profits I'm guess'n. Anyway, it was her that carried the story to the town. Seems like the banker, he refused to open the safe. Told the men to get out before he got angry. Who'd have ever thought that of an old man like the banker? That just made the robbers more angry. Ma, she backed into a corner and told the clerk to get down on the floor. The robbers, they kept a'whopp'n on the banker, like I also just said. Then, that old man, he pulls a small handgun from his jacket pocket and shoots one of them fellas.

"The banker, he was pretty stove-up, what with the punching and the kicking and the whack on the head with the butt of a gun. Still, he somehow got off that shot. Ma says the robbers, they kicked him a couple more times, cleaned out the little bit the cash drawer held, and then dragged the clerk out. They told Ma to tell you that if you follow, they'll kill the clerk. Anyway, you had best come to town."

Rory turned back into the cabin and was out in a few seconds with his tied bedroll and his saddlebags holding some trail provisions he kept at the ready. He had pulled his gun belt, carrying the two holstered weapons, around his waist.

Key, just starting to relax and get his wits about him, made the mistake of looking around the yard. Now, adding greatly to his unsettled mind, there were two Jamison girls listening. Only they were no longer on the porch, they were right beside him. Right there beside his horse. Why, he could have reached down and touched either one of them, almost, a thought that both thrilled and terrified him. Seeking distance, he gently heeled his mount sideways, ready to follow along as the sheriff walked to the barn.

By ranch country figuring of age, Key was a man, expected to do a man's work. The fact was that he had been working since he could walk, doing one thing and another, like all pioneer ranchers expected of their offspring. Past the age of twelve, he had been working the herd along with the crew, who watched over him as he learned. Although still slim and slight of build, the making of an adult body showed through his shirt, emphasizing good shoulders and arms that could be trusted to hold up their end of any task. Under his hat was a thatch of whitish-blond hair, cut roughly by the cook back on the homeplace. The barber in town had twice tried to put some shape back into it, but Key figured it needed at least one more period of growth before he could put the memory of the cook's well-meaning efforts behind him.

He had ridden away from home, knowing there was much the world had to offer that he would never come to know if he didn't pull away from the isolated cattle outfit for a year or two. He had stopped in Stevensville only to gift himself with a break from his own cooking. As he worked his way through one of Ma Gamble's lunches, Dusty Macklin, owner of the Roundup Ranch Supplies Store, looked over at him and asked, "You hunt'n work, young man?"

Key raised his head at the sound of the voice and glanced around the room. The stranger seemed to have his eyes fixed on him. Wondering if the question was directed his way, he looked the room over and decided there was no one else present that the question could have been aimed at. Without invitation Dusty Macklin stood and walked across the room, carrying his coffee mug, taking a seat across from Key. They talked, and Key decided that perhaps it was time to stop for a few weeks. He had clerked in the store since that day, although he was holding out the possibility of something more exciting to spend his learning time on.

And now, here he was on the Double J Ranch, bearing a message for the sheriff, who was older than him by only a couple of years. And right there, standing so he would have to ride past them to get out of the yard and back to town, were the Jamison girls. He was thrilled and terrified, all at the same time.

When the sheriff started walking toward the stable, Key nudged his animal into movement and followed, hoping for some safety in gaining distance from the girls.

Within a few minutes, the two men were riding out of the Double J Ranch yard, heading to town. When Key said something, using the title sheriff, Rory corrected him.

"The name's Rory. I'm guessing you have a name. Mind sharing it?"

"No, of course not. Key. That's what they called me, Key. Don't altogether know why they would choose that, but there it is anyway."

Rory had always wondered about his own name. He had thought from time to time to change it, just start calling himself some other name, legal or not, but decided against it. "We live with what we're given, Key, although there's really nothing to stop us from changing it, calling ourselves whatever we want."

"I suppose. But my folks would get pretty upset if I did that. Key, that's short for Keyman, which means strong or something close to that in another language. That's not my folks' language either, so it seems strange. But I guess I'll carry on with it for a while anyway."

"Well, Key, it doesn't sound like there's any real hurry to get to town, the robbers are gone, and the banker will be cared for by now. But I'm thinking we'll step it up a bit anyway."

A half-hour later, they rode onto the dusty, crowded street of Stevensville, Colorado. The short winter was little more than a memory. Any snow left in the shaded spots would soon be gone. It wasn't hot on the street, but neither was it cold. By the calendar, it was spring, with snow still capping the westward mountains, adding a chill to the air and ready to maintain a moderate climate for the summer months. There were buds forming on the trees, just aching to burst into the greenery of spring and summer. The youngsters of the town would soon bid farewell to the kitchen tables their mothers kept them at while she worked over their letters and numbers with them, hoping to ease them into a civilized manner before they cut the apron strings altogether. The newly released youngsters would soon be heading to the river with long willow poles and cans of worms. The older ones would be seeking some way to put a few coins in their pockets, preferably some way that included horses.

Sheriff Rory had eased through a quiet time, with no new crimes and no new challenges to brighten up his first few months as an appointed county deputy sheriff. He had made several trips to Denver to assist in the investigation of Mike Wasson's crimes and to attend his trial. Wasson was the rustler Rory had tracked down and dragged out of the bush the fall before with the help of Ivan Ivanov. Other than that, Rory was more of a rancher than a sheriff. But the excited crowd on the boardwalk of their little town told him the pause in the crime wave was over. It really hadn't been much of a crime wave. But for the totally inexperienced young deputy sheriff who was not yet old enough to vote, it was as much as he wanted for his first case.

Knowing the quiet time was over filled Rory with some apprehension and wondering. Chasing after men who carried guns and had already broken several laws, from bank robbery to serious assault on the banker, to horse theft, to kidnapping, could offer a clear downside.

These would be dangerous men to corner. Desperate for distance and freedom.

Before Rory and Key reached the crowd, they heard the pound of horses' hooves behind them. Without turning around, Rory said, "That will be the girls. Can't hardly keep them off a horse or out at the ranch. It's a caution how they like to get to town."

Key turned to look, and then, with a deep intake of breath, he said, "I'd best get back to the store."

Rory grinned as he watched him ride through the crowd.

2

RORY'S FIRST STOP WAS THE DINING ROOM AND A VISIT with Ma Gamble. It took but a few minutes to confirm the story Key had relayed on the ride back from the Double J. Ma emphasized the fact of her surprise that the banker, no longer young, but not really old, either, and beginning to show just the leading edge of a bit of weight on his otherwise rail-thin physique, had managed to dig the .32 out of his coat pocket while trying to duck the onslaught of punches and kicks laid on by the robbers. The crack on the head that laid the banker out cold on the floor hadn't come until after he shot one of his attackers. Ma had been afraid they would kill the man but instead, with his partner shot and no longer concerned about anything but his own survival, the man who slugged Jesse Ambrewster hoisted the slightly built bank clerk to his feet and dragged him from the room as a hostage. The man who was shot was already struggling onto his horse. They rode from town at a full gallop with the terrified clerk hanging onto the saddle horn with two hands, his horse being led by one of the thieves.

Rory listened until Ma ran out of words. He could almost feel the tension in her voice and sense it in her jerky hand actions. Rory thanked her and suggested, "Why don't you lock up and go home for the day, Ma? Maybe read a good book or take a walk. The rest would do you good."

"And lose all this business? Look at them all out there. As excited as if it was two Christmases, one day after the other.

"I expect there will be a good crowd for dinner this evening. Sonia and I can handle it. And you want me to go home. Shame on you young folks. Don't know what it is to have to deal with whatever comes in order to earn a dollar to keep body and soul together." She flashed a big grin at the sheriff after saying it.

Rory answered, "Well, I'll just take a gander around town, see what the doctor has to say, and perhaps come back for lunch. I doubt I'll still be here come dinnertime."

Before going to the doctor's office, Rory crossed the street to assure himself that someone had locked the bank door. Tippet, the livery hostler, saw him rattling the doorknob and hollered over, "Locked 'er up tight, Sheriff. Done 'er myself. Done 'er up first thing. Wouldn't want ol' Ambrewster to lose track of the twenty-four dollars and seventy-six cents that's mine in that big vault of his. Feller's got ta look after hisself, don' ya know."

He capped off this exchange of information with one of his typical cackling laughs.

Rory just waved his thanks and set out for the doctor's combination home and office.

With a slight knock on the front door, the sheriff

turned the knob and let himself into the small waiting room. "Doc? You here?"

"Come on in, Sheriff. I'm sure the patient will be happy to know you're on the case."

From the other room came a voice struggling to be heard, "I'm happy enough just to be alive, Doc. And I'm not too sure I wasn't at more risk from your not-too-gentle ministrations than I was from those two beating on me."

"It's not often I get a chance to work the kinks out of a banker, Jesse. I sure wasn't about to lose out on this one opportunity. Anyway, except for that conk on the head, the rest will just take time. You'll develop some interesting shades of blue and pink over the next few days, but that's nothing to worry about. You take those pills I gave you for headaches. If your headaches get worse, or you feel as if you're going to black out or get dizzy to where you fall down, you get yourself back over here. Now, pull your pants on and get out of here. And dig into one pocket or another and pull one of those shiny coins out and pay the wife as you leave. That's another thing I don't often get to enjoy, having a banker spending money right here in my very own clinic."

The banker, full of possible replies but remaining silent, swung his legs off the side of the gurney and tried to stand up. When it was clear that he needed steadying help, the doctor grabbed one arm while Rory reached for the other. They got him steadied but hung on for just another few seconds. The banker, trying for dignity that was in short supply, with him standing there with only a towel wrapped tightly around his slowly expanding middle, said, "If I could have a bit of privacy…"

The doctor grinned at Rory and said, "You get

dressed, Jesse. You show up on the street looking like that and no one will ever bank with you again."

Whatever grumbling came from Ambrewster was blocked out when the doctor closed the door. Rory eased the door back open just enough to say, "Come to the dining room when you're done up here. I'll buy you a coffee, and you can tell me your story."

A half-hour later, the two men were sitting together, leaning across the table to where they could commune in whispers. Ma, true to her prediction, was doing a brisk business. Rory figured it would only get busier as the clock rolled around to lunchtime and then, later, to the dinner hour. It seemed the little town was ready for some excitement, something to talk about. That a man was missing—kidnapped—only added a grimness to the day. There had been mention of a posse, but Rory put an end to that as soon as he had reached town.

The story relayed by Key on the ride from the ranch was confirmed by the banker. He also confirmed that the amount kept in the drawer for daily business was small, causing little concern. The banker, showing more emotion than Rory had believed him capable of, had two concerns. The first was for his clerk, a young town man named Andrew Speth. The second was for the banker's own health. Even as they talked, Rory could see the man fading. As he tired, he began to slightly slur his words, and his eyelids were falling into a sleep position.

"Mr. Ambrewster, how would it be if I was to get Tippet to bring his buggy around and give you a ride home? The bank can stay closed this one day. Or even for a few days."

Ambrewster raised his head, looking directly into Rory's eyes, as if he was trying to focus on the words.

Finally, he just nodded, and again dropped his eyes, and his head.

With a slight goodbye wave to Ma and Sonia, Rory left the dining room and walked to the livery. Tippet swung into action, going immediately for the buggy horse. Rory tightened the cinch on his own gelding and stepped into the saddle. The townsfolk had agreed that the thieves left town heading toward the river. So, the river it would be. Now, the question was, east or west. Knowing little about the geography in either direction, Rory could easily make a time-wasting mistake. As he rode, he tried to think through the alternatives.

There was really only east or west. For sure, they would turn off the road. To carry on would only lead them to the big city, more curious folks and more law, which they would be wanting to avoid. But after leaving the road, there would be multiple choices.

West would take the traveler into the high country where there were endless watercourses to follow, canyons to conceal the wary, and ample wild game to keep a man fed. Remembering what he and Ivan went through, tracking down and capturing the cattle rustlers a few months before, Rory wasn't anxious to repeat that venture through hills and valleys, forest and lighter brush, and endless possibilities, some of them offering to lead him into false trails, away from the fugitives.

If the thieves took the river route to the east, there was much open country. Only along the river's lightly forested course would they find bush or rocks enough to offer concealment and water for themselves and their animals. But the river wound around like three snakes in a tangle, almost coming back onto itself in numerous places. Actual forward travel would be slight if they followed the river. It was probable they would take the easier path of riding from point to point as the river wasted time and energy in its many turns. That made a problem for anyone following. Of course, it was also possible the men could have gone to ground anywhere along the river. Rory would have to sort it all out, leaving no twist or turn unexplored.

One thing in the sheriff's favor was that the wounded man would need to seek medical help. That would slow them down if they stopped to heat wash water or find healing herbs among the many plants along the stream. It could also cause them to become careless if the man was sick enough.

Rory found his mind turning to concern for Andy Speth. The bank clerk would quickly become a burden. Would the fugitives continue to drag him along on the escape, or would they turn him loose? And what of the third, more grim option?

West, the shallow river valley soon became a mountainous canyon, difficult on foot and nearly impossible for horses in some areas. They would soon realize they had to find another way. Several pioneering settlers had made grass claims in the rugged up-country, but there would be no towns or settlements where they could logically hope to find a doctor unless they swung to the south, to the mining areas. If they did that, they would eventually find a doctor. Whether or not they would find one quickly enough to aid the gunshot victim was an open question. And again, what of the clerk? They couldn't hope to drag him into a strange town and keep him hidden from the townsmen. The fate of Andy Speth was becoming a burden in the sheriff's mind, overshadowing the bank theft itself.

To the east, out in the sparsely settled cattle country, there were towns, or at least small villages, but nothing close enough to find immediate attention for the bullet wound. They would have to ride clear into Kansas or Nebraska to find a town, or far northern Colorado. Any of those choices represented days of fast riding.

Rory's travels had been to Idaho and Montana, and a single ride through Wyoming. But his knowledge of eastern Colorado was slim, at best. He guessed there could be a town he didn't know about. He had heard mention of an army fort somewhere to the east, but the rumors were that the army had abandoned it.

Only a few minutes ride from Ma's dining room took him to the river crossing. Rory acknowledged that he knew little about tracking, but the thieves would have been desperate to get away. Perhaps they had been careless, leaving tracks that even he could follow.

As he neared the narrow wooden bridge that crossed the river, he swung his horse to the west. A careful study of the riverbank, and even back up the trail over one hundred yards, showed no disturbed grass, no broken limbs on the bordering brush, no sign at all of the three horses being ridden by the escaping thieves and their kidnapped hostage.

He walked the gelding to the east side of the trail and followed the same routine. Nothing. No disturbance of any sort. It wasn't until he crossed the bridge and looked again to the east that he saw the trail. The broken sod and turned-up, dried-out leaves caused by the running horses were plain. *Plain, even to me*, thought Rory.

Having learned caution on his long ride home from Idaho, and again while seeking the rustlers the previous fall, he stopped and took a careful look. Brush and small trees bordered the stream, most of it too short to hide a man on horseback, but tall enough to conceal a frightened thief who was prepared to fight off pursuit. Still, it was doubtful the men would ride at full gallop from town only to pull up this close to potential capture. Watching for any discernible sign of travel, Rory cautiously urged his gelding down the bank from the road to the shortgrass prairie. It wasn't until he had ridden another few yards that he could plainly see the tracks of the three horses moving directly east, more or less following the course of the river, but avoiding the many loops.

Considering the time it took Key to ride to the Double J and for Rory and Key to ride back into town, and then for Rory to talk with both the banker and Ma Gamble, no less than two hours had passed, possibly closer to three. So, he was a bit late on the trail.

Rory had heard all the tales, some of them beyond credence, of men who could track an eagle across the sky or tell the age of a hoofprint within a minute and then tell you what color the horse was to boot. But he assigned none of those skills to himself. Still, logic said these were tracks made in the rush and the panic of escape. He could safely move forward in the belief that the men would not really begin sorting out their options this close to town. Here they would be trying for distance.

As noon passed, Rory recognized that by studying every bend and twist of the small river, he was falling behind the travel of the fugitives. But he had the advantage of a fresher horse that had not been hard ridden, or a companion hoping to remain alive with a bullet in his shoulder. He was free to ride long hours, where the wounded man would need to stop and do whatever he could to reduce the pain or slow the bleeding. But as long as there were visible tracks, Rory could simply keep riding.

On the long trail to Idaho, when Rory and his father had left the Double J in the care of his father's brother, and Rory was still a bit short of his fifteenth birthday, the young man had several times complained about the time in the saddle and the miles of the trail. His father had a simple answer, *A man never arrives at his destination riding only half the distance, Rory. When you know you're right and that your goal is still ahead of you, the choice is simple, keep riding or face failure. Which you choose will set the pattern of your life.*

The crime was behind him, and the fugitives were up ahead somewhere. There were still tracks to follow. Rory, county deputy sheriff by means of a one-year appointment, would keep riding.

By midafternoon, it was nearing six hours since the holdup at the bank. Rory studied the sun to confirm what his inner clock was telling him. Both he and the gelding were tiring a bit, more from pushing through bush and soft ground than miles covered. The tracks had either disappeared or become faint from time to time, depending on the firmness of the prairie sod. Still, by simply moving forward, Rory had somehow managed to find them again. Now he was watching for signs of smoke, hoping the desperate fugitives had finally stopped to treat the wounded man. But he had seen nothing so far. Midafternoon turned into early evening, and finally, faint but visible, a half mile or so ahead, a slight mist of smoke rose into the air.

Rory's big gelding was tiring after the many hours of steady plodding. He could logically believe that the fugitives' mounts were no better off.

3

IN AN EXCESS OF CAUTION, RORY DISMOUNTED, TOOK THE reins in his hand, and moved forward on foot. In a further expression of caution, he moved to the offside of the animal, changing the reins to his left hand, putting the animal between himself and the river valley. He would hate to have one of the beautiful Double J Ranch blood-red bay horses shot, but rather that than taking a bullet himself.

At this point, the river flowed through a small, treed, rocky canyon, looking from a distance to be about a half mile long. It was the roughest portion of the river's travels he had seen so far and the first that offered any real cover. The obvious problem was that the fugitives had to know anyone following would also recognize it as such.

Rory proceeded for another few hundred careful yards and stopped. Considering his options, he loosely tied the gelding to a small bush he would be able to free himself from if Rory failed to return. He lifted the carbine from the scabbard, checked the loads, reached into the saddlebag, lifted out a handful of replacement loads, stuffed them into his jacket pockets, and took a careful look around. He was still a bit more than a quarter mile from where the smoke was showing. To appease the nagging in his stomach and in recognition of the truth that he had eaten nothing since he rode away from the Double J, he broke off a corner of hardtack and stuffed it in his mouth along with a bite of cheese. It wouldn't solve the hunger problem, but the softening of the hardtack would give his saliva something to do and might help to keep his mind on his business.

Height. Elevation. A bird's eye view. That's what he needed. He needed to gain some advantage. The north side of the small canyon offered that, as well as the first opportunity for shelter for the fugitives. The south side of the canyon was wider and more spread out, offering less elevation but more shelter from trees and under-brush. Moving far enough from the horse so the geld-ing's tearing of grass couldn't be heard, Rory stood still and listened. There was nothing at all if a fella ignored the very faint gurgle of the stream and the lapping of the water as it rounded a rock on its journey to join the South Platte.

Making as little sound as possible, Rory removed his boots and socks, held them in one hand, with the carbine in the other after rolling up his pant legs, and waded into the shallow stream. A dozen careful but quick steps placed him on the north bank. Stepping far enough from the stream to find dry land, he sat and replaced his footwear. He then set out for the height of rocks in the near distance.

Coming parallel with the visible smoke, Rory turned to the rocky bank. Approaching from the north, he was in no danger of being seen, but sounds travel when there is little wind and where nervous men are listening. He made his way through the sheltering trees and, after another careful glance around, placed his foot onto the first rock that was jutting out of the embankment. That step, followed by more, soon put him near the crest of the ridge. Removing his hat, he eased up the last few feet, rising to where he could see over the top. At first, with the smoke swirling through the overhanging branches and leaves, he didn't spot the fire or the men. It was the movement of the bank clerk that first grabbed his notice.

The clerk was down on one knee, bent over a man who was stretched out beside the fire. What he was doing, Rory couldn't see, but there was a blood-covered shirt lying in a crumpled heap and a small cooking pot edged into the fire with steam rising from it. The third man was sitting on the turf with his back against a small tree. He held his carbine across his lap and appeared to be constantly twisting his head from one place to another, looking for pursuit.

He thought he might be close enough to hear their talk if he remained quiet and if the river held its thoughts to itself. He eased a little higher, bringing his eyes and ears to where there was nothing between them and the small camp across the river. The first sound he heard was from the wounded man.

"I got to go back, Slade. There just ain't no other way about it. I'll die out here by morning, and what for? Less than fifty dollars in that drawer and nothing more. You go on. I got to go back."

"You go back, they'll have you in jail."

"Jail is preferable to the grave."

"Anyway, you'll never make it. You can't even stand. How you going to keep a horse under you and heading true?"

"I'm going back, and this here fella you grabbed outa the bank is going to take me. You don't need him anymore. He wore out his usefulness a mile from town. You go on ahead. Maybe so we'll meet up again somewhere."

The man named Slade stood, took a few steps to the side, and raised his Colt. Taking aim at the bank clerk, he said, "You're right on that one thing anyway, Bronc. He's for sure no use to me now. So far as that goes, you're not much use to me either."

Rory had no way of knowing if the threat was serious or just a gambit, but he took no chances. Lifting his own carbine carefully over the rocks so there would be no warning sounds, he took quick aim at Slade's hand and fired off a single shot. Slade's Colt flew through the air, and the gunman dropped to the ground screaming in pain. The eyes of the wounded fugitive turned to where the curling smoke of gunpowder was drifting off on the breeze. The bank clerk dove for the nearest brush and was out of sight.

Rory stood to his feet, still pointing the carbine.

"Don't move, any of you. Sheriff Jamison here. You move, you die. Believe it. Now, I'm coming down. Don't do anything you'll regret for all eternity."

He placed his hat back into place and swung his legs over the crest of the short canyon wall. Gripping the rocks behind him with one hand while he held the carbine with the other, he slowly, carefully worked his way down, rock by rock, grasping trees for support as he went.

When he neared the bottom, there was a three-foot drop with no footholds to aid him. He had no choice but to take his eyes off the fugitives' camp while he made the drop. That, or risk injury that would do no one any good at all. When he was again standing firmly on the grassed riverbank, he looked back over to the little camp. Slade was on his feet and running. Rory fired another shot, but Slade was in the riverside forest and ducking between trees. There was no chance for another meaningful shot. He stood there frustrated as he listened to horse's hooves pounding across the prairie turf.

For the first time the bank clerk spoke.

"Safe to come over, Sheriff. I've taken this fella's guns from him. That's them lying there on the grass. Anyway, he's too sick to do much but whine and complain."

Back on the south side of the river, this time allowing the cold water to have its way with his boots, socks, and pant legs, he approached the fire carefully, listening for the sounds of a returning horse, in case Slade decided to come back and shoot it out.

"He won't be back, Sheriff. Cowards, the both of them. Wanting nothing more than wealth other men worked for and an easy way through life."

The clerk was showing more grit than anyone in town had ever given him credit for. When he arrived in Stevensville, offering no explanations for his presence, he had been taken as a man unfit for ranch or frontier life and more or less ignored. Rory found himself admiring him.

"Never really were introduced. I know you as Andy is all."

" The name is Andrew Speth. Known as Andy to the one friend I had back east. You can take your choice."

"Alright, Andy it is. Now, tell me what's happening here and what needs to be done to get this fella back to town."

"I guess, Sheriff, that what should be done and what needs to be done are perhaps not quite the same thing.

What should be done is we should snug a rope over this fella's foot and drag him out into the open where the varmints can get a clear go at him. But I'm guessing what you're going to do is load him up and take him back to town, wasting money and time for the doc, trying to pull him together enough to put in prison, or hang, after the law finds all that he's done in times past."

While Rory was studying the situation with the wounded man, Andy picked up the cast-off gun belt and strapped it around his own waist. He lifted the Colt from the holster, spun the cylinder to assure himself that it was loaded and clear of grass or dirt, and returned it to the holster. Rory looked on in dismay as he caught just the last bit of this action.

"Might be best if we were to hang that rig from my saddle, Andy."

"No. I've been put upon enough for this one day. Should Slade poke his head back around, I may just decide to see if I can still hit anything with a Colt. After you get first opportunity, is what I mean to say, Sheriff. I don't intend to be taken again."

"Do you know how to use one of those, Andy? You don't seem to be the type."

Rory immediately regretted his words, recognizing the barely hidden insult in them.

In answer, Andy turned his back to Rory, flipped the .44 from its holster, held it waist-high, banged off three shots, sounding as one, and peeled bark from a slender, white-barked aspen with each shot. He reloaded from the ammunition belt and returned the gun to its holster. Only then did he turn back to face Rory.

Rory's only comment was, "Let's get this man onto a saddle."

The blood smell had the horse prancing and fidgeting. The wounded man's screams of agony didn't help. But finally, Bronc, as the wounded man named himself, was aboard with a one-hand grip on the horn. Rory said, "You hold on and keep quiet. You'll have help sooner if you cooperate and don't do anything stupid."

He then turned and said, "Andy, I'm going to trust you to take this man back to town. Get him to the doc just as soon as you can. The bank is closed for today, so you hang around the doc's office. When he's done what he can do, you take Bronc over to the jail and lock him in. You stay with him until I get back. Ma will lay out a plate for him if I'm not back by mealtime."

"You going after the other one?"

"I am, and the sooner I get started, the better. Did either of them say anything about where they hoped to go?"

"Nothing at all. All I got from them was that they rode into town broke last night. Slept down by the river and woke up hungry. They had no intention of robbing a bank when they arrived. It just seemed to happen. They were broke and hungry, and the bank was there. That's all the explanation I was able to get from either of them. And I'm not too sure I believe even a single word of it."

"Alright, get going. And don't give in to temptation with that Colt. I don't want to be having to track you down."

Not bothering to answer, Andy kicked the stolen horse into movement and tugged the wounded man's gelding along.

Rory walked back to his horse, watered it and himself, and set out again on the trail. The tracks of the running horse were plain. He even thought he could see where the fugitive had the animal in a gallop and where he had slowed to rest him. Could it be possible he was learning just a bit about this tracking business?

And now, he had more information. Slade had no food in his saddlebags. He might catch a fish in the river, but that would take time, and the cooking would require more time and a smoke-generating fire. He could shoot something, but again, he would need a fire. Slade, riding hungry and desperate into the bare eastern grasslands didn't bode well for the few settlers out that way. Rory had met only two small ranchers during the rustling matter the previous fall. He knew nothing at all about Earnest Fisher, the rancher that gave him directions to the Flint/King ranch, the K Slash brand. Could the man defend himself, or would he be vulnerable?

He knew Lavinia Flint had spent the winter in town. They hadn't talked recently, so he had no update on Ambrose King, his wife, Katie, or the children. Mrs. Flint, Katie's widowed mother, had originally thought Ambrose and Katie would leave the struggles of the small ranch and take up some other occupation. She had stated that Ambrose was a good man, a good husband and father, but not really suited for frontier ranching. If Slade rode that way, he may find a peace-loving, young family man, or he may find empty buildings and no welcome at all.

4

WHEN THE RIVER TOOK A SLIGHT TURN TO THE SOUTH, THE fugitive, obviously believing there was more to offer in the north, crossed the stream. His tracks left no doubt that he hadn't even stopped to water his horse. Rory followed him across, but he stopped to water both himself and the gelding. With another small square of hardtack stuffed into his cheek, along with his usual bite of cheese, he continued.

To the sheriff, one small rise or fold in the grassland looked much like another. He would have placed no bet on his location. He had tried to liken his ride to the one taken the previous fall, out to the K Slash Ranch, and came up short of a convincing comparison. But the trail, now more difficult to follow on the hardened turf, with the sun setting behind the Rockies, leaving only the hour or so of twilight that separated day from night, continued its northeast direction. Rory stepped up his pace knowing the K Slash had to be off in that direction. If he lost the trail, he would scout it out again in the morning. His concern now was for Ambrose

King, Katie, and their two little ones. There was no telling what the desperate Slade might bring to their doorstep.

With most of the day's light faded into memory, Rory saw a dim outline of a ranch yard a short mile ahead. He didn't see the lighted window until he had ridden another quarter-hour, and then there could be no doubt. He had stumbled, more by good fortune than wisdom, onto the K Slash Ranch.

Not knowing what to expect, he rode slowly, casting his eyes in every direction. Only once did he see someone passing between the lamp and the window, casting a shadow across the darkening glass. There was no telling for sure, but it looked like a woman, probably Katie King. If that was true, it would at least confirm that she was alive and able to move freely. Or perhaps she was preparing the evening meal under the threat of Slade's gun. He slowed the gelding to a cautious walk, easing toward the corral and barn. Through the nearly total darkness, he saw three horses in the corral. They had all turned at the sound or the horse smell rising from his own gelding, staring over the top rail as he approached. He had not seen what Slade was riding, so he could pass no judgment on the horses. But seeing nothing further except a narrow band of light seeping past the ill-fitting barn door, and hearing no unnatural sounds, he carefully stepped to the ground, tying the horse to the corral rail.

He had just turned toward the house, wondering what his next step should be, when a voice from the deep darkness shrouding the small barn said, "That's far enough, stranger. You shuck that gun belt. I can see just enough to know what your hands are up to. You set a hand to lift a weapon, and it will be your last move. Drop the belt and step away from the horse. Then tell me who you are and what brings you to the K."

Rory recognized the voice right off. Thankful for the realization that Ambrose seemed to be in control of his own ranch yard, he ignored the demand about the gun belt, saying instead, "The last time I was out this way, Ambrose, I carried you, screaming and hurting, out of the house and onto a wagon. Then took a long night's ride to town and the doctor, fighting wind and snow the whole way. Unless you've lost a sizable amount of weight since that time, I'd not welcome the challenge again.

"Evening, Ambrose. Rory Jamison here. Wondering if you've had any visitors this afternoon."

Seemingly satisfied with the introduction, Ambrose relaxed, although Rory couldn't see the slight drop in the man's shoulders. But the tension left his voice, replaced by a welcome note.

"Good of you to come by, Sheriff. There'll be no need to carry me this night. The doc patched me up pretty good. Still don't have full movement in my shoulder, but I'm learning to live with it."

The barn door creaked on rusty hinges, spreading light onto the ground outside.

"Come here, Sheriff. Guessing at what brought you out here, I've got something you might be glad to see."

Rory approached carefully until he had Ambrose fully in view. The single lantern hanging from the nail jutting from a rafter was inadequate to cast more than minimum illumination, leaving many corners and stalls in darkness, causing Rory some concern. Ambrose lifted the lantern down and beckoned Rory to follow him. As they walked the center aisle of the barn, with the weird and bouncing shadows cast by the swinging lantern, each stall was lit enough to satisfy the sheriff. Finally, coming to the last stall, Ambrose held the lantern high and nodded toward a well-tied bundle of misery lying on a bed of straw. Of course, it was Slade, but a much-diminished Slade, with all the fight seemingly gone from him, and appearing as if he wanted nothing more than to sleep.

As the two men were talking, a large gray dog walked slowly down the aisle of the barn, taking the measure of the sheriff, the hackles on his back standing straight up, deciding on his choice of actions. The animal finally brushed up against Ambrose's leg and received a reassuring stroke on his head in return.

Ambrose bent and pulled the filthy saddle blanket off the curled-up form of the man. Slade didn't move, didn't even open his eyes. The fugitive's shirt was in tatters, with one sleeve gone altogether. The exposed arm was a mass of scratches, tears, and bite marks, most of them dripping blood and some kind of pale-yellow liquid. One ear was chewed cruelly, and the cheek below that ear would never look right again. The eyelid was torn and hanging over the eye.

Looking at the hand that was wrapped across Slade's chest, cradling the much-abused arm, Rory could see that it, too, was chewed and bleeding, as if he had used that hand to fend off whatever it was that was attacking him. Looking more closely, Rory could see that two fingers on Slade's right hand were missing, and half of his thumb was hanging loose. That had been the hand Rory shot the gun out of back by the river. It looked as if Slade had wrapped it in his kerchief, as a portion of the red material was still clutched in his remaining folded fingers.

There was a loop of rawhide wrapped around the man's one good wrist. The trailing end of the tie disappeared into the bed of straw, reappearing as a loop fastened securely to a rail in the next stall. His feet were similarly tied. There was no chance at all of Slade getting loose unless he managed to chew through the strip of leather. Rory decided that Slade was in no condition to do anything of the sort.

"What happened here, Ambrose?"

Wishing to make a bit of a story out of it, Ambrose started back a few months.

"You know, it's strange how things happen. Things a fella has no designs on at all. Few months back, this dog straggled into our yard. Cold day it was. Threatening more snow. Big fella. Short haired. Good-looking animal. Half-starved, beat up, and cold, one ear hanging almost torn off, as if he had come a close second in a disagreement with a couple of coyotes. If'n it had been wolves, they'd have killed the dog and had him for lunch. But, of course, a coyote, now, he's a coward. Turn from any fight he's being bested in and run like he's hearing his mamma calling somewhere over the next hill.

"That dog, he walks right up to the kids playing in the yard. Scared their mother half to death, her thinking the worst of the desperate animal. But that dog, he walks up to where the kids are playing, and he lays right down beside them. The boy, he starts to pet the dog while the girl, she runs screaming for her mother to come see.

"I'd been watching from the corral, concerned a bit myself at first. But when I saw there was no danger to the kids, no signs that he was rabid or aggressive, I put down what I was working on and walked over. Katie, she dug some leftovers from lunch out of the cold pantry and laid them before the animal. He swallowed those down in a single gulp and looked for more. With another bite of food and some water, that dog lay down as if he had found his way home and intended to stay right there.

"Lavinia, that's Mrs. Flint, Katie's mother, she got out her sewing stuff, and she sewed that torn ear back into place after I trimmed off some putrefied flesh. Then, the two women, they soaked that poor beast down with soapy water and rinsed him with cold well water. I don't believe he enjoyed it one bit, but he tolerated it. When they were finished, he smelled like a dog is supposed to smell, after the wet dried away, of course. Bedded him down here in the barn. As I said, it was a cold day. But the straw and a saddle blanket seemed to be all the beast needed for comfort."

Rory was tempted to interrupt this lengthy dialogue until he realized there was no real hurry. Ambrose was enjoying the telling of it, and Rory was through traveling for this one day. He would find a place to sleep, probably in the loft, and if he was offered dinner and breakfast, he would accept with gratitude. So, Ambrose continued uninterrupted.

"Sheriff, you never seen the like. That dog, he barely tolerates Katie or me but those kids! Why, he never leaves their side. Sleeps on the back porch when the weather is fine, his rump never more than inches from the door, his eyes scanning the yard for intruders. I fixed up a couple of folded, worn-out saddle blankets for him under the stoop for when it's raining.

"Now, the point of all this is, Sheriff, this here fella," Ambrose kicked Slade's foot to identify who he was talking about, "he steps down from his horse, and he walks right up to where those kids were playing. Katie, she saw it all from the window. She was about to wipe her hands clean from the dinner biscuit dough she was forming into shape and go out there, when this fella, he gets too close to where the boy was digging in the dirt. I was walking over from the barn.

"He had his warning, this fella did. Dog, he stood to attention, bared his teeth, and growled a threat that should have been heeded. Instead, Katie heard him say, 'Kid, where's...' with that, the growled warning grew, sounding like it came from the very pit of the animal's being. This fella, showing what was probably a lifetime of misjudgment, he swings his leg as if to kick the dog. He starts again with, 'I asked where...' but that's all he got out before this catamount was on him. By that time, Katie was shouting for me, all the while running across the yard, her apron flying in the breeze and the shotgun hanging from her hand.

"By the time I got there, running from the corral like I done, the boy, he had pulled the dog off, but it was really pretty late in the game, as you can see right here." He kicked Slade's foot again for emphasis.

Rory studied the young rancher, considering all he had just heard. He couldn't really find it in himself to condemn the man or the dog but, still, he felt a note of caution.

"There's not much I can say to that, Ambrose. Be kind of tough, though, if a friend should ride up all unaware and get the same treatment."

"You're right on that, Rory, and I've been thinking on it. No solid answer yet, but in fairness to the dog, he didn't move until this fella swung his foot at him. Most folks wouldn't do that, understanding dogs like anyone working stock would do."

Rory was slow to condemn or criticize, but he still had a question.

"Ambrose, I can clearly see the damage the dog did. The pain and discomfort from that must be considerable. But he didn't get that lump on the head from the dog. I suspect that's what's got him lying here not knowing if it's summer or winter."

Ambrose replied, "When the dog was pulled off him, he set out to curse the entire world and everyone in it, especially here on the K Slash. Even so, when he took a staggering step toward his horse, we might have let him go, but he wasn't finished with the foul talk. He turned and aimed a nasty threat at the boy, and that done it. It was more than Katie was about to tolerate. She was standing kind of off to the side, her dough-covered hands slippery on the shotgun, but still, she managed to swing that old double twelve in a fine arc, connecting with right where you see that lump on his head. Kind of put an end to the talk and everything else. I doubt as how this fella's seen anything but stars since that moment. I'm just glad she didn't up and pull the trigger."

The two men stood looking down at Slade, with Rory feeling just a bit sorry about how the day had ended. It was true the two men were would-be bank robbers, and they had stolen a horse and forced Andy Speth to ride with them, but Bronc, back in town by this time, had a badly shot-up shoulder and arm. And Slade, although he would very likely recover from the whack on the head, would never fully mend from the awful chewing he had suffered. It was a heavy price for a spur-of-the-moment bad idea. If, indeed, that is what it was. Rory was slowly losing his naivety about folks. Just the few months in the lawing business, on top of the shooting at the gold camp, had taken the edge off his trust.

Katie had not called dinner yet, and Ambrose seemed to have nothing particular that needed doing. As if in wordless agreement, the two men shunted a bit to the side and settled onto a couple of upturned buckets.

Curious at the difference in Ambrose from the gentle man Lavinia Flint had described the first time Rory had been at the K Slash, a man she described as a good man for another, more settled age, he finally decided to lay his thoughts out.

"Ambrose, you've changed some. From the time the rustlers ran off the K Slash stock to today, you've changed. I'm thinking it's more than being thrown by that horse last fall. I come here today, and you've got that fugitive safely bound up in the barn, and you're belted with a Colt. That's not the man that was described to me by your women folk."

Ambrose was slow to answer, first studying the sheriff and then glancing around to where he could see Slade wrapped in pain and an old blanket, lying on the straw-covered floor. Finally, he seemed to gather the words he wanted.

"No, I guess I'm not, Sheriff. What happened, I suppose, is that the truth of the situation finally became clear to me. That and the realization that I am now the only man on the K Slash. Katie's father, my father-in-law, is no longer here. He's the one that settled this place, of course, not me. This is his belt and holster I now carry. With his death, I've got a wife and kids to protect and a ranch to run."

Still hesitating, it was a few seconds before he continued.

"I wasn't always so peace-loving, Rory. I was raised in a tough town by a tough father. A small coal town back in Kentucky. Hardworking men, my father and the rest. Good men, but tough. Would take no nonsense from anyone. I bit into more than my share of situations before I came of age. And then, when I did come of age, I was just in time to poke my nose into the last two years of the war.

"You're young, Sheriff. Too young to have seen war. I don't know what other history you have or how it affected you, but the first time I pulled the trigger and watched a man fall, I changed. Changed in the very heart of me. There lay a man dead from my lead. A man about my own age. A man with hopes and dreams, just like I had. We spoke the same language, worshipped the same God. In another situation, there would have been nothing stopping us from being friends. But he was dead, and I was alive.

"Of course, that scene was repeated too many times in the months till the end of that foolishness. I was in battles where good men died on all sides and all around me. I shot until the barrel of my gun was too hot to touch. I picked up another, there were enough lying around, and kept shooting till powder and lead were gone, used up. And still, I lived. Me and some others. Lived among the corpses and the pitiful crying of the wounded. No matter what you hear about that time, Sheriff, believe this—there wasn't a man among us that wasn't changed. Some for the better but many for the worse.

"I came away from it sickened at heart. I never wanted to see another gun or hear another cry for help. But after you put your life on the line for me and mine, and found the men who stole our herd, or the most of it anyway, returning a big part of the value in cash money, I was shamed. So hopeful for peace, I had stood by and done nothing while thieves hid behind a made-up law to steal our herd.

"When I recovered from the injuries that wild horse laid on me, I found I couldn't hardly look my womenfolk in the eye, wife or mother-in-law, either one. I decided if we were going to ranch in an unsettled country, I had better be prepared for what came our way. I hope to never shame myself again. And I live in the hopes that my kids can someday hang this gun belt over the mantle in remembrance of a father and grandfather who had to wear it, thankful that those days were gone."

AMBROSE HITCHED his team to the wagon early the next morning as a loaner for Rory. Together they threw some bedding straw in and then backed the wagon down the center aisle of the barn. Slade was awake and hurting. Rory got him onto his feet and helped him to the privacy of the next stall. Giving him enough time to do what he had to do, Rory then said, "Climb in. Sit or lay as you please. But I'm going to tie those leather ribbons again just so you won't forget you're a prisoner. And if you give me even one moment of trouble, I'm going to lose my good sense of humor."

As Rory was tying his and Slade's animals to the back of the wagon, Lavinia Flint came from the house and climbed onto the wagon seat. When Rory gave her a questioning look, she said, "Good excuse to go to town. Visit some friends. Pick up a few things from the mercantile. Bring the wagon back tomorrow, or mayhap in a day or two. Visit a neighbor or two on the way home. It's for sure I'm not needed around here. Be good to get away for a couple of days."

RORY DROVE the wagon down the front street of Stevensville just past noon. Several people stood on the boardwalk watching, but no one spoke until he neared the marshal's office. Andy, freed from the closed bank and acting as jail guard, watching over the patched-up Bronc, stepped outside to greet the sheriff.

"You got him, did you? He still in just the one piece?"

"One piece, Andy. How's Bronc doing."

"He's deep into repentance, saying they never intended to do what they done and it's all Slade's fault. Myself, I might forgive them the theft of less than fifty dollars, not that it was my money nor my option to forgive, but I take my kidnapping personal and serious. And the fella whose horse they took, he just didn't see any humor in that at all. You want help bringing Slade in here?"

"Slade needs the doctor pretty bad. I'm thinking I'll have to handle that first. That is, if the doctor will even let me bring another prisoner to him. I'm thinking he might have seen enough of me for the next while."

RORY LISTENED as the doctor expelled several big breaths through the small gap in his upper front teeth, causing a whistling sound as he looked Slade over.

"Don't even know where to start. This fella looks like he spent the night in the lion's den with no angels to look over him."

"It was something like that, Doc."

"Well, leave him with me."

"Can you get your friend that helps you sometimes to come and sit guard? I don't want this one getting up and running away."

"Elias. Yes, I'll get him. But this one's not going anywhere. Not for a while, anyway. A dose of ether will have him sailing around the moon in just a few minutes. You go now. Leave him with me. He'll be here when you get back."

5

SONIA AND RORY WERE SITTING TOGETHER, WORKING ON coffee and a slice of apple pie each. Sonia was on her afternoon break from serving in Ma's dining room.

Rory had nothing special on his mind, but Sonia certainly did. Her problem was in how to move the conversation into her preferred direction. Rory had been great company when they were alone on their several buggy rides after church on Sundays. But when he was in his sheriff mode, as he was at the moment, he could be silent and unresponsive, mentally trying to sort out something that faced him. Something he needed an answer to. Those moods pushed all else into the darkness of the future.

Just as Sonia was forming the first word of her suggestion for another buggy ride, Rory, unaware, said, "Being a two-day ride from the nearest lawyer's and judge's court is a real problem. When Ivan and I captured those rustlers last fall, one ended up dead and the other injured. Ivan suggested that no one would much care if the second one was to be buried up on the mountain, along with the first. It would make our jobs easier and kind of clean things up neat and done."

"That's my brother for you. He always has an answer. It may not be a good or wise answer, but he will have an answer."

"Yes, well, anyway, we brought the man down, and he's behind bars in state prison for a good, long stretch. Now, I don't know what to do with these two. Neither one can sit a horse for two days, and I don't want to be saddled with a wagon, nor the trouble of holding them safe overnight on the trail."

Forgetting about the buggy ride for this time, Sonia suggested, "Perhaps you should take the stage. You'll still have an overnight stop, but you won't be driving a wagon."

"That's probably an idea worth thinking about. I'll have to see if they'll let me on with two prisoners."

Sonia thought she might have found her opening.

"Do you think you'd be leaving right soon, or will you still be here on Sunday?"

Rory smiled, seeing through her question.

"I'll check with the stage when it comes through tomorrow and let you know. What did you have in mind?"

"Well, I was just thinking that I don't really find making a picnic lunch too much trouble. And perhaps, if it doesn't rain, we could go down along the river some-where. Now that you've been down that way chasing bank robbers and such, perhaps you spotted a nice place to stop for lunch."

Right at that time, a group of townsfolk came into the dining room for an early dinner. Sonia rose to her feet and said, "Back to work."

"Thanks for sitting with me. I enjoyed it, and I'll let you know what my plans are right soon."

WHILE RORY WAITED for the doctor's decision on the treatment and recovery of Slade, he rode out to the Double J. After enjoying his usual family gathering and a night's sleep, he rose while it was still dark. He required only a few minutes in the barn to have the big bay gelding saddled and ready. Rory returned from the tack room with his bedroll and carbine to find his uncle George stroking the animal's neck, waiting for an explanation for the early departure.

"One prisoner in the jail and one at the doctor's house. I need to be there. Probably should have stayed in town. Be better sometimes if the Double J was further from town so's I wouldn't be so tempted to ride out every chance I get. My work is in town or out in the county. Pretty soon, guilt is going to get under my skin, so I had best tie this bedroll in place and point this horse south."

HE WENT FIRST to the small marshal's office only to find the door standing open. He quickly swung off his horse, dropped the reins, and rushed across the boardwalk. Fearing for the well-being of Andy, who he had left in charge of the prisoner, he called out but received no response. He stepped carefully through the door with his Colt leading the way. Andy lay on the floor in a crumpled heap, with dried blood edging the trickle that ran down his forehead and cheek from a swelling slash below his hairline. Quickly glancing further into the small office, he saw no one. The cell door was open.

Holstering the gun, he bent to Andy. There was no response to his name being called out, but it was clear he was still breathing. And still bleeding. Hoping the young man was simply knocked unconscious, and seeing no more serious wounds, he stepped back and out the door. As he neared his horse, Tippet, the liveryman, hollered out, "What's happening, Sheriff?"

"Andy's down. Not bad, I'm thinking, but you need to come and watch over him. I'm going over to Doc's."

With no further talk or explanation, he swung aboard the gelding. With a short fifteen-second run, he was at the doctor's small house. The sun was casting its early glow onto the scene, but Rory could see there was a lamp burning in the back room of the little house. Not bothering to knock, he rushed inside, calling out for the doctor.

"In here!" came from the office portion of the house. Rory moved quickly, again lifting his Colt to lead the way. He found the doctor on his knees, dabbing a bloody skull wound on Elias.

"What happened? I found the same thing over at the marshal's office."

"What happened is your prisoner is gone, although I don't know how he managed it, as cut up as he was, and still recovering from the ether. Ether is a wonder drug when it comes to painless surgery, but there's nothing easy about what it does to the stomach as the patient is waking up. How your guy managed to overcome Elias in the condition he was in is beyond me. But he's gone, and here lies my friend. I dragged him in from the yard, but I'm going to need help getting him on the table. Give a lift here."

6

A COUPLE OF HOURS LATER, ELIAS AND ANDY WERE
drinking coffee and sharing the stories of their mutual
bad night, or early morning if you prefer the absolute
truth. With the risk of more danger nowhere evident
and with Doc's patches looking strangely similar on both
men, they were somehow able to see the humor in the
situation. Ma Gamble came from the kitchen to sit with
them for a few minutes, wanting the story firsthand.
Rory had already listened carefully to what each man
experienced and had taken notes.

Elias glanced sheepishly at Ma, wishing none of this
had happened. It was more difficult to tell this good
woman of his carelessness than it was to tell the sheriff.
When he finally got his courage perked up, he said,
"Totally my fault. I'm ashamed to have to say that. Might
just as well come out with the other truth too. I'm no
longer getting old. I am already old. Old and often
wishing to believe better of my fellow man than what
they deserve. I moved out here from the big, busy, dirty
city back east. Came for the peace and quiet and the

forever view of the mountains. But mostly for the peace and quiet. Doc, he and I play a game of checkers from time to time, and when he asked me to sit night-watch last year after he had seen a busier than normal day, I couldn't see a problem. Sat watch many a night since. Came to where I thought I'd seen it all. Sick folks. New mothers. Bullet wounds. Mostly a bit of everything. Never once had a hand raised against me.

"Was still some time before the dawn this morning when that Slade, he who was all dog chewed, he wakes up from whatever it was Doc gave him so's he could work on him. Saw me sitting there half snoozing, with the lamp turned low, and he says he needs to get to the outhouse. Feeling mighty upset in his stomach. Doc told me he'd wake up hurting and sick. Probably have a killer headache. So, I wasn't surprised.

"Slade, he was so cut up and banged around I didn't think he'd hardly have strength to get outside, let alone tackle me and make for the hills. He put on a great show, needing my help to get out and down the path. Of course, I waited, staying close by but still giving the man some privacy. The retching I heard from him could not be anything but real. He was sick, as Doc had said he would be. But he was far tougher than I ever expected.

"I made the mistake of standing to the offside of the door so that when Slade pushed it open, it hit me full on the face, knocked me to my knees. No doubt he had hoped for that result. He had pushed the door about as hard as anyone could. Far as Doc could tell, when he found me an hour later, Slade, he thunked me on the forehead with a fist-sized rock that was still lying there and made his getaway. His first stop was obviously at the marshal's office, where he somehow surprised Andy here, and treated him to the same ministration as what he laid on me. He released his friend. Took off for the hills, I'm guessing.

"End of the story is that both men are gone. Slade must have pulled on some old clothes that had been folded into a box in the marshal's office for giving away. Grabbed up their own gun belts, he and Bronc, plus a couple of long guns from the rack, snuck their own mounts from under Tippet's nose and rode away."

Ma listened carefully, pushed back her chair, and stood. She looked from one man to another, a wry grin on her face.

"There's this about it, fellas, you have a story to tell your grandkids someday."

Elias returned the grin, saying, "That's not likely for me, seeing as how I've never been married, nor fathered any kids."

Ma didn't figure that conversation needed any further detailed discussion.

RORY SADDLED up immediately after seeing that Doc had the situation under control and that neither Elias nor Andy was in any danger of further complications from their head wounds.

How either escaped prisoner could ride far in their condition was a mystery. They were either tougher than they had first appeared or desperate beyond Rory's understanding.

If what Bronc had said was true, that the bank robbery was a spur-of-the-moment decision, and they had never done anything like that before, the desperation seemed somewhat excessive. But what if the men were lying? What if they were criminals of long-standing? That would make their reckless escape more under-standable.

Where to look? That was the first question on the sheriff's mind. It seemed possible that they might take to the river gorge in a repeat of their run after the robbery. There would now be a familiarity to the area that may appeal to Slade, who Rory accepted as the leader of the two. At the thought of a leader, Rory's mind went back to Slade's words, the words that caused Rory to make the decision to shoot Slade's gun out of his hand. *"You're right on that one thing anyway, Bronc. He's for sure no use to me now. So far as that goes, you're not much use to me either."*

Would Slade really shoot his partner? It had looked awful much as if he would. So, what about now? Had Slade broken Bronc out just so no court could get a confession out of him? A confession that may go hard on Slade as well.

These thoughts ran through Rory's mind as he rode hard for the river. A careful scan of both sides of the trail showed no new markings. There was no turned-up sod as if from running horses. Rory circled his horse back to the north and through town at an easy trot. Folks were beginning to crowd the boardwalks as the town came alive.

Browning was sweeping the walkway in front of his mercantile. Rory lifted a hand in greeting and meant to ride on, but Browning called him over.

"Just now heard what happened, Sheriff. I don't know if it means anything or not, but just before daybreak, I heard horses heading to the north. Couldn't see how many and thought nothing about it. Lots of folks up early and doing around here."

He pointed with a raised thumb at the second-story window facing the street.

"No reason you should know, Rory, but that's my bedroom right up there. Hear most things happening in the street come nighttime."

The information didn't really mean much, but Rory thanked the man and bid him farewell, continuing on to the north. He passed the gate to the Double J, allowing his eyes to scan right and left, hoping to see new tracks while also hoping the tracks wouldn't turn toward his home ranch. He didn't need fugitives hiding out among the buildings or the few bush-filled hollows that dotted the Double J pastures.

It wasn't until he had ridden a full five miles further that he saw the disturbed grass on the west side of the trail. Early morning dew was still clinging to some of the bent grass. Other grass had found the strength to stand back up. Rory guided his gelding along the trail, slowing as he approached a small hollow ringed by pine trees and miscellaneous undergrowth. He knew from previous times that the hollow was bottomed by a pleasant little pond that was fed from an uphill trickle. Beyond the pond and the hillside it sheltered under, stood a much larger and higher rocky slope. Although there was access to the west and the series of valleys and progressively higher foothills, from this exact spot, there was no opening suitable for horses. Neither of the fugitives was in any condition to move out on foot. That meant they were most likely lying low, beside the pond.

Rory swung to the side and entered the pines, using them for cover as he approached. Fearing exposure if he rode closer, he stepped down and tied his horse. He lifted his carbine from the scabbard and proceeded on foot, stepping as carefully and silently as possible. As he broke through a shelter of undergrowth, bringing the pond into clear view, he saw the two tied horses but nothing more. He dropped to a kneeling position and studied the area around the pond. There was no smoke that would indicate a fire. There was no one right beside the pond. The horses were resting peacefully, sensing no alarm. The men had to be further back into the pines and behind the undergrowth.

Rory began a wide circle of the area, peering carefully into every likely hiding place. The growth was too thick to move in the duck walk he had used on previous occasions, so he stood and moved from tree to tree, hoping to minimize his risk of being shot. He saw no movement and heard no noise.

It wasn't until he was right against the hillside that he saw the two men. One was stretched out on the grass, holding to a fetal position, one hand gripping his opposite shoulder. That would be Bronc, suffering as if his shoulder wound had broken open again. The second man was leaning against the bole of a large cottonwood, a tree that loved the water and was often a signal that groundwater was available to the traveler that didn't mind a bit of digging. That would be Slade. Although Slade's eyes were open, moving from side to side, as if he had heard something, neither man was totally alert or sensitive to his surroundings.

They looked sick. Done in. Beat. The little bit of compassion Rory still maintained for the defeated rose to the surface but didn't last long. These were fugitives. Bank robbers. Kidnappers. Horse thieves. These were, and could be again, dangerous men.

Rory was unsure what his next move should be. Bronc was clearly out of it, although he had a handgun lying close by. Slade might still have some fight in him. Hoping a shock might bring Slade around to the sheriff's way of thinking, Rory steadied his Winchester against a small cottonwood. Holding still while he sleeved sweat from his eyes, he took careful aim. He squeezed the trigger gently, holding his sights on the bark of the cottonwood just inches from Slade's head. Bark flew in every direction, much of it scattering itself against Slade's face, blinding him for just a moment. The thunder of the heavy shot was a startling noise in the quiet morning. Several birds bolted into the air, and then the pond fell to silence.

Slade, frantic and still brushing the bark fragments from his face, lifted his Colt from the ground, pointing it in the general direction he had heard the shot come from. Before he could locate the shooter, Bronc spoke. He had his own Colt pointed at his partner.

"Slade, you pull that trigger, I'll shoot you myself. I'm done up, and so are you, only you're not smart enough to figure that out. Now, put the gun down."

Slade brushed his eyes some more while he continued to hold the gun. But finally, his hand lowered, and the weapon slipped from his fingers. Bronc held his Colt steady until Slade was no longer armed. Only then did he lower his own hand and say, "I expect that's you out there, Sheriff."

"That's me alright, boys. I'm coming in, and I don't want to see any threats from either of you."

Rory stepped from the cover of the forest and moved forward to where he could be heard without raising his voice.

"You aren't looking so good, fellas. I'm thinking you were better off right where you were, in the lockup and the doctor's office. I'm going to step forward and relieve you of your hardware, and then we'll get you on your horses. If you wish to be under the grass tomorrow, why, all you have to do is reach for a weapon. I'll shoot you and make you as dead as you'll ever be. I'll not enjoy it, but on the other hand, I'll not particularly care either. But it's sure I've taken about enough of your nonsense."

The fugitives' horses were grazing close to the pond. It appeared as if the men had slipped off their mounts and flopped to the ground. They hadn't bothered to tether them or loosen the saddles. Rory stepped toward the men, relieved them of their Colts, and then took up the reins of a big, black gelding. He remembered from the time by the river that it was the horse Bronc had been riding. He walked the animal over to where Bronc was stretched out on the grass and dropped the reins.

"Come on, Bronc. Let's get you aboard. I have no intention of lifting you, so you've got it to do."

He stood by, holding his carbine on Slade while Bronc struggled with what Rory figured was probably the last of his strength. Slade sat where he was, his eyes open, watching every move the sheriff made. He offered no resistance when his turn came to stand and rise to the saddle. Rory stood far enough away to be out of reach in case of a last-moment flare of bravery by Slade. Bronc was barely able to hold his head up, so there was no danger from that direction.

When they were all mounted and the horses were steadied down after the fumbling of the two fugitives as they rose to their saddles, Rory said, "Lead out, Slade. I'm not letting you get behind me, so I can't lead those animals. If you kick the horse into a run, there'll be a dead man in the saddle. But I'm thinking you already know that."

Looking around the small pond and the light forest surrounding it, Rory said, "You men picked a nice spot to rest in, even if you weren't very well hidden."

"We weren't exactly hiding," answered Slade. "We

were kind of waiting for you. Or for someone. We could go no further, and we knew it."

"You could have turned back to the jailhouse."

Slade glanced over his shoulder. "I thought of it but just couldn't bring myself to do it. Just couldn't."

"I might even understand that, although I have no sympathy for you. You two caused a lot of harm and trouble in just a few hours. And caused me to ride many a mile. There's sheriffs that would have shot you down by the river that first time. It would be a lot easier. With a bit more experience with your types, the types that are a waste of space on this earth, I might someday get to that point."

The remainder of the ride into town was taken in silence. When they pulled up to the rail in front of the small marshal's office, Andy was sitting in the chair on the boardwalk, his head bandaged and a coffee cup in his hand. He did not look happy, but he perked up a bit at the sight of the two prisoners.

"Got them, did you, Sheriff?"

Rory let the question slide past. The evidence spoke for itself.

"You up to helping me get these two out of their saddles, Andy?"

Without a word, Andy rose to his feet, stepped off the boardwalk, still carrying his coffee mug, reached for Slade's dog-chewed arm that was hanging loosely by his side, and pulled. The would-be bank robber awakened from his half-stupor and screamed as he slid from the saddle. Slade dropped to the dust of the road in a heap and lay there whimpering in pain. Andy made to reach for Bronc, but Rory quickly said, "Perhaps you should leave this one for me."

Andy went back to his chair and sat down, leaving

the moaning prisoner lying in the dust of the road. He still had a half cup of coffee that he hoped to continue enjoying. Rory studied Slade for a moment and then glanced back at Andy, thinking, *that's a man who's taken about all he intends to take.*

Tippet heard Slade's scream and looked across the space separating his livery from the marshal's office. "You need help over there, Sheriff?"

He was already walking toward where the commotion was taking place. Others were looking on from nearby.

"I guess I could handle it, Tippet, but if you feel up to it, you might try to get that one on his feet." He was pointing with his chin at Slade, who was making as if to crawl away.

When the men were locked down safely, Rory thanked Tippet again and then took a seat beside Andy. As Tippet led the horses toward his livery, Rory and Andy sat in silence for a minute before Rory chuckled. "I have to say, you got the job done with Slade, Andy. What I asked you to do, is what I mean. I'm not sure your method would be recommended in the sheriff's training manual."

"I never heard of any sheriff's training manual."

"Well, neither have I, for that matter."

7

For the first time, Rory had access to everything Slade and Bronc had on their persons or in the saddlebags. Sharing the single cell, lying on two cots, the men were trying to sleep. Entering the cell, Rory kicked each of them on the foot to waken them.

"Empty out your pockets, fellas. Turn them inside out so I can see you got it all. Shirt pockets too. And money belts if you're wearing one. If you should happen to forget about a knife or a holdout gun, I would be an unhappy man. That, in turn, would have the result of you becoming unhappy. Or dead."

He had stripped their gun belts from them before leaving the pond.

When that chore was completed, he double-checked the lock on the cell door, dropped the gather on the desktop, and walked to the livery. Rory went directly to the tack room and lifted the saddlebags and bedrolls from the prisoners' saddles, carrying them back to the marshal's office. He unrolled the bedrolls, finding nothing of value. He dumped them both on the ground outside the back door. He figured they hadn't seen a scrubbing with soap and water in many a month. As far as that went, judging by looks and odor, the blankets just might be past their redemption point.

Like so many other occasions and so many different circumstances, the dirty bedrolls reminded him of his father and how often the two of them had cleaned and scrubbed their own blankets in their Idaho gold camp. *Wouldn't tolerate the likes of this*, was the thought that flitted through Rory's mind as he carried the stinking blankets out of the office.

The saddlebags, dumped out into two separate piles on the desk, proved to be of more value. Along with the few dollars in coins taken from the men's pockets, there was a roll of bills in each saddlebag. The men were nowhere near as broke and hungry as they had first implied. Glancing at the men through the iron bars, holding a roll of bills in each hand, Rory said, "Been a lot better all the way around, fellas, if you'd gone to Ma's and paid her for a plate of side meat and eggs. Then you could have just ridden off. Headed for somewhere offering more than fifty dollars in small bills and change from the bank's day drawer and a two-by-twice cell. Too bad. For all of us."

Digging further, Rory found a couple of letters in each bag and some other private correspondence. He looked through it all and then turned to the cell with a grin.

"Slade Duhamel and Bronc Liken. Well, well, fellas. I don't know what drew you to our little village. From what I've read in the newspapers, you two are into bigger things. Yes. Yes, of course, I've heard of you. Didn't twig until I read your last names on these letters. Even way out here, some news does manage to penetrate from time to time. There seems to be a toss-up about you two. Which of you is the nastiest piece of work, and what state wants you the most. I'll let others answer those questions. Me, I'd just as soon as never hear your names again."

Rory went outside and sat back down beside Andy. He studied the young man, who was in truth older than Rory, and asked, "Can you sit here another short while? I have to make some inquiries. I'll be back just as soon as I can."

"I'll stay."

"Please don't shoot the prisoners, even though I'm sure they deserve it."

"I promise."

"I'll have you sit inside then, where you can watch their every move."

Andy moved inside while Rory walked to the mercantile.

"Afternoon, Mr. Browning. I've got a couple of sure enough fugitives in the lockup. If I can clear it with the stage company, I'm going to put them on the next run south. Take them down to the big city. I'll be away for most of the week. Is it all right with the town if I leave Andy in charge of the marshal's office?"

"You do what you think best, Rory. You haven't made any mistakes yet that I can pin my mind on."

Rory went from there to the dining room. He had missed both breakfast and lunch. And he wanted to talk to Sonia. But the lady didn't get a chance to sit with Rory until he was nearly finished with his meal. She brought a cup of coffee for herself and flopped tiredly onto a chair across from him.

"Busy today?"

"You could say that and double it. Ma hasn't been off

her feet all day, and this is the first I've taken a break since seven this morning. I don't know where everyone is coming from. Does no one cook at home anymore? And what's this I hear about you had to recapture those two prisoners?"

"Hardly worth the telling. But I have to get them down to the city. I plan to use the stage, but I need help. I'm thinking to ask Andy to ride up tomorrow and fetch Ivan. If it was about time for your break, this would be an opportunity for you."

"Why aren't you going up yourself?"

"I don't feel good about leaving the prisoners to Andy. As it is, he's only doing me a favor until the bank opens again. And riding up to the I-5 is considerably less risky than minding two wanted men in a hammered-together excuse for a jail. If you were ready for another visit, I'm sure you would be safe with Andy. He's a good guy and far tougher than I expected a bank clerk to be."

With a strange look on her face, Sonia stood, picked up her coffee mug, and said, "I'll let you know."

If the troubled look on Sonia's face had registered in Rory's mind, he found a way to brush it aside while he considered, again, the problems of being so far from the city.

TWO MORNINGS LATER, Rory and Ivan had secured the two prisoners in the back seat of the stagecoach, their hands and feet tied firmly. With the rope from their feet trailing to a metal bracket that held the seat in place. Rory had convinced two of the three passengers who came in on the stage to lay over in Stevensville for one night and connect with the next stage through. Catching a glimpse of the rough-looking men being led from the small jail, those two had readily agreed. The third man, saying he had no time to waste, climbed to the high seat and rode along with the driver.

Rory and Ivan took turns throughout the two-day run and the one long night in the stopping place to rest and sleep while the other held a twelve-gauge double-barreled shotgun loosely in the direction of the back seat. The prisoners said not one word on the long, wearying trip, having been warned ahead of time by Ivan that he wanted no talk.

Arriving in the big city, the driver went off his prescribed route to stop in front of the county administration office. Rory stepped down and stretched to take the kinks out of his body. He then opened the door to the office, walked wordlessly past Bertha, the officiously unpleasant office clerk, ignoring her efforts to waylay him, and went directly to the office of Oscar Cator.

Too tired to trust himself to words of greeting, Rory dropped both sets of saddlebags on the desk and asked, "Do you think anyone still wants Slade Duhamel and Bronc Liken?"

The county administrator's reaction caught Rory completely off guard. He leaned back in his chair, swung one foot to the desktop, folded his hands behind his head, and laughed. Finally, he said, "Caught you some bad ones, did you? I hope you buried them deep so's we have no more trouble with them. Been problems most everywhere you can think of with those boys. Be like them two to find some way to clamber back out of the grave and go to raising Cain again."

"Come with me."

Oscar dropped his grin, swung his feet to the floor, and put on his hat. With Rory leading, the two of them were soon on the street, both men ignoring the seriously flustered Bertha. Ivan saw them coming and swung the stage door open. He stepped to the sidewalk himself and stood back. Oscar stuck his head into the doorway and studied the two pathetic men holding down the back seat.

"Well, hello, Slade. Bronc. Imagine meeting the two of you here. Where have you been the past year or so? I've missed hearing about your escapades. Now that I eye you a little closer, boys, don't either of you look so good. Rough life you chose for yourselves. Well, let's get you down to the lockup."

He stepped into the stage and took a seat. "Lockup's a ways away, fellas. We might just as well ride."

Rory climbed in, followed by Ivan, who Rory finally introduced to Oscar. With no instructions, the stage driver pulled back into traffic and headed down a side street. Seeing a question forming in Rory's mind, Oscar said, "No worries, my young friend. Tate knows where to go. He's brought along more than just one or two bad ones over the years."

When Slade and Bronc were ushered into the lockup and out of Rory's care, he felt a great burden lift. Oscar said, "Thank you, Sheriff. And you too, Ivan. If you want to come to the office, we'll get the particulars of this adventure sorted out and written down. The federal marshals will want first crack at your prisoners, but we'll need some detail."

"Tomorrow morning is soon enough, Oscar. Right now, I need a meal, a bath, and about three days of sleep. I'm thinking Ivan might feel just about the same."

THAT EVENING, after the baths and the afternoon sleep, Rory and Ivan were in the dining room taking on a good feeding. Rory grinned at Ivan, saying, "This is the exact spot where you met the Strombeck sisters, Allie and Polly. Sure be something if they happened along again and with us having nothing at all to do and all evening to do it in."

The look on Ivan's face said he would be just as content if what Rory was suggesting didn't happen. Rory grinned a bit before saying, "We were so busy with our prisoners that I forgot to remember to ask you. I'm assuming Andy and Sonia arrived alright."

"I guess she was alright. Looked alright anyway. But I can never figure her out. Her or the other few females I've met, either. I asked who she was with and where you were. She looked at me as if she hated the whole world and stormed into the house. Never did speak with her."

"I can't altogether figure them out either, Ivan. Maybe it's best that we can't."

TWO DAYS LATER, after a morning spent answering Oscar Cator's questions, the two men arrived back in Stevensville. Little had been said on the long ride, but an idea had been working its way through a maze of questions in Rory's mind the whole way. The stage pulled to a stop in front of the hotel, and they stepped out, calling their thanks up to the driver. Rory said, "I'm riding out to the ranch for just the one night. It's too late to head up to the I-5. Why don't you take the cot over in the marshal's office? It's as comfortable as the hotel beds. Ma Gamble will feed you and charge it up to the sheriff's account. I'll pay it off at the end of the month."

While he was talking, he reached into his pocket and pulled out a roll of bills. He peeled off two tens and held them out to Ivan. "For your help. And thanks."

"That's a lot of money. You taking that from your own pocket?"

"Well, it's from my pocket in one sense, but it's not my money. I kept the rolls of money Slade and Bronc had on them same as I did with those two you and I chased through the hills. I cleared it all with Oscar Cator. It saves me paying and then trying to collect back from the county. Bertha handles the expense claims and the wages. I'd rather not face that. This way, I pay myself, too, on the trust Oscar has in me. You take the money and thanks. If you hang around a bit tomorrow, I may see you when I come back to town."

On his way to the Double J, Rory stopped again at the mercantile, leaving Mr. Browning with a suggestion.

8

IVAN WAS TAKING BREAKFAST THE NEXT MORNING WHEN
Mr. Browning and Hip Dawson, Stevensville's mayor,
came in. It surprised Ivan when the two men came
directly to his table and sat down without invitation.
With his fork held halfway between the plate and his
mouth, he stilled himself, staring intently at his visitors.

"I believe you to be Mr. Ivan Ivanov. That is, if I
understood the sheriff correctly. I'm Browning, from the
mercantile, just down the street. I know your parents
from their dealings in the store. And, of course, we all
know Sonia. This is Hip Dawson. He's the town mayor.
And more importantly, if your tastes run to a sweet
tooth, he's the town baker. I'm led to understand that
you have been assisting the sheriff. You have the town's
thanks for that. That will also mean that you know
something of the sordid past regarding our town
marshal's office. We're still trying to sort that mess out.
Now, Hip has something he wishes to talk with you
about."

61

As this short conversation was going on, Lydia Andres, the town woman who filled in at the café when Sonia was away, had laid a cup of coffee before the two town councilors. Hip Dawson said, "Thank you, Lydia." and turned back to Ivan.

"Ivan, I need to get back to the bakery, so I'll cut this short. We're just a small town here, but we're growing. This is good country. Ranchland and uphill country, both. Outside folks are starting to see the merits of settling here. Back when both Browning and I could name off every person in town or in the country close around, we felt we didn't need a marshal. We hammered that simple marshal's office and its single cell together with whipsawed lumber, hoping we would never have to use it. Now, we recognize those days are past. We need a marshal. A better man than the last one. The one you had a big hand in running down. The thing is, Ivan, we'd like to offer you the job. It pays about the same wage as a working cowboy gets, and you have your own living space over at the office. Ma will feed you, and the town will pick up that cost. Or, if you prefer, you could eat down at Sonny's from time to time. That's the cantina down at the south end of town. We'll pick up that cost, too, but we don't pay for drinks."

With that said, and Hip now silent, Browning let the silence continue for a moment while he studied Ivan, looking for a reaction. Finally, he said, "Does that interest you, Ivan?"

Ivan laid down his fork, picked up his coffee mug, and leaned away from the table. He held the mug to his mouth while he studied the two men, but didn't sip. He'd had little to do with town men, or women, either one, until Rory had dragged him away from the remote ranch and into the edges of the lawing business. He hardly knew how to respond to this sudden offer, but he knew he had to say something. He took a drink of coffee and set the mug down.

"I've never lived in a town. I know cattle, grass, forest, wildlife, and a bit about the dangers of weather and livestock diseases. I know nothing of town life."

"But you know right from wrong. Rory has attested to that. And you have a firm opinion on the matter. Now, you think on our offer. You talk it over with Rory, knowing that if you take the job, any one of us will help you meet the town folk and learn the ropes. And as we go along, we'll figure out just what all the position includes. But both Hip and I have to get back to work. We'll hope to get your decision in the next day or two. Talk to Ma too. She's on the town council, and she's a wise woman."

The men returned to their businesses, and Ivan sat alone for another few minutes with thoughts he had never struggled with before working their way through his mind.

When each of her patrons had their meals before them, Ma came from the kitchen and joined Ivan. She studied him until he felt she was looking right through him. She finally asked, "Is your future going to be on an uphill ranch, Ivan, or have you been thinking further afield? Rory has had you down to the city twice now. You've chased fugitives through those hills you know so well, and you've spent some time in town. I'm sure, in your mind, you've contrasted all that with the quietness of the ranch.

"I've never seen any of those uphill grassed valleys, but Sonia has told me about the beauty of the place. The only problem for you and Sonia both, is that you don't own any of that beauty for yourselves, nor the cattle to turn a piece of it into a profitable holding. And how are you going to get the funds to start your own operation if you don't set out to do something on your own?

"I think you would be a good marshal, but you talk it over with Rory and with Sonia when she comes back to town."

~

RORY DIDN'T SHOW up back in town that day. Ivan spent the time walking the main street, looking into one business after the other. He then saddled up and rode the side streets. It wasn't far out of the way to ride down to the north bank of the river. There he dismounted in a sun-warmed spot, watered his horse, and sat, leaning against an old, peeling, and badly disfigured poplar tree where he could see the river and the land to the south. Enjoying the noonday warmth, he figured on everything that had happened to him since Rory Jamison had come into his life. If nothing else could be said about those times, it was at least true that they hadn't been boring.

Now, contrary to his own thinking and what old Kiril, that mysterious loner with connections to the same old-world country his family had come from, had warned him about, he found he liked the town. He liked Rory, too, and enjoyed being with him. His sister, on the other hand, appeared to be angry at the sheriff and perhaps at himself as well. He didn't dwell on those mysterious facts. He didn't understand women and didn't really expect to ever understand them.

Ivan soaked in the sun for an hour, thinking thoughts he had never allowed himself to think before. Thoughts of independence, of leading his own unobstructed life. It wasn't that his father was a hard or difficult man. It was that he was the owner and boss of the I-5 Ranch. He had his ways, but he seemed to be missing any tendencies to change in his makeup at all. If something was fixed in Grigor Ivanov's mind, it was fixed and had become virtually immovable. In town or riding with Rory, Ivan was finding a sense of freedom he had never before known or even dreamed about. Although his new thoughts troubled him at first, he had been forced to let go of a few of his own firm beliefs, including his first opinion of Rory.

Further to all this was the truth that the I-5 was unlikely to ever grow to where it could pay either Ivan or his brother a wage that would set them financially free. Although they never talked about it, Ivan thought his sister, working for Ma in the dining room, was making more spendable money than he was on the ranch. Thought led to thought until his mind was like a ball of earthworms dug out of the kitchen garden in the warming days of spring, leading to a jumble of confusing options and hardly knowing the head of one from the tail of another.

Hunger finally put him back in the saddle, heading toward town at a slow, worry-free walk. He had seen the hand-painted sign for a small establishment that morning. He knew it to be a lower-end eating house, so he headed that way. Entering, he was surprised to see the room was divided between the café and a bar or small saloon on the other side. Never having drank himself, he hadn't considered that there was no saloon in town. But, for sure, there had been more than enough of them in the city. He had been introduced to that side of life the first time he accompanied Rory, taking Mike Wasson, the previous town marshal, now a prisoner himself, to the city and jail. Rory wasn't a drinker, but he wanted to talk with a cowboy who had helped him before, so they visited a couple of saloons looking for the man. Neither the drink nor the atmosphere had appealed to Ivan.

After a jalapeno-saturated, sinus-clearing lunch that fell a good bit short of Ma's offerings, he made his way back to the marshal's office.

The next morning, early, Rory rode back into town, shaved and looking rested. He had left the big bay gelding at the ranch in favor of a smaller black animal. He rode directly to the marshal's office. Ivan was sitting in the morning sun, just as if he was an old hand at these things. He was holding a coffee cup and sucking on a toothpick. Rory rode up to the hitch rack and grinned, looking down at the man.

"You look right at home there, my friend. I'm taking it that they offered you the job, and you accepted."

"Half of that is true. They offered me the job. I have yet to decide."

"Well, let's talk about it as we ride up to the I-5. I promised Sonia that I would come for her the first chance I got."

With a sly grin, Ivan said, "You are just exactly one day too late. The banker rode up yesterday. They were back in town in the afternoon. Both of them were smiling, but they said nothing at all to me, so I don't know what they were looking so happy about."

Rory involuntarily turned his eyes toward the dining room and then back to Ivan. The only thing he could think to say was, "I thought the bank would be reopened by now."

"It is, but somehow the young banker talked Jesse Ambrewster into giving him the time."

Rory wasn't completely convinced that was a good thing, but he let it go. He had no real choice in any case.

As he was thinking of other things, one small portion of his mind was accepting the possibility that this would not be a good time to discuss a picnic after church.

He glanced once more toward the dining room before saying, "I have a small bit of banking to do myself, Ivan. You sit tight for a few minutes, and then we'll discuss that offer over coffee."

ENTERING THE BANK, Rory said, "Morning, Andy. Jesse in?"

Before Andy could answer, they both heard, "Come in, Sheriff. I'd as soon as not stay seated. Let you do the walking."

Rory entered the back office and shook hands with the banker.

"I'd say you're looking almost as good as new there, Jesse. A bit of rest and the doctor's treatments have brought you right around again."

"Well, it was both of those things, plus the good food and care Ma Gamble brought up to the house. She's a caring woman, that one. I guess I never saw her that way before."

Rory smiled at what he suspected might not have been included in those few words. Instead of commenting, he said, "I thought I should come by and bring you up-to-date on the bank robbers."

The telling took only a few minutes. Much of the story was already known around town. Andy had relayed as much as he knew to his boss, repeating it to Ma Gamble. From there, it seemed to spread on the wind, reaching every back door and listening ear.

Andy, thought Rory, *seems to be just about everywhere these days.*

On the way out of the bank, Rory held out two ten-dollar bills. "Your pay for the time you put in at the jail-house, Andy. And again, thanks for helping out."

"No trouble. And thank you. For the pay, I mean."

9

RORY AND IVAN WERE SITTING IN FRONT OF THE marshal's office discussing the town's offer to Ivan when the sound of pounding hoofbeats broke into the silence. They both looked up to see a rider heeling his sweating mount into a final quarter-mile effort as they approached the town. Rory rose to his feet, suspecting that the rider was coming with news. He stood there until the rider was within one hundred yards and then stepped off the boardwalk with his one arm raised in a signal to stop.

"You the sheriff?" the man hollered.

"I am. What's happening?"

"Sheriff Anthony Clare said I should come and get you. He needs your help. There's an almighty big fuss going on a few miles out. Seems those prisoners you hauled down to the city were a part of a larger gang. They somehow got broke out of jail and are on the run. Running for the rails, I'm thinking. Sheriff Clare and a couple of others think they have them in sight, but they're outnumbered. How soon can you be ready to ride?"

And just that easily a man's plans for the day, and perhaps his life, are changed. A visit and talk with Sonia, a further discussion with Ivan, a much-delayed family conflab about the future of the Double J Ranch and Rory's part in it, all were pushed to the back of the sheriff's mind as he said, "Ready this very minute."

As usual, Rory had his bedroll tied behind the saddle, and there were a few bare necessities in the saddlebags, amounting to little more than a few broken pieces of hardtack and a moldy block of cheese. But the important things, extra ammunition and two full canteens, were there on the saddle. With that, he would ride. He knew the black to be a good steady animal that loved to run but still, he wished for the big bay. No matter. He would ride.

As he untied his animal, he asked the rider, "You got a name?"

"Clem. Folks call me Clem."

"Well, Clem, you lead, I'll follow. That is, if your gelding has any run left in him. Or you could trade him for one at the livery if he's done in."

To Rory's surprise, Clem, staying with his own mount, rode to the south of town and then turned east. He had naturally thought the fugitives would have ridden for the high country, but Clem was riding full speed into the rolling hills of the eastern ranchlands. He had no thought but to follow.

Patting his spirited gelding on the neck, Clem hollered over the sounds of the wind and the hoofbeats, "He's good for a while yet. If I have to fall back, I'll point you the way. Can't hardly get lost out on this grassland."

ONCE PAST THE TOWN, Clem swung to the northeast. Rory immediately thought of the King Ranch, but if they stayed on the chosen direction, they would skirt it a bit to the west. After a steady mile, Clem dropped to a walk to rest his animal. Riding close to the man, Rory asked, "How long ago did you leave Clare to ride for Stevensville?"

"Just over an hour ago by the sun. I've got no time-piece with me, so that's a pretty close guess."

"So, an hour heading back to your starting place. And they would have moved on from there. They'll have at least a two-hour jump on us, plus the extra miles they've made since you left them. That's a good piece of country to make up."

"It is, but perhaps not quite so much as you suppose. They were a ways from it yet, but Clare figured they were heading for some rough lands along the Platte. Says it's not much cover, but it's better than this open country. And those two you brought in were all shot up, as you well know. They'll need to rest themselves and their horses."

"When did they break out?"

"Three days ago. Almost as soon as you brought them down. They had nearly a full day on us before we located Clare and found their tracks again. Our mounts were fresher, and we made good time. Closed the gap considerably. We know that because, at one point, we saw two riders swing off to the east. Left the others, it seems."

Splitting up seemed strange to Rory. He didn't know this east country well at all, but he was fairly certain there was little cover anywhere short of Nebraska, other than that bit along the river. Any meaningful cover was far away. But as he thought of this, he wondered how settled the country was out that way. Desperate men will take desperate measures. And desperate men had been known to take hostages or otherwise cause mayhem with isolated ranchers. It was true that most settlers were able to care for themselves, up to the point where they were taken by surprise or were shot and put out of the picture. Then, their families would be at the mercy of the escapees.

Rory called out again to Clem. "Will you know the point where those two left the bunch?"

"Land don't have much for markers but right about where they turned off, there was a small gathering of brush and some few larger trees. Seemed to be leading into a valley or coulee of some sort. Might be an offshoot of the river valley. At least it was some time after we waded through a running stream. I figure that stream was winding its way to the river, less it simply dies out somewhere along the way. Don't know any name for it. And I don't know this country, so can't tell for certain sure."

"You tell me when you see the spot. Now let's pick it up again. There're miles to cover, and our friends could be in trouble."

An hour and a half later, after several times alternating between walking the horses and running them, Clem hollered, to be heard above the pound of their horses' hooves and the wind. Pointing, he said, "There. Right there. That's where the group broke up."

Rory answered, "Alright. You keep going. Do what you can to help Clare. He'll do better now with the runners broken up. That will balance the game considerably. I'll find the tracks of the other two and see what I can do about those fellas."

Rory pulled to a walk, scanning the ground for tracks, while Clem again pushed his weary animal into a slow run.

~

MILES TO THE EAST, Tex Hunter and Rob Grant, the two outlaws that had swung off the original trail, were sitting in the kitchen of the Gridley ranch house. Horace Gridley sat slumped in a chair. There was blood running from a gash above his ear, and his face was horribly abused, his nose was broken and dripping blood, and one eye was closed almost entirely, with the surrounding skin turning color. He appeared to have no fight left in him, but Rob was watching closely. You could never tell for sure about these pioneer ranchers. They were known to be tough men. Most had no quit in them that anyone ever saw.

The two men had burst into the house with guns drawn. Gridley heard them coming and armed himself with a stick of firewood, the closest thing to hand. He never wore his gun in the house, and it was well out of reach. He had managed to lay Tex on the floor with a single blow to the belly followed by one to the forehead. But those were the only blows he delivered. Rob Grant hit Gridley with a balled-up fist and followed in with the butt of his Colt and then several more blows to the face. It was all over in too few seconds to bother counting.

Grant turned around after hitting Gridley the final time, as Mrs. Gridley screamed and was about to swing the stove poker at him. He swung his hand up in protection and caught the woman by the wrist. He jerked the poker from her hand and threw it in the corner. He followed that action with a backhand swat across the woman's face, sending her reeling and falling into the corner, landing awkwardly on the woodbox.

Rapid steps were heard on the stairs and a young woman, the Gridley's twenty-year-old daughter, Julia, ran into the kitchen hollering, "Mother, what's..."

Grant saw her and said, "Just you shut up, girly. We'll not hurt you if you sit down and shut up. On the other hand, if you go to causing trouble, we may have other plans for you. Tex there, he has a liking for the women. And he ain't going to be too happy when he wakes up. So best you keep your mouth closed.

"All we want is a meal and whatever fresh horses you have on hand, and we'll be gone. You get your mother back on her feet and get whatever's close to hand and fry 'er up. We've got no time to waste."

Julia bent first to her father, who was still out cold. With assurance that he was breathing, she moved to her mother. The older woman wasn't cut or bleeding, but the backhand had clearly disoriented her. Julia said, "Come, Mother. Back on your feet. Sit here in this chair while I get some grub out of the cold pantry. I'll cook up a meal, and these men can get on their way."

Adding her strength to her mother's, Julia soon had the woman, still dizzy from the experience, safely on the chair. Julia heard her father groan and stepped over to him. Again, with her assistance and encouragement, he rose to take a seat by the side of the stove.

In the meantime, Grant had managed to get his partner on his feet and then moved to a chair beside the big table. No one spoke as Julia went to work. She glanced from time to time at her parents, her mother on her left and her father on her right. Her father was awake and staring hatred at their intruders. Catching his eye, Julia warned him with a very small shake of her head. She then, pretending to wipe the hair out of her eyes, lay her finger across her lips, indicating for her father to remain silent.

As Tex came to awareness of the situation, he glanced around the room, looking first at Gridley and then at Gridley's wife. Only then did he focus on Julia. He glared at her with lascivious eyes, causing the pretty young lady to squirm in fear.

～

RORY NEVER PRIDED himself on his tracking ability. Nevertheless, he managed to find the fresh tracks heading east. They were clear in the otherwise unbroken expanse of the ungrazed shortgrass. He followed at a good lope without losing them. But the day was quickly turning toward evening and darkness. That troubled Rory, as he knew he could do little tracking in the dark of night. A bright moon would help, but he couldn't be sure the drifting clouds would make space for that. Well, he had some time, he would keep going as long as the bent grass and scuffed soil led him onward.

He saw signs of grazing here and there, and a couple of times, passed small herds of longhorn-cross animals. And far on the horizon to the north, he twice noticed ranch buildings. There was a single, small soddy to the south, with a corral and a stand of horses off a short distance.

Coming over a small rise, after an hour of riding, two ranch layouts came in sight. One was a bit off the trail and to the south by about two miles. The other was directly east and a bit further away. Perhaps three miles. When the tracks veered to the right, heading toward the closest ranch home, Rory pulled up, staring all around, looking for a better way to approach without being seen. Back a bit to the west, he saw a small fold in the hillside. Nothing in the grassland was far off the level, but neither was it flat, as some had claimed. Turning his horse toward the fold, the best cover he could see for a man on horseback, was right before him. He slid behind the low hill and into the slight cover. He could no longer see the house, so logically, anyone at the house would not see him. He lifted the black back up to a lope.

It took only a few short minutes to ride close to the ranch layout. He stopped when he was behind a corral holding what appeared to be riding stock. Among them were two saddled animals. In the lower land, a bit further to the east, were cattle. He still couldn't see the house. But ahead, he could see a clear path to the east, with even a few stubby trees sheltering the continuing fold in the land.

Not really knowing what kind of men he was dealing with or how to approach the house without causing the ranch family's situation more harm than good, he pondered on his choices. An idea came to him. It would delay his actions by a few minutes, but it might also gain him an advantage. And it might keep the ranching family alive if it worked out. Deciding to follow through on the idea, he pushed forward, heading east while he was still hidden. A ten-minute ride put him within easy sight of the second ranch. Taking a chance that the fugitives had not come this far, he rode up to the buildings and around the small barn. A voice said, "That's far enough until you identify yourself."

Rory pulled the black to a stand and turned his head toward the voice. The man was standing in the corral, sheltered between two horses.

"Rory Jamison, sir. Deputy county sheriff."

As he spoke, he kneed the horse to a slow walk. The rancher watched his every move. Rory pulled up outside the corral fence and spoke quietly. "This your ranch, sir?"

"Now, who else's would it be? Do you see anyone else out here doing any work?"

Rory smiled at the man. "No, sir, I don't. And since I've done a good bit of that kind of work myself, I do believe I would recognize such a thing if it was to come into my view."

"Deputy sheriff? Never saw a lawman so young. You wouldn't be lying to me now, would you?"

"No, sir, I'm not lying. First thing I said when I was offered the position was that I wasn't even old enough to vote. They gave me the job anyway. Said it wasn't about voting. It was about keeping the peace and running down the few bad ones that found their way into my jurisdiction. So here I am, on the trail of some fugitives that broke jail down in the big city. You don't seem to be under any threat, so I suspect they stopped at your neighbors. I thought that when I saw their tracks heading for the yard. The two saddled horses in the corral over there must be theirs. Rather than taking a chance on making the situation worse, I hoped you might be able to tell me what I'll face over there. Is there a family? Wife? Kids?"

"That's the Horace Gridley place. His wife Dinah and his daughter Julia. Just the three of them now that the boys have grown and started their own places. Julia, she's about your age, I'd guess, although it ain't polite to ask. Horace, he's a good man. Tough. And that woman of his, Dinah, why she's a pepper pot. Tackle anything that brings a threat to the place. Kills her own rattlers. Unless they're under the gun or dead by now, they'll stand up for themselves. Wait while I saddle up, and I'll come with you."

"I appreciate the information, sir, but you stay here. You'll maybe need to protect your own place, and if I'm alone, I won't worry about shooting you by accident. There's not much light left in this day. The darker it gets, the easier it will be to come up on them. But now I see a buggy over there under the shed. I'm hoping you'll lend me that, and a horse broke to harness."

"Sure enough. What do you have in mind?"

"Something I'm still working out myself. Might work. Might not. Let's get that buggy put together."

Privately he was hoping that his ruse would at least get him a glimpse into what the family was facing. If he used the daughter in that effort, it could well have the secondary effect of getting her out of harm's way.

Making no effort to hide his approach, Rory drove the buggy up to the front garden fence at the Gridley ranch house. He tied the horse to the fence, and with a lightness he didn't feel forced into his steps and a smile on his face, he opened the gate and strode up to the porch. Commonly, country folks seldom used the front door, reserving that for company. Rory hoped his attempt to appear to have come courting would be seen as company and provide cover enough to get into the house without gunfire.

He knocked on the porch door just the once, and then, as if he was familiar enough with the family to take some liberties, he twisted the handle and let the door fall open about halfway. He called out as happily as he knew how, "Evening, folks. Lemuel here. I promised Julia a buggy ride this evening. I hope she's about ready."

He stepped into the seldom-used parlor and moved toward the kitchen. He could see the two fugitives sitting at the table, apparently waiting for whatever the two women were preparing at the stove. He thought he saw the furthest away fugitive hurriedly sliding a Colt off the table, but he couldn't be sure. Everyone in the room looked startled at his intrusion, but no one spoke. He smiled at the men and doffed his hat, as if he wasn't seeing what was obvious right before him. Ignoring the blackening eyes and the bloody shirt fronts, he said, "Oh, sorry folks, I see you've got company. Don't mean to intrude. If Julia can just grab a sweater for the cool of the evening, we'll be on our way."

Rory had purposely left his light jacket on the buggy seat. He wanted the men to see he was well-armed, and if there was gunplay, he didn't want anything in the way of his movements. Still, he made no threatening gestures. He simply stood there, waiting for the younger woman to make a move. He carried a smile that was coming close to hurting the muscles of his face. So far, the daughter had kept her back to the visitor, concentrating on something on the stove.

Finally, the older woman, obviously the mother, and who had just as obviously been hit and hurt, figuring it out, nudged her daughter and said, "You go along there, Julia. I'll finish up here. You go with Lemuel and have a nice ride. Don't be out too late."

The men looked from one to the other, but finally decided to say nothing. They had both been studying Rory, paying special attention to his gun belt and the twin .44s it carried. Clearly, there was nothing to be said or done that wouldn't fill the kitchen with lead, powder smoke, and dead bodies. And there was no telling whose bodies those would be. Best to let it alone. In any case, Rob Grant seemed to remember something he'd heard. Something about a kid lawman who carried two guns the way this kid did. If what he had heard was anywhere near the truth, he wanted nothing to do with it. They'd best let it go and get out of there themselves. But Tex was hurt and hungry. And he had been holding his eyes on the younger of the two women, letting the want in him grow to where it would soon be uncontrollable. If he didn't get a plate laid in front of him pretty quickly, there was no telling what the man might do.

Julia wiped her hands on her apron, untied it, and laid it aside. She then turned to Rory and smiled, saying, "Sorry, Lemuel, I'd forgotten that this was to be our evening for a ride. Let's go. I'm ready."

Rory was startled by her attractiveness and her joyous smile. Tall, like her mother, who stood beside her, slim and yet fully feminine, Rory found himself almost without words. To keep from sounding like a fool, he kept his mouth shut.

He followed Julia out of the house after bidding everyone good night. The two young people said nothing as they walked through the yard and climbed into the buggy. As Rory turned the rig back the way he had come, Julia waved back at the house, although there was no one in sight there to return the wave. They both remained silent until they were far enough away to speak without being heard. Only then did Rory say, "Rory Jamison, Julia. Deputy county sheriff. I want those two men, but I didn't want to tangle with them in the house with all of you there. I'm glad you saw through my ruse and cooperated. You're safe now."

"I'll know I'm safe when this is all over and those men are dead, like they deserve to be. Or at least gone."

She seemed to pause, thinking, and then said, "That was an almighty big bluff you pulled off there, mister. There was more than just the one thing that could have gone wrong. But now my folks are back there at the mercy of those two. I need to go back. There's a shotgun in the barn."

"You'll do no such a thing. You leave the fighting to me. You stay out of it." He knew she was suddenly angry. Whether at him, for his telling her what to do, or at the thought of her parents unarmed and alone, he couldn't tell. Nor did he really care, not right at the moment he didn't. Breaking into her silence, he asked, "If this was a real buggy ride, would we go this way, past the corral and down that fold in the land?"

Stiffly she said, "We could. But if you're worried about those men, I doubt if they've ever been here before or would know the difference, no matter where we go. I also doubt if they're watching. But they'll be in a rush now in case we come back with help."

"I'm going back, Julia, but you're not. As soon as we're out of sight, I'll drop to the ground, and you take the reins. You stay out here and be safe. I'll take care of the rest as best I can."

She didn't like it, but she said no more. Without a word, he passed her the reins and turned to look back at the lamplit house windows. As soon as the lighted windows disappeared as they drove down the slight grade behind the barn, Rory picked his Winchester off the buggy floor and jumped from the slowly moving rig. After a cautious but hurried walk, picking his way through the unfamiliar yard in the dark, he eased onto the back porch of the little house, dropped to his knees, and carefully crawled to the window, staying below the sight line. Only then did he remove his hat, lying it and the carbine on the porch floor, and rise high enough to see inside. It appeared as if no one had moved, although both men now had their Colts lying on the table with the muzzles pointed menacingly at Horace and Dinah Gridley.

The men were eating in a rush, scooping one forkful after another, while Julia's parents sat silently, staring at their captors. It would have been a simple thing for Rory to shoot both men, but he couldn't justify that action. He didn't want that kind of a reputation, whether he was a sheriff or not. Instead, he lifted one of the big .44s from its holster, carefully checked the loads in the slight light coming from the window, replaced his hat, and stood. There was no time to waste. The light would outline him, and there was no chance the men could miss that.

Aiming by instinct, as he usually did, he shot the Colt in front of the closest man, knocking the weapon into a spin that carried it to the floor between the two men. The ricocheting lead tore cloth and, perhaps, a bit of flesh from Rob Grant's stomach.

Window glass flew in all directions. As fast as he knew how, Rory again squeezed the trigger, this time knocking the second Colt across the table and beyond, to lay harmlessly on the floor, out of reach. The dinner plates were smashed into a scattering of pieces, mingled with bits of food, and thrown in every direction. Everyone in the room reacted to the startling shots. The fugitives jumped to their feet, knocking their chairs over in the process. Both men looked to the now broken window and automatically reached for weapons that no longer hung at their sides.

Horace Gridley jumped up and swung his fist at the closest intruder, the one who had laid a beating on him such a short time before. He delivered a solid hammerblow to the man's recently lead-grazed belly and followed that up with more damage from his hard fists.

Dinah Gridley grabbed up her trusty stove poker and swung at Tex.

Rory's vision was blocked by the outside wall of the house as he took the two steps necessary to reach the back door. He smashed through without bothering with the doorknob.

Whatever he had intended to do was unnecessary. Horace Gridley was in the process of laying a severe beating on Rob Grant. Dinah was, in turn, wielding the stove poker, and wielding it with purpose and good effect. She was whapping her man across the head time after time, as he fell first to his knees and then onto the floor. And still, she swung the poker. His ear was split to the core. Blood ran freely.

The man who had fallen under Horace Gridley's fists covered his head with his hands and struggled to his feet in a bent-over position. With a mind fixed only on escape, struggling through a roar of pain and fear, he charged into the parlor and slammed out the front door. Rory ran after him and was in time to see him met by a load of buckshot as he reached for the gate. Even with the weight of lead that met him, his momentum carried him forward, to fold over the top of the fence and lie still. Rory didn't have to look more carefully to know he was dead. No one could survive a load of buckshot delivered from a mere ten feet of distance.

As a troubled silence fell over the ranch yard, Rory saw the buggy and horse standing a few yards away. And there, still holding the shotgun, stood Julia. She looked to be in shock, staring at the man who was dead by her hand. Rory said, "It's all right now, Julia. It's all over. I'm going to walk out to you. Don't shoot anymore."

Slowly he made his way to the distraught girl and gently reached for the gun that still had one live load resting beneath a pulled-back hammer. She resisted just a bit, but as he lay his hand on her shoulder, she seemed to relax just a little, and Rory felt the weight of the gun fall into his hand. Turning the muzzle to the sky and using only his thumb, he eased the second hammer to the safe position, thankful that the girl hadn't pulled the other trigger when he ran out of the house. It seemed the most natural thing in the world for Rory to slide his arm across her shoulder, saying, "It's alright now, Julia. It's all over. The other man is down too. It's all over."

As if it was also the most natural thing in the world, Julia leaned a little toward Rory, slumping just a bit, as if her strength was leaving her, as she laid her head on his shoulder. He squeezed a bit tighter and assured her again that it was all over.

With a voice that was little more than a desperate squeak, she said, "I. I killed him. He's dead. I killed him."

Rory turned her away from the sight of the dead man, again saying that all was well. When she seemed to have settled a bit, he led her through the gate, staying between her and the corpse draped over the fence, and into the parlor. He led her to a big, overstuffed parlor chair. With no words, she sat, now folding her hands in front of her face. Rory thought he could hear a quiet weeping as he stepped toward the kitchen.

Horace had led his still upset wife to a chair. She continued to hold the stove poker, which was now badly bent, staring threats at the unconscious man, as if he might rise from the blood-stained flooring to further combat, and she would have to put him down again. Horace had pulled his chair over close to hers to hold her and, perhaps, to temper her instincts.

Into the hush, Horace spoke. "I don't know who you are, young man, but thank you. I'm assuming Julia is out in the field, safe, with the buggy. I'm also assuming someone with you was waiting with a shotgun and that the fight is over. I certainly hope so, at least."

Rory said, "Something like that." and bent to the badly beaten man on the floor. There was still a sign of shallow breathing. Rory came close to wishing he was dead but then corrected himself with some recrimination.

10

WITH THE LITTLE FAMILY SETTLED TO WHERE GRIDLEY felt he could leave his wife, and Julia had quit crying after slowly, between great shuddering breaths, explaining the true situation with the man who was still draped over the front fence, Rory nodded for the rancher to come with him. They left the house with Rory asking which horses the fugitives had ridden in on and if Gridley could lend him a horse.

"Left their mounts in the corral. Didn't even unsaddle them. Thoughtless of man and beast both, those two. I'm not short of horses, Sheriff. I'll pick you a good one. But you're not riding out tonight, are you?"

"Just as soon as we can get those fellas laid across their saddles and I have a horse under me, I'll be out of your hair, and you can start putting your house back together."

To fetch the horses and get the two men tied across their saddles took up a half hour, in which time Julia, who was slowly recovering from her shock, had managed to prepare a cup of coffee and build a fat cold beef sandwich wrapped in a piece of newspaper for Rory. He drank the coffee while standing beside the horses, with the sandwich stuffed into a jacket pocket, to be eaten as he rode back west seeking Sheriff Anthony Clare and the posse.

Julia stood by him as he drank. She was silent until he passed the empty mug back. Then, knowing he was leaving and she may never see him again, she said, "Sheriff, you're a bit pushy and rather strong in your opinions on the limitations of women, but I, that is, we, owe you our thanks. I am so very glad you came by and that your bluff to get me out of the house worked. I couldn't begin to repeat the plans those two had for us. My mother and me especially. I'll shudder every time I think on it.

"If you're out this way again, please stop in. You would be very welcome."

"Thanks, Julia. I wish we had met under different circumstances. Perhaps we can have a short visit when I come back for my horse."

"He'll be here for you. I'll bring him up when I take the buggy back tomorrow."

Rory grinned for the first time in hours. He looked somewhat haltingly at Julia and said, "Actually, I owe you a buggy ride. I hate to make a promise and then break it. But we live miles apart, and I don't have a buggy."

She grinned back as if the two were hatching a private conspiracy.

"I'm guessing Mr. Williamson would make the loan of his buggy if he were to be asked."

With a look of mutual understanding, the two young people turned back to their duties, Julia helping her mother clean the kitchen and Rory to his sheriff's tasks.

HORACE GRIDLEY WAS CHECKING the ties on the two men. If one came undone, Rory would have a time getting the body loaded again. Although Tex was still alive, he would never have been able to sit a saddle. Horace lifted his head up by the hair and looked at the badly damaged face and head. Addressing Rory without taking his eyes off the man, he said, "Won't live to get wherever you're going. Be dead before morning. And a good thing it is too." He spoke with no compassion in his voice. Rory found himself harboring the same feelings.

Rory had already explained where Clem said he thought the rest of the sheriff's posse had cornered Slade, Bronc, and their accomplices. With a nod, Horace said, "Know the area well."

He had followed that comment with a bare outline of the shortest route to that area, hoping it would ease the sheriff's overnight ride.

He dropped Tex's head as he wished Rory good hunting. Again, he said, "Thank you, young man. You'll always be welcome in our home. Come anytime."

As Rory swung into the saddle, Horace held up his hand. Rory stopped, waiting. Haltingly, Horace said, "Sheriff. Is it going to be necessary to give the exact details of what happened out here? You know, who exactly did what?"

Rory was unsure what his response should be. In his short time in the lawing business, he found himself continuously opening new doors, it seemed, constantly making decisions he wasn't sure he should be making. But Horace wasn't going to be satisfied without some kind of an answer. The image of the two women being forever known as the killers of the home invaders did not make for a happy picture in the sheriff's mind.

"I'll have to think on that, Mr. Gridley. I'll keep the women out of it if possible. Actually, I doubt that there will be anyone asking for the details."

11

MILES TO THE WEST, SHERIFF ANTHONY CLARE AND HIS posse had run the fugitives to ground. It appeared to Anthony that the prison breakers had convinced themselves that they had time to stop at the river's edge for a rest, watering of the animals and coffee, and perhaps a bite for themselves. But they were careless in their choice of firewood, creating enough smoke for the sharp-eyed Clem to see.

At the first mention of smoke, Clare was doubtful. He studied the slight upward change in the color of the overcast sky and said, "Looks to me just the same as the clouds, only a bit more windblown, perhaps."

"You keep watching." was all Clem said.

It wasn't but a few minutes later that Clare swung his horse to point him directly at the smoke.

"I do believe you are correct, young man. Good eye. Now, what does that good eye tell you as to distance?"

Clem, having already thought it through, quickly said, "Five miles or a bit less."

"Then let's kick these rides into a bit more speed. Keep an eye out for a posted guard though."

Even moving at a good trot, the distance was not being reduced quickly enough for Clare's liking. Knowing that if the rested fugitives were to again take to the trail the posse might lose them, Clare said, "It's run or rest time, fellas. I'm thinking we have no choice but to take the last of the run from these nags. We're either going to get those men here, or we'll be on a long trail after we rest these horses. These are strong animals. We'll take what they still have to give and hope it's enough.

"We're a bit to the west from their camp, so they'll have whatever brightness leaks through the overcast in their faces. Still, we'll have to look sharp. Let's not get ourselves trapped."

They moved out at a good, ground-eating lope, Anthony Clare in the lead, followed by Clem, Pike, and Cyrus. They closed on the river camp spot, still directed by the smoke. A half mile out, Clare hollered over the pound of hooves, "We'll charge directly into the camp. Hold your fire until we're sure who's there. If it's the ones we're looking for, take no mercy. These boys are not going to surrender or give up. It's all or nothing, and everyone involved needs to understand that. If you hesitate, you may die. If you're going to have doubts when a man falls into your gunsight, drop out here. A fast ride through the camp and get out, looking for cover if we don't get them all on the first pass. If one of you spots their horses, drop out and drive the animals off."

Every man in the posse rode with his sidearm in his hand except Clem, who much preferred his Henry. Ready for action, they drove forward, toward the hollow the fugitives were hunkered down in.

Clare broke over the top of the shallow riverbank, charging through the brush as if it didn't exist, and turned to follow the river to the campsite. The campers had heard them coming. As Clare closed on the bunch, they were scrambling to their feet, reaching for their sidearms or rushing to their saddles for carbines. A single look at the activity was all the posse required. There was no doubt about the identity of the campers.

The ride through the site took only seconds. Clare fired at the closest man as soon as he was in range. He was moving too fast to know if his shot had taken effect or not. The other posse members took up the battle immediately. Still, the return fire was also making its mark. Clem was struck in the left shoulder with one of the first shots. He gripped his Henry tightly in his right hand but was unable to lift it again. He got off just the one shot at a man who was frantically trying to pull his carbine from the saddle scabbard. That man dropped onto his face beside the saddle and didn't appear to be moving. Hunched in pain, Clem kicked his horse into even greater speed, looking for a way out of the campsite and into cover.

One man, who Clare identified as Slade Duhamel, rose from his position behind a small rocky outcrop just in time to be run over by the sheriff's charging gelding. As Slade flew several feet and then fell to the ground, Clare rode past, pointing his handgun directly down at him. He fired two fast shots, not knowing if he struck flesh or not. Clare turned his horse to the cover of some brush thinking, *Slade might still be alive, but he'll be hurting.*

The shots tapered off as the posse made its way out of the hollow. Only Clem had been hit, and Pike's gelding was bleeding from a slash along its flank.

As the bedlam quieted, Clare led his posse to a hollow

along the river's edge, much like the one the fugitives had chosen. They were out of six-gun range, but a good man with a rifle could still do them damage. The same would be true the other way. They all swung to the ground, turning their horses loose. The animals went immediately to the river's edge and dipped their muzzles into the refreshing water.

Sheriff Clare said, "Down behind these rocks, boys. Cyrus, you know a bit about gunshots. See what you can do for Clem. Pike, take up a position behind that sand ridge beside the water. Warn us of any movement from the camp. Watch that bunch of horses by the river. It appears as if ours and theirs have mingled together before we could drive theirs off.

"If they attempt to mount an animal, theirs or one of ours, shoot man or horse, either one, but don't let them get away. I'm going to worm up onto the other bank. See if I can find a shot into their camp."

It was less than a minute before both Clare and Pike opened fire with their .44 caliber Yellowboy carbines. Clare downed a man with his first shot, dropping him beside the fire. He fell on his face and immediately rolled over and tried to sit up for another shot. Before he could complete his turn or take aim, Clare squeezed off another shot. Even as the man fell, Clare could see that it was Bronc Liken. That he was dead was beyond doubt. As he flopped onto his back, one arm fell into the fire. He made no move to extract it.

Pike took aim at a man who had just put his foot into the stirrup on the one horse that remained in the fugitive camp. As he was swinging his other leg over the saddle, Pike's bullet took him above the hip. The man screamed and fell forward, trying for a grip on the saddle horn. Pike's next shot drilled through the long, shaggy hair, sending hair and a big part of his scalp and skull flying after his hat, which was tumbling through the air, landing several feet away. The lifeless body of the man named Homer hung to the saddle of the terrified horse for two or three jumps before falling to the sand. The horse kept running, encouraging the rest of the small remuda to break away from the posse's animals and follow suit.

Slade, always the noted leader of the gang, was showing his merits. Seemingly ignoring the dog-chewed arm, which must have been hurting abominably, and the abuse suffered under Clare's horse, he charged out of the little hollow where the fire was smoldering and took aim at the sheriff, firing shot after shot from the hip. His charge was effective. Sheriff Clare went down, curled up in pain, but still gripping his Colt. He managed one shot that must have hit Slade somewhere, although Clare didn't know where. Sheriff Clare was able to quickly roll behind a rock with some covering brush while Slade stumbled once and then dropped to one knee, taking hurried, ineffective aim at Pike.

Another fugitive, later identified as a man named Wally, had been only a few steps behind Slade, looking off in all directions for the enemy. Pike steadied his Yellowboy for a shot at Wally, now the only gang member in sight. The two men pulled their triggers at the same time, Pike's shot knocked the man to his knees, although Pike couldn't be sure where he had been hit. Pike had somehow avoided injury. Slade took another hurried shot in Pike's direction, then immediately moved to the side of Wally, lifting and dragging his friend as he dropped over the sand ridge separating the two camp areas. Pike saw Slade flinch as he shot at him, but again, he saw no obvious wound, and Slade didn't stop running, dragging Wally along with him.

With the disappearance of Slade and Wally, the shooting ceased, and a nervous calm overtook the area. Looking around the small clearing Pike went first to Sheriff Clare.

"How bad is it, Sheriff?"

"Took me in the upper chest. Lungs alright, I think, but I know I'm bleeding."

"Can you move, Anthony? I'd like to get you down below, behind the rocks."

"You give me a bit of help, and we'll get 'er done."

With that completed, Pike went to Cyrus, who had been hit somewhere along the line, Pike couldn't be sure when. So now Pike had three men losing blood and little enough for bandages. His next half hour was a scramble between ripping shirts into pieces for bandages and glancing over the sand dune to see what was going on in the other camp. Slade apparently was in no position to pursue the fight, and neither was Pike. Slade and Wally had hunkered down alongside a big poplar and were nearly out of sight. After studying the men for a half minute, he decided they offered no immediate risk.

But now there was another problem. Pike knew for sure that two of the fugitives were dead, but that left two alive, although injured. They were still men to contend with. Additionally, he had three injured men in his own camp that needed medical attention. Their horses were close by, but he wasn't sure if he could bring them in without exposing himself to deadly fire, or if any of the men could sit a saddle. Unsure of what to do, he did nothing, other than what he had already done to staunch the flow of blood, for fear of causing further hurt to the posse members.

Slade knew where they were, so there was no hiding from the other camp. From where Pike was sitting, he could see most of what was going on over there. Finally, he reached down inside himself and routed out the courage and determination to crawl through the brush toward the other camp. It was slow going as he attempted to approach silently. Reaching his goal, he very slowly scooped a small notch in the ridge of sand, just enough to get a glance into the campsite. Two bodies were crumpled on the sand where Slade must have dragged them. Slade himself and one other man were leaning against the biggest tree in the camp. Both were clearly beyond forming up another attack. Satisfied with the situation, and not being able to justify simply shooting the two, he backed away and made his way back to his own layout.

Knowing he could do nothing else, he figured he might just as well boil up a pot of coffee.

12

USING THE DIRECTIONS SUPPLIED BY HORACE, RORY headed west, into a land lit only by a partially clouded-over moon. The two loaded animals plodded faithfully behind on leads tied to Rory's saddle horn. Rory didn't ask more of the horses than a steady walk. To trot or lope would be to risk the loosening of the tie ropes or cause injury to the burdened horses with their unresponsive loads.

Thankful for the satisfactory conclusion to what lay behind him but concerned about what he may discover ahead, Rory found himself wishing he knew more about the law-keeping business. So far, he had gone on instinct. That his efforts had worked out reasonably well was more a credit to good fortune. Good fortune, and the ones he had been working with—Ivan, Andy Speth, and Anthony Clare. He wondered how matters would have turned out if he had been on his own.

He also found himself wondering if he wanted to continue being sheriff. His one-year appointment would be ending in a short while, and he would have to decide. It would be necessary for the county to either hold an election or go back to where they had no resident county law at all. But the rate of growth within the broader West, as well as his own county, would soon demand organized law, whether the people wished to find the funds to hire a sheriff or not. As he allowed these and other random thoughts to filter through his mind, he was studying the land ahead. Every small bit of brush, every slight fold in the terrain, could hold a threat. He was sure the men he sought would be further west, but he couldn't take the chance of being wrong.

His wandering mind brought him back to the events of the past few hours. What Julia had said about the threats in the Gridley home had shaken him to his core. He partially understood theft. A man down on his luck and feeling he was out of options might do almost anything to feed his family. A lazy man might think he could get through life by taking the gains from hard-working men and women. A rustler might think a rancher wouldn't miss a few head. A bank could probably spare a few dollars out of the large amounts on hold. Rory in no way approved any of that, but he might be able to understand it. Even the actions of the phony judge might have an explanation.

What he couldn't understand was the simple terror and horror brought about by men such as those that raided their gold camp in Idaho and murdered his father. Murdered that good man and put a permanent dent in his own skull, that place, normally covered by his hat, where hair no longer grew. And even worse, for desperate men to enter a home and make vile threats on the women was beyond anything he could make sense of. Those men, the murderers, the home destroyers, the corrupters of women, those men had to be stopped. But did he want to be the one doing the stopping?

Rory would not have considered himself skilled at judging time by the movement of the moon or stars. He did alright in the daylight hours. The sun's movements were pretty obvious. Even on a cloudy day, a hint of extra brightness could usually be seen, to track the time. His father had tried to teach him about the stars during the three years in Idaho, but there were limitations in that often cloudy country with mountains and forests all around. Nevertheless, doing his best with what he remembered from his father's teachings, Rory figured he must be close to where Clem had said he'd last seen Sheriff Anthony Clare. The stars told him the clock would have moved past midnight by one or two hours. He had his father's pocket watch with him, but to read it, he would have to stop and strike a match. Caution held him back. Even a match flare, as small as it was, could be just enough to give away his presence. It didn't really matter anyway. *It is what it is*, he thought to himself.

After a long ride, Rory was glancing back to the east from time to time, looking for that tell-tale rim of brightness that would rise over Kansas, lighting that vast grassland, before bringing the promise of morning to Colorado and Nebraska. With the miles he had covered, he wasn't sure where he was. He would have said Colorado if asked but finally decided the exact location didn't really matter.

The now weary horses plodded along. He was nearing a full twenty-four hours since he had last slept. His tired eyes finally picked up a faint, unnatural glow on the western horizon. It had to be a campfire. No, he decided, he had that wrong. There were two small glows, close enough together to appear as one at a casual glance. He could not see the fires themselves, just the small glow rising above them, reflecting off rocks or shrubbery or whatever the campers were sheltered behind.

Well, he was making little enough noise. He doubted anyone could hear his approach. And the darkness assured him that he couldn't be seen. He would proceed. But he would be cautious. The glow said the fires were all of a half mile away and that they were both sheltered in a hollow or by a growth of trees or brush. And separated. He could see that much from the irregular shapes of the lit area. There must be some rougher land or perhaps some treed cover. He didn't think they were close to any river or small body of water. The horses would have told him if they smelled water. He again reminded himself how important it was for him to locate a trustworthy map of the territory.

One fire would almost certainly be the sheriff and his posse. The other would be the escapees. But to be camped that close together and for both to keep a fire glowing in the dark of night meant that something had happened. He thought of three choices. The sheriff could have the men captured and under control. The opposite could also be possible. Or they knew where each other's camp was, but there had been a battle, and neither camp was in a position to pull out or to continue the fight, so the men had simply hunkered down for the night. Or, of course, there could be no one there. Just the final smoldering of dying fires after everyone had pulled out. In the worst case, they could all be dead or seriously wounded.

Stopping his mind from wandering and inventing possibilities, Rory decided he would tie the led horses to the first shrub he saw. He would then proceed to the closest fire, cautiously, as silently as he could on horse-back. He had no intention of being caught on foot. He would invent his next steps when he saw the situation. Then his horse's head came up, alerting Rory to something on the wind. The easterly wind had seemed to follow him on his entire night's journey. Now, with a shift to the northeast, the night seemed to cool almost immediately, and even he could sense moisture in the coolness of the predawn air.

Perhaps he had been wrong in his judgment. Perhaps there was water. The animals had sensed it before he did, but not by much. There was definitely a change in the air, along with a freshness and a faint trickling and gurgling, that could only mean water.

As he rode closer, he could clearly see the moon shining off a small body of water, but he couldn't imagine its source. As he had before, he regretted his unfamiliarity with the territory. But for the moment, the source of the water didn't really matter. What mattered was that the shoreline was heavily bushed, the water lay a few feet below the slight rise that surrounded it, and the fires were on his side of the water. Forgetting his plan to rid himself of the led horses, boldly, perhaps foolishly, he thought when it was already too late, he rode right up onto the bank and looked down at the first dying fire. The camp was close to the river or stream. Three men lay sprawled on their blankets. They were obviously wounded, if not dead. There was enough light for him to clearly see that one of them was Sheriff Clare. Another was Clem. There was a fourth man sitting on the ground, leaning against a big rock. That man was wide awake, and his rifle was pointed at Rory. He was awake and alert. He looked as if the fight was gone from him, although Rory sensed a cautiousness in the man's gaze. He held his rifle steady but made no threats.

Rory backed his horse away, dropped the reins of the led animals, and turned to the other fire. There he saw much the same situation. Two men were sitting up, apparently watching and ready, while two others lay sprawled much like those at the first camp. One of the awake men was Slade Duhamel. His dog-chewed arm was heavily bandaged and hung in a blood-splashed sling. Unable to handle a rifle single-handedly, he held his Colt in his left hand. The second man held a rifle snug under his arm, its butt on the ground, and the barrel pointed to the sky. He appeared to be unhurt, but not particularly vigilant. Both men were staring at him. It appeared to be a standoff. No one spoke. Rory and the two fugitives simply stared at each other.

Finally, the silence was broken when Slade, his voice quiet and strained, said, "Where you been? I've been expecting you. You're like a nail in a man's shoe. Nail don't amount to much on its own. But it'll nag a man half to death until he just has to stop and rid himself of it."

"You don't look to me, Slade, as if you're in any condition to do much about anything at all. And I can see that arm has bled through the wrapping again. Just lay down that gun, you and your buddy there, too, and we'll get you to some help."

"Naw. There's no more help for me. You already know that, Sheriff. Not for me nor Wally here, either one of us. There's nooses tied for both of us, tied and waiting, in more than one courthouse around the country. We can't, either one of us, let you take us again. You want us, you've got it to do."

"So, tell me, Slade, what made your bunch head north? South you would have New Mexico, Arizona, or even Texas to choose from. Seems like the prospects for hiding out would be better in any of those places."

"Didn't want to hide out anymore. Decided I was done with rid'n and hid'n. Head'n to the steam cars. California. Los Angeles. Always summertime out there. Got a good bit of loot stashed away in the bank out there. Enough to hold me for years. These others, they just decided to come along. As tired of it all as I was, I guess. Too late now."

With that bit of talk, Slade appeared to be fading even more. His speech became so quiet Rory could barely hear. He was lisping his halting words. He was gasping for breath. But he never took his eyes off the sheriff.

"You can still throw in your hand, Slade. I'll get you to whatever medical help is available."

"My answer ain't changed, Sheriff."

Rory wondered what Wally would do. At first glance, he looked fit and uninjured. But even in the short time since he had ridden to their camp, Wally seemed to have faded. Certainly, his attention was no longer on Rory. He seemed to be staring at the two men on the ground. Why that was so, Rory could not have guessed.

Still not willing to simply shoot the man down, Rory dragged his right hand .44 and put a bullet so close to Slade that sand and bits of rock flew up into his face.

Slade responded with a shot that sailed off into the night, coming nowhere close to the sheriff. It seemed he wasn't particularly adept at handling a Colt with his left hand. Wally hadn't moved. The thought flashed through Rory's mind, *they're both more dead than alive.*

Rory spoke just loud enough to be heard. "You're a tough man, Slade, but you're more dead than alive. And you'll be altogether dead if you move. Or if you fire again. I think you know I mean what I say, Slade. Throw the guns away, you and your partner both. Then turn your backs to me."

Slade gently laid his weapon on the ground. He then lifted the carbine out of Wally's hands and tossed it a few feet away. As if it had been the carbine that had been holding Wally vertical and giving him purpose, he simply folded at the waist and slowly lay over sideways, out of the fight.

There appeared to be no opposition left in either man. Rory couldn't imagine the intensity of the battle that had wounded or killed these men on the ground and had so taken the fight out of the others. But he now intended to end it.

He stepped out of the saddle, tying the horse to a bush, and walked carefully down the slope toward the campsite. Only once did he take his eyes off Slade as he looked where he was placing his feet. But that was enough opportunity for Slade to pick up his Colt and put another shot his way. It missed, but it was a close thing. Rory was conscious of the whine of the lead as it frighteningly whistled past the brim of his hat. The thought flashed through Rory's mind that he had so much to learn, should have insisted that he throw the gun away as he had first instructed. But now the only possible response was to raise his own .44, which he still carried in his hand, while he cradled the carbine in his left hand, and put a bullet into Slade's chest. Slade dropped the gun, slowly closed his eyes, and fell sideways to lay against Wally.

With very careful steps, watching the men lying on the ground as well as Slade and Wally, Rory took the final step onto the river's shoreline.

He went first to Slade and Wally. He thought they were both dead until Slade cracked his eyes open just a slit and whispered, with bloody froth on his lips, "Dangdest thing. Rode the trail all those years and then got bested by a dog. A dog. Man never can tell."

Those were the last words the man would ever speak. A quick check assured Rory that Wally had also said his final words.

After checking to see that the two men on the ground were dead, Rory left them where they were and climbed back up to his horse. A while later, after watering the horses and taking a mouthful of the refreshment himself, he stepped into the saddle and was soon back in the other camp.

Dismounting, he stepped to the top of the grade. The guard by the rock said, "I'm hoping you're the county deputy we were told would be along. Did you end it?"

"Rory Jamison, deputy sheriff. It's ended. You can relax. Catch some sleep if you wish. There's a bit of time before first light."

Rory then stepped down the shallow grade and went directly to the wounded men. The guard came to where Rory was kneeling over Sheriff Clare and said, "He took one through the flesh below his collarbone, but he'll be alright. Seems to have missed his lungs. Those others, too, should be alright. They need a doctor, but they'll live if we can find our way to a town in the morning. Lost a lot of blood, all of them."

Rory stood and looked the man over. He was strong, fit, and clearly willing to help, but it had just as clearly been a long day. He looked about done up, in need of food and sleep.

"Do you have a name?"

"Pike. There's more to it, but that'll do."

Rory asked, "Do you have the horses somewhere close by, or did they run off."

"I managed to catch ours up. They're tied off down the river a ways. Those others, their horses ran off almost first thing. Mingled with our own mounts at first and then just ran off. It was just as well. Clare, he figured we'd ridden about as far as he intended to go. 'It stops here,' he said before we attacked the camp. I'm expecting daylight will show those nags taking their fill of river water and whatever grass they can find, somewhere close by."

Rory was staggering with weariness, but he said, "Pike, we're going to have a time of it getting these men to the help they need, with just the two of us. Seeing this river helps me a bit in placing our location. If I figure this correctly, there are a couple of small places, trading posts and such, perhaps a stage station. But I don't know if they'd have a doctor or not. And it's a far ride back to Stevensville. You'd best grab an hour of sleep. I'll round up some horses."

Pike had his eyes firmly fixed on the two horses Rory had led into camp, focusing on the tied-down bodies, but he said nothing. When Pike turned to his bedroll, Rory walked over and took a look at Tex. The man was dead. Well, that was as expected.

13

AFTER CATCHING AN HOUR'S SLEEP, RORY WAS DRIVING A
half-dozen horses back into camp when he heard the
rumble of an empty wagon and the crunching of bunchgrass under steel-rimmed wheels. He left the horses
where they were and rode out of the shallow river valley.
Looking carefully from behind the bush rimming the
river, he studied the wagon. Friend or foe. That was all
he cared about now, in his exhausted state and with the
chore facing him and Pike that day. He could see one
man driving the wagon and four, no—five outriders. He
recognized no one, but he sensed no threats. The travelers looked like ranchers, working men, going about
their day's business.

He didn't expose himself until he recognized Horace
Gridley holding down the driver's seat. Only then did he
ride out to meet the men. The men and one woman, as it
turned out.

Gridley waved from a distance. They were still too
far away for talk. Rory waited, wondering. As the bunch
drew closer, one rider broke from the rest and spurred

toward Rory. She was now close enough to identify. Julia, of course. Who else would it be, riding beside her father's wagon? And then Rory identified Williamson, the neighbor who had loaned the buggy. He had no idea who the others were.

Julia pulled her horse close to Rory and sat there with a big smile on her face. There was just enough predawn light showing to see the other riders clearly.

"How is it, Sheriff? We heard shots. Did you find the men you were looking for?"

"I did. They're right close by. Just down by the river. It's not a pretty sight, though. You'll not want to go down there."

"Are you trying to protect me again, Sheriff? What in the world am I to read into that?"

Rory was spared the agony of coming up with an answer when Gridley pulled the team in close and stopped. Speaking around swollen lips and seeing with only one eye, he said, "Morning, Sheriff. We thought you might could use a bit of help. Gathered up a couple of neighbors and came right along. The women and kids are forted up at our place in case there's more hard cases skulking around. Sorry about bringing Julia. She wouldn't be left behind. Haven't never been able to figure womenfolk. Now, with the boys gone off on their own, that's all I have around is womenfolk. Makes for some long days.

"So, what's been happening?"

Rory, trying all the time to keep his eyes off Julia, gave a quick, bare outline. He ended by saying, "Got three men that need doctoring. Do you know where the closest help might be found?"

"Sure enough. We're not all that far from the old fort. Bunch of folks settled in there, seeing the value and beauty of the country, I suppose. Nice spot. Few folks have even got fruit trees growing. Got an old army sawbones. I ain't heard anything bad about him. Of course, when in need, any doc at all looks like a gift from the Almighty.

"Let's load them up. Got a good bed of hay in the back. Lead on, Sheriff."

"I need to catch these horses again. I was just bringing them in when I heard the wagon. We have some dead men too. I figure to carry them on their horses if we can use the wagon for the injured."

Horace turned in the seat and said, "Williamson, how about you and these others catch up the horses down by the water. Bring them to where you see the wagon."

With that, he slapped the team into action, expecting Rory to move ahead as guide.

With the wagon in place, Julia and her father both walked to where the wounded men were lying. Anthony Clare was awake and hurting. He looked up at Rory, then flashed his eyes to Julia, and then her father.

"Good to see you, Sheriff. I see you brought along some helpers too. And one is downright pretty."

"Never mind that. You need to remember you're a shot and hurting man. And a married one too."

"Oh, I remember. Doesn't stop me from remembering other times. Olden times."

Horace asked with a grin, "You remember how to walk? We've got a wagon here to tote you in."

"I can walk. You help me onto my feet, and I'll show you."

With Clare in the wagon, comfortably laid out in the hay, the men turned back for the other wounded men. Julia stayed at the wagon. The other ranchers were at the outlaw camp loading out the dead bodies. When they were done with that, Williamson reported back to Rory.

"Those horses are loaded and waiting. And I'm hoping to not have to repeat that job any time soon."

Rory said, "Thank you. I was afraid I was going to have to leave them lying there while I got these others to the doctor."

Before they headed out, Rory untied his own horse from the back of the wagon and gratefully mounted the black he knew so well.

Four slow hours later, the wagon and outriders pulled into the old fort. Horace Gridley led them to the doctor's office. Williamson asked the liveryman where to take the bodies.

With both of those matters cared for, the order of the day was sleep and food. Or food and then sleep, if we wish to be exact. But first, Rory had a job to complete. One he had done before, in a different situation, but still hated the very thought of.

He went alone to the shed where the bodies were laid out on the floor, took several deep breaths, and bent to the first man. A half-hour later, he had been through the pockets and clothing of all the men, putting each stash into a separate paper sack he had gotten from the mercantile store. He then went to the livery where the horses had been stalled and untied the saddlebags from their saddles, throwing them over his shoulder. He would go through them later. But first, a good scrub with hot water and soap to get the stink of death and dried blood from his hands. Then food and sleep.

14

Everyone involved in the affair was gathered at the livery the next morning. By first looks, it was evident that food and rest had done wonders for the bunch. Julia was holding her horse's reins, standing uncomfortably close to Rory. Not that she was uncomfortable, but Rory certainly was. He enjoyed her presence but had no idea how to respond.

Just before separating to go to their individual hotel rooms the evening before, Williamson had sauntered over to Rory and whispered, trying to obscure the movements of his lips, as if he was divulging a conspiracy of some sort.

"You can borrow the buggy any time you wish."

Rory had looked at him in total surprise but could think of no meaningful words. He had simply nodded his head and turned to the hotel stairs, leaving a grinning Williamson enjoying the sheriff's youthful embarrassment.

Now, with the ranchers ready to point the wagon back to the east and home, and with Rory and Pike left with the chore of driving the fugitives' horses and the horses of the posse members who were still under doctor's care, taking them south to Stevensville, the parting was imminent. Rory had shaken hands with the ranchers, and there was nothing left to do but rise to his saddle and move out. Nothing but finding a way to say thanks and goodbye to Julia without making a fool of himself in front of her father and the other men. Horace Gridley helped him out of his dilemma when he said, "Come visit us sometime, Rory. We can assure you of a welcome."

Julia simply smiled in agreement, and Rory nodded silently, as he found himself doing so often. He had used the money found in the pockets and saddlebags of the fugitives to pay for the meals and hotel rooms, plus the charges at the livery. The doctor's and undertaker's charges were also covered with the impounded cash. He had slipped each man a ten-dollar coin as he shook hands, showing his thanks. When Julia insisted on a hug in place of a handshake, he was in a dilemma over how to slip her a coin. Rory, always thankful when someone came to his rescue, managed to give her a coin when she broke from the hug and somehow ended up holding his hand.

Pike was having trouble keeping the rested horses in a bunch. They were in danger of joining the ridden horses or the wagon teams of ranchers going about their daily business. He finally spoke loud enough to be heard over the other noise of the village.

"We've got it to do, Sheriff. Best we get 'er started."

With no further words, Rory kicked his black into motion and gathered up the couple of horses that had broken from the others. Once underway, the saddled but unridden animals grouped themselves and led the way south. Three hours later, the loose horses were in Tippet's corral with all the saddles safely in the tack room. Rory and Pike said their goodbyes, with Pike promising again to let the families know that the men left under doctor's care up north would be just a few days recovering before they caught the stage home. Pike headed further south, pushing the posses' horses ahead of him.

WHEN RORY WALKED UP to the marshal's office, Ivan came out to greet him, somehow looking as if he belonged there.

"Can I take it that you accepted the town's offer?"

"For a look-see anyway. I made no long-term promise. We'll give it some weeks or months. See what happens."

15

LEAVING THE FUGITIVES' SADDLEBAGS LOCKED IN THE single cell, under Ivan's watchful care, Rory rode to the Double J. They had ridden past the gate on the way to Stevensville. The temptation to turn in was strong but not realistic. Now he was back. There was still law work to do but first, home and ranch responsibilities.

The family, as always, greeted him with food, news, and questions. Aunt Eliza was working over her pots and pans on the big wood burning stove, preparing the evening meal. Nancy and Hannah could hardly hold back their excitement at the news they had to share.

"We had visitors while you were gone."

The happenings of the past couple of days had tested Rory as he hadn't been tested since he buried his father and turned his back to the gold camp. Everyday matters had fallen considerably in his thinking.

Somewhat distractedly, Rory asked, "And am I supposed to guess who they were, or are you going to just up and tell me?"

"What do you think, Hannah?" asked Nancy. "Tell him or make him guess?"

"I'm for telling him. If I have read our cousin correctly, I don't think he particularly cares. If you don't tell him, he'll most likely just let it drop."

Nancy studied Rory across the table with a mischievous grin on her face.

"I shouldn't really tell you, Cousin, but since they came to see you and then got diverted into another direction, I might just as well tell you that the Strombeck family was here. Mr. Strombeck, I believe he said his name is Gale. Him, his two daughters, and one son. The girls were Allie and Polly. Quite attractive. Perhaps a bit forward, if I was to confess to the truth."

"Why don't you tell him the son's name, Sis, since he interested you the most?"

Rory glanced at Nancy, waiting.

"Everett. That's his name. Quite a pleasant man, overall, for a backcountry hillbilly. Pretty old for me, and Hannah already has her man picked out. If he ever really becomes a man, that is. She's still waiting for that to happen. And hoping."

The last half of that statement interested and confused Rory, but knowing nothing was to be gained by pursuing it, he avoided making a comment. When he was sure the girls were finished with their chirping, he asked, "How is it that they were way down here? They don't live anywhere close to Stevensville."

"Said they had some dry cows and a few grown steers they didn't manage to dig out of their hiding places in the bush last fall. They pushed about one hundred head to Cheyenne. Came by here on the way home. The girls were pretty upset to find you gone. But Dad and Mr. Strombeck had a good visit. Dad rode him around the ranch showing the upgraded bulls and telling him his plans. Mr. Strombeck ended up asking if Dad would sell half of those bulls. I don't have to tell you how that conversation ended. They were sitting here having dinner at the time, so we heard the talk. Mr. Strombeck laughed and said, "Well, I had to try."

Nancy looked at her sister and suggested, "You tell him the rest, Hannah."

Hannah hesitated a bit and then said, "Well, I don't know what your relationship is with those two girls, Cousin, but they were sure all eyes when Henry and Thomas rode in. The boys had been to town and got back just in time for dinner. They stomped their way into the kitchen, hung up their hats, and turned around, noticing the company for the first time. I don't know whose eyes bulged out the furthest, the guys or the girls. My brothers, they were so taken, they started pulling out their chairs to join the meal, looking nowhere but at the girls. Would have just sat down, too, if mother hadn't reminded them that in this house, we wash our hands before eating. They were some embarrassed, but they soon got over it.

"The upshot of it was that, after dinner, the four of them tightened their cinches and rode out to look at the ranch. I doubt as if any of them really saw much of the ranch. And then, it turns out that the Strombeck ranch is not far from the Triple T, where the boys used to work.

"All in all, they looked like a happy foursome for the time the Strombecks were here. Headed out to the hotel in town for the night. If you have your eye on either girl, Rory, you may have to pull up your socks and shave a bit more often if you hope to stay in the race."

"I'm not in a race. The girls are fun to be with, although, from time to time, they seem to be skirting danger without hardly even trying. But they're too old for me. Anyway, I have no serious interest in girls. Given my age and responsibilities, I don't plan on having that interest for a long time yet."

Nancy couldn't let that conversation drop without saying, "Sonia might be a bit surprised to hear that. I do believe she's been making plans, in her own mind anyway."

To stop any further talk in that direction and to show a bit of discretion, which Nancy wasn't particularly adept at, Hannah said, "The other bit of news is that we're opening a school in Stevensville this fall. It will be held in the church for a start, and I've been hired as the teacher. I've already got some class plans put together, and I've started identifying families with school-age children. Mind you, some of those children, as I've just now called them, are actually closer to being adults. But perhaps they can still benefit from a few months of study."

Rory continued to sip on his cooling coffee mug as he stored all this chatter into his memory. The girls' mother finally came to Rory's rescue.

"Girls, I think it's time you got about your own chores. The chickens need care, and there's probably other things you could put your efforts to."

Rory took the break in the conversation as an opportunity to retreat to his own cabin for a rest.

16

KNOWING THE BUSY TIMES THAT LAY BEFORE HIM, including another trip to the city, delivering the news of the fugitives' deaths, and the delivery of the saddlebags and the evidence they contained to Oscar Cator, Rory encouraged the family to sit after the evening meal, to discuss the ranch.

"When we last talked, you were all considering the herd, and if you should put out the funds for a better class of animal. What's become of those thoughts?"

George, the family patriarch, now that Rory's father was gone, brought what had been a long family discussion over the past few weeks down to just a few words, knowing that was all Rory was really interested in.

"We've spent hours on this, Rory. The decision we came to was that if we are to grow and prosper on the Double J, we must upgrade the breeding stock. We've been there in our minds before, of course, but it finally came down to being the only option unless we were to keep the place as a one-man ranch.

"We are only left with three questions. The first one,

only you can answer. That is, how much you're prepared to invest into the ranch to hold your half share. We'll talk about that another time.

"The second question is, where do we sell the present herd? We have just over three hundred fifty cows out there, and all but two have a calf at foot.

The third question, which you also have knowledge on, is where do we go for new stock?

"Let's leave the question of your investment until after we discuss the rest. As to selling the current herd, we wondered about the ranches that had their animals rustled. Do you think Ambrose King on the K Slash Ranch would be interested?"

Rory was already becoming impatient with the discussion. He was beginning to understand how much he had changed during his short time as a law officer. When chasing fugitives, there was no time for long discussions.

He said nothing, but he thought, *the K is only a few hours' ride to the east. One of them could have ridden out and talked with Ambrose.*

"Why don't one of you ride out and have a talk with him?"

There was silence around the table while this question pushed its way into their thoughts. While the family was silently tossing this around, Rory picked up on the question of making a purchase of new stock.

"The bulls came from the Galen Farm. Aunt Eliza can look up her account book for all the information on Mr. Galen and his cattle. The only thing to be wary of, I would think, is that we don't want animals that are closely related to the new bulls. In a closed-in ranch like the Double J, inbreeding could become a problem.

"The second breeding farm up that way is the Washington Hereford Farm. And there are others if you don't find what you want in those two. My suggestion is that one of you ride to Cheyenne and buy a ticket east. Make a deal and get 'er done."

"As to my financial input, you do the deal. I'll cover my half, like I promised. That will be about the end of my possibles. The ranch is going to have to stand on its own, but I can't imagine a problem with that. The market is demanding a better grade of beef. If we have the breeding stock on offer, with a good calf crop, there will be no end of takers."

George looked around the table at his family, ending with his eyes on Eliza, his wife of many years, and the one who kept the ranch accounts straight. Eliza closed the meeting with a comment.

"As Rory said, 'Get 'er done.'"

Nancy couldn't hold back her laugh. It wasn't often she heard her mother making such a no-nonsense comment.

17

GEORGE WALKED INTO THE BARN JUST AS RORY WAS readying his horse for the long ride to the city and the state offices of Oscar Cator.

"Looks like you're packed for the trail, Rory."

"Don't want to do it, but it can't be avoided. Six jail-breaking fugitives dead and buried. You'd think that would be the end of it. But the state people need their records, and I've got all the belongings left behind by the men. I'll leave the horses, saddles, and other gear until I get directions from Oscar. But until the county is organized and we have a court established here, the papers, money, and whatnot found on the bodies and in their saddlebags, has to go to the state lawyers. That's something I've had to do with each arrest. What they do with it doesn't interest me. So long as it's off my hands.

"I need to stop and see Sheriff Anthony Clare's wife on the way south, so I figured to ride. Anyway, I don't really enjoy bouncing around in the stage, hours on end."

"Let me saddle up. I'll ride along with you for a mile or two."

The two men lifted their horses to a trot as they left the Double J ranch yard. Eliza, watching from the kitchen window, wondered where her husband was going, but she was too late to ask.

Easing out of the driveway onto the state road, George ventured into the conversation he had been holding back on, waiting for some alone time with his nephew.

"Your year as deputy will be up soon, Rory. You've had some adventures, seen some country, and met some folks. You've also been in a couple of tight scrapes and taken some chances. You've always been a quiet man. Take after your father in that. Jacob was the quiet one in the family. It's not a bad way to be. Mind you, most folks quiet down with maturity and responsibility. Some days I long for the time those two girls, who are not really in any way still girls, take on some responsibility away from the family home. They chatter like a couple of birds at dawn sometimes, but down inside, they're both serious and responsible young women. They just haven't found their challenge yet."

George pulled his gelding to a walk, wanting to talk. Rory followed suit.

"You've a decision to make, Rory. And you have choices and opportunities. The Double J is half yours. You would be welcome as the flowers in May any time you wanted to ride home and settle in. With the proceeds of the gold claim, you have other choices as well. You could start a town or city business. You could go east and attend a college of some sort. Maybe become a lawyer. That way, you could face the bad guys in court instead of over the sight of your rifle. There's no end of choices.

"Or you could take up the law business full time if

the county was organized. Of course, there's nothing stopping you from moving to another county either and seeking election. And who's to tell. Being elected sheriff could easily lead to a life in politics. As far as that goes, studying the law often enough leads into politics too."

The two men rode side by side for several minutes. Rory was sorting out what his uncle had said, knowing the man had waited until they were alone before he spoke. He was mixing his own thoughts with George's, trying to pick out the meaning. He had some fairly firm thoughts, but he hadn't voiced them to anyone up until that time, wondering when the right time would be, or if there even was a right time. Perhaps now?

On a peaceful day such as the current day was, with the sun shining warmly, the trees and trailside shrubbery all greened out for summer, the birds and unseen ditch-side wildlife chirping, clacking, rustling, and buzzing through the grass and low-lying branches, it would be easy enough to make a decision without giving heed to life's other realities. One of those realities was that not every day in the saddle was like this day. He had ridden through thunderstorms, soaked to the skin. He had longed for food and drink. He often needed rest but couldn't stop until his job was done. He had ridden through blinding snowstorms, never quite sure if he had lost his direction.

He had shot and been shot at, every time laying his life on the line. He had watched men die as powder smoke still curled from the barrel of his weapon. Only once had he sought out men with the intention of either bringing them to justice or inflicting his own brand of justice on them if the law wouldn't act. That had been for the men who had shot him and murdered his father.

All other actions were either to save his own life or to act in the name of the law.

He was not immune to feelings as he watched men die, or when he hauled them to prison. If he stayed with the law business, would he become hardened? If he made the move into a different life, would he look on from a distance, smoldering within himself every time he heard of an injustice being done, with no retribution being taken by the authorities, and wishing he was there to do it himself?

His uncle George was certainly correct. There were several paths open to him. The decision he would make when he sat down with Oscar Cator, when the time came to organize a vote, forcing himself into deciding, would point him onto one of those paths. He could help organize the county and then seek election as sheriff. Or he could listen as Oscar laid out the opportunity and say thanks, but no thanks. In such a simple way, his future could be decided.

"I've tried to think of all that, George. There's no denying that I'm young and inexperienced. And not really knowledgeable of those several options you mentioned. But this is a young country. There are men my age who own and run ranches. There are military officers not much older than me. I have seen responsible cowboys everywhere I go, men my age who have the trust of their ranch bosses, taking care of herds on the move or being taken to market. The streets of the big city are busy with men my age or close enough, all carrying responsibilities. I can't run from it. And I don't wish to run from it."

"That's all true, Rory. And it's also true that the decision you make doesn't have to be the final or permanent decision for your life."

"I know that too, George. Our three years alone in the gold fields left my father and I many an hour to talk, discussing all manner of things. While that was helpful in understanding life from an academic point of view, I'm afraid I was pretty naive about life on the open frontier. That started changing, of course, with Father's murder. Still, I somehow came to believe that crime was mostly focused on financial gain, robbing banks, rustling stock, etc. Then I saw what that crime had done to the families that had been robbed. A bit more naivety melted away. On this last hunt, I tracked down two thugs that had pushed their way into a ranch home, holding father, mother, and an adult daughter at gunpoint.

"Together, we managed to put the two gunmen down with no real harm to the family. But later, when the daughter told me the threats the two had leveled against her and her mother, I was shaken. What kind of men can come up with such vile threats and still call themselves civilized human beings?

"I came away from there knowing men like that had to be found and stopped. And I suppose it sounds rough and perhaps even unchristian, but I no longer see any place for that type on this earth. Prison isn't going to change or fix them. They belong in the grave. And preferably before they can do more harm than they've already done.

"Knowing and understanding this still leaves me with the question of whether or not it's my job to do. I'm working on that."

Following another couple of minutes, as the two men listened to the horses' hooves falling onto the hardened dirt of the trail, Rory said, "This isn't really fair to you, George, and I don't mean to pin you down, but do you have a suggestion, coming from your more mature and experienced view of the world?"

"No one can make your decisions for you, young man, but seeking good counsel is the wise way through life. That direction is certainly found in the Scriptures, and I have sought out others myself on more than just the one occasion. Whether or not I can give wise counsel is an open question, but assuming it to be so, I will say that from my observations and the few things others have said, I believe you're cut out for what you're doing, at least for this time. I think you would regret the decision if you were to come back full-time to the Double J, or some other ranch. Although, saying that, you have also shown keen insight into cattle and ranching.

"If you chose to help set up the county and run for sheriff, you can depend on the support of the family. And, I suspect, the support of most of the town folks, especially the young ladies, who, privately at least, have their hats, if not their traps, set out for you. There may be more danger there than in chasing fugitives."

George grinned as he said this, but Rory had no real response.

Finally, George pulled his ride to a stop and half-turned toward home, looking directly at this young nephew of his.

"I have no need to go to town, Rory. I just wanted a few minutes away from the others where we could talk in confidence. I'm not trying to live your life for you. Just wanted to discuss options. You've a long ride to the big city. Use the time wisely to sort all of this out. Do what your heart and head agree on. You'll find full support from me and the others."

The two men shook hands before each turned to ride on to his own destiny.

18

RORY HAD DECIDED TO MAKE A BIT OF A GAME OUT OF charging right past Bertha as she attempted to hold all visitors to verbal ransom before allowing them into the inner county offices.

"Good afternoon, Bertha. It's always good to see your smiling face when I visit the big city. It's one of the things that makes an otherwise dreary ride worthwhile. No, don't bother getting up. I'll find my own way."

With that, he stepped past the sputtering woman and walked directly to Oscar Cator's office. The door was already open. Having clearly heard the greeting at the front counter, the county administrator sat behind his cluttered desk with a big grin on his face. Saying nothing, because voices could easily be heard throughout the office space, he simply stood and offered his hand in greeting, grinning the whole time. The two men took their seats before Oscar spoke for the first time.

"You are always full of surprises, Sheriff."

His continuing grin told Rory the short statement

had more to do with Bertha than it did with law or county work.

"Well, that I'm again in the big city comes as a surprise to me. Every time I come down here, the ranch looks sweeter and more welcoming when I get home. I look forward to having the telegraph someday soon. And the steam cars. Apparently, the roadbed is being prepared for a line down from Cheyenne. That would save me considerable riding. But for now, I have news and some evidence to share."

He set a single saddlebag stuffed with the accumulation of letters and such found in the many saddlebags left behind by the dead outlaws on the empty chair beside him.

"Other than horses and saddles, here are the entire estates of Tex Hunter, Rob Grant, Bronc Liken, Slade Duhamel, Wally, and Homer. The family names of those last two may be somewhere in their junk, but I didn't bother going through it all. They are all safely underground up at the old fort. They left some wounded posse members behind them, but that's another story. We can get to that, but first, tell me what I should do with the horses and saddles."

Oscar Cator held his keen eyes on the young deputy for a long time before speaking. Finally, he said, "For a lightly populated and unorganized county, you seem to have more than your share of work. I'm wondering though, after the rest of the gang broke Bronc and Slade out of the city lockup, why did they flee north? The chances of disappearing would seem better to the south."

Rory was surprised to hear about the city lockup.

"I somehow believed that they were in the state prison."

"They would have been in another couple of days.

Their transfer was being arranged, but the gang got to them before the move could take place."

Accepting that explanation, Rory reverted to the question of why north. "I asked Slade about fleeing northward just before he died. He was already mortally wounded but still able to talk. He said he was quitting. Heading for the rails. California. Said he had a large stash in a bank out Los Angeles way. The rest of the crew was just following along. That might have been the truth but also, perhaps not. We'll never know for sure. You might mention the bank matter to the Federals, though. I don't think there could be that many banks out there yet. They might recover some loot."

Oscar took all of this in with a nod.

"Well, whatever the truth is, the main fact is that the reign of theft and killings is over for that bunch. And, I must say, you have the knack of bringing it all to a conclusion in a way that leaves little to do but write the report and clean up the details. Or swab the deck, as an old sailing man friend of mine used to say.

"As to the horses and saddles, and whatever money you are returning in that saddlebag, that all belongs to the county you represent. There may well be rewards to collect. That, too, would belong to the county. My advice would be to check the brands on the horses. They could be stolen animals. If you were to return one or two to their owners, you would earn a thank you, if nothing else. Otherwise, sell the beasts and the rigging and hold it aside for county expenses. The same for whatever money you have in that saddlebag.

"Now, let's you and I walk down the street. There's a new place opened that makes the best apple pie. They're serving it with a scoop of ice cream. I had never heard of that before, but I am becoming addicted to it. We'll sit over coffee and pie and plan out your future, young man."

Standing, Oscar said, "Bring that bag with you."

At the front counter, Oscar took the bag from Rory, laid it on the counter in front of Bertha, and said, "Bertha, I would like if you would take everything out of this bag and sort it all out. It's the final estates of six dead fugitives. Set the money aside, and we'll return it to the sheriff here before he rides for home. Now, write down the names Rory gives you."

With that, he nodded to Rory and waited. From memory, Rory recited the names while Bertha wrote them down. Satisfied, Oscar led the way to the café.

RORY RETURNED to the Double J Ranch with several answers and a few more questions. He had visited the Anthony Clare home to assure Mrs. Clare that her husband hadn't been badly wounded and should be home soon.

He opened a bank account in Stevensville, explaining to banker Jesse Ambrewster that it was county money. That led to a brief discussion of the need to formalize the county and for Stevensville to apply for the position of county seat. Anxious to get back to the ranch, Rory found a way to cut the conversation short.

A single day of rest, with more of Aunt Eliza's cooking than he really needed, and Rory was back to his sheriff's duties. He went first to Mr. Browning at the mercantile. There the two men talked about county matters, with the store owner promising to talk with the other councilors. At the news of the bank account holding county money, Browning said, "You've proven yourself to be trustworthy, Rory. You manage that money as you see fit, always doing whatever is good for the town and territory."

He went next to the livery, where he walked among the captured horses, writing down brands and descriptions along with any other helpful information about each animal. He would make up an advertisement for the city newspapers and send it down to the city by mail. If the horses hadn't been claimed in reasonable time, he would use the county authority to sell them, and the saddles.

The word from the Stevensville town council came more quickly than Rory might have expected. The council met in Ma Gamble's dining room for a midafternoon discussion with the sheriff.

Hip Dawson, town mayor, said, "Rory, we are agreed that organizing the county should have been undertaken well before this date. Now, we have a proposal for you. We would like if you would ride across the miles of the county, taking names of ranchers and farmers, and counting heads. We will need to have some idea of numbers before we proceed. Gathering names of town folks is probably beyond the need for now, but the total number of people in each settlement would be good to know. As you go, you could try to identify the men carrying influence in their areas. If you could more or less map out the locations of the ranches and farms, as well as the settlements, big or small, that would be a good start on organizing the county.

"Of course, you would be identifying yourself as sheriff and keeping an eye on things as you ride. Organizing the county is nowhere as important as your law duties. We appreciate the work you've done in the past year and hope you will decide to stay on."

Rory replied, "I'm leaning that way, but the county will have to organize, hold an election, and put up the funding. My state job ends this coming fall."

Ma Gamble, who had found time away from cooking, had joined the group. She grinned at Rory and said, "Well, then, I'm guessing you had best get at it."

The meeting broke up on that informal note, and the businessmen went back to their duties. Rory stayed, at Ma's invitation, for another cup of coffee. She had nothing particular to say. In fact, she almost appeared to be biding her time until something else happened. She rose from her seat as Sonia finished collecting the cost of a meal from the last customer.

"Sonia, perhaps you could get Rory a warm-up of coffee while I put some things together for the dinner hour."

As she walked away, her purpose in delaying his departure became clear. She didn't really intend to meddle. But perhaps she was, just the same. She would face that matter another time.

Sonia brought the coffee pot and a clean mug for herself. She poured and then took a seat. The two young people looked into each other's eyes. Neither spoke for an uncomfortable, stretched moment. Rory finally said, "I've been gone a lot lately, Sonia. How have you been? It seems to me that we had more or less agreed on a buggy ride after church before I was called away for that day."

Sonia turned her mug in circles as she studied the oilcloth-covered table, looking down rather than into Rory's face. When she didn't say anything, it finally became clear to Rory that she was not happy with him. As always seemed to happen, he had no credible idea what to say or do. But when Sonia still didn't speak, he figured he might just as well bull in and see where the pieces landed.

"It's a large county, Sonia. I'm just now beginning to understand how large. That business the past couple of weeks had me almost riding the shoes off my gelding. I didn't mean to be gone so long, but that's the job."

"I missed you, but I'm glad you got home in one piece."

Although the words were there, Rory wasn't sure about the feelings.

"I'm sorry we missed our buggy ride, and I apologize for not being here to take you up the hill to the I-5. Ivan tells me that you did manage to get home for a few days."

Sonia twisted her mug, the coffee forgotten. Without looking up, she said, in a flat voice that was impossible to read, "Andy got some time off and rode up with me."

Their relationship had started out very casually, and Rory was hoping to keep it that way. But as he hesitated, he could almost see Cousin Nancy shaking her head and saying something like, "You have so much to learn." Well, he guessed he did have a lot to learn. But at the moment, he was busy learning the sheriff's job and something about the law. Buggy rides had dropped into another place in his mind. A place that didn't seem so important anymore, although he was sure that day would come.

Almost as if she had to get it off her shoulders, Sonia, still staring at the tablecloth, said, "Andy and I went for a buggy ride too."

As if in need of presenting a justifying excuse, she quickly said, "I had the sandwiches, and the lemonade and all, already made. When you didn't turn up after church, one of the other girls said, 'There's more than one fish in the creek.' She said it loud enough that folks turned to look. One thing led to another. And, well…"

Rory had been struggling inwardly, silently, as he thought of Julia Gridley, off to the east on their far-flung ranch. Hearing that Andy had stepped in at the moment of seeming need put Rory's mind to rest. Almost.

Somewhere he found a smile.

"It would have been a waste to let that lunch go unappreciated."

Sonia finally lifted her head and looked at this smiling young man across from her.

"You're not mad or anything?"

"No, Sonia, I'm not mad or anything. I like you a lot, Sonia. Respect you. You and your family. But I have a traveling kind of job, and it looks like I'll be traveling even more for the rest of the summer. Andy appears to be a fine young man. And if I am to be honest, I believe we're all too young to be thinking about more than an innocent buggy ride with a chicken sandwich and a glass of cold lemonade. We all have a lot to learn before we get serious and settle down."

The look on Sonia's face said she might have some doubts on the subject, but she said nothing.

19

Armed with a pencil and a paper tablet provided by Hannah, from the supplies she was putting together for the next school year, Rory headed north. He would go first to the old fort. Perhaps he could find a military survey map of the area. There hadn't been one available in Stevensville. Stopping often to talk with settlers along the way, noting names and numbers of residents at each place, he was a full three days reaching the old post. He was unable to find the map he wanted, but he did get a reasonably accurate count of the local population from the ranch supply store owner, Grady Stiles, who had taken it upon himself to keep track of such things. He also noted down the names of the movers and shakers in the community, again as laid out by store owner Stiles.

He was surprised to find that the old fort actually had more residents than Stevensville held.

Grady Stiles proved to be a source of all kinds of valuable information helpful to the process of the organization of the county. When the man mentioned having the post named as county seat, Rory said nothing, preferring to avoid that politically hot topic. He would leave that to others.

When Rory had enough notes to fill several pages in the tablet, and the conversation began to wander, he closed the tablet and stood. But Stiles wasn't ready for the conversation to end.

"I don't know if you received any thanks, or adequate thanks anyway, from the town folks, young man, but we owe you a debt of gratitude for cleaning up that mess of hard cases a couple of weeks ago. Those boys are exactly where they needed to be, under several feet of gravel and dirt."

Rory had no response. Into the silence, Grady spoke again.

"Horace and Dinah Gridley were in a couple of days ago, filling in some gaps in the story. I don't know as I've ever heard more thankful people. They sang your praises till I was starting to wonder if you had walked across the river dry-footed too. And Julia, well, I couldn't begin to describe her admiration, although she did mention something about you being somewhat bossy."

He said that last bit with a broad grin on his face.

Rory's comeback was, "The sheriff and his posse did most of the trailing and the actual fighting. Took down the other four. Got shot up themselves in the process."

"That they did, Rory, but to have two men of the roughest sort take over the Gridley home and threaten terrible violence was in a class by itself. Not many men, even of the criminal element, will disrespect a good woman. The praise for your actions stands. And will stand, so long as local memory holds."

Rory had no logical reply, and he certainly wasn't going to tell this talkative man that it was the women that finally subdued the two men, even if it was Rory who had set up that possibility. So, he moved the subject to a question about Sheriff Anthony Clare and his posse. Stiles' response was, "Doc had them back on their feet in a couple of days. From there, it was just a matter of hotel rest and good food to get their strength back. Left here on the stage a few days ago. Mostly just suffering from loss of blood anyway, so Doc says. Three or four days of lolling about, eating heaped helpings of Amber's roast beef and garden truck, over at her Town and Country Café, had them ready for home in no time. It's a fright how that woman dishes up the garden stock. A complaint will be met by a lecture on the good the greenery does a man, so it's simply easier to do as you're told at mealtime or go down to the Mex's chili house."

This short outburst was met by a chortle of glee as Stiles thought of the many times he had watched cowboys question the wisdom of eating such as carrots and cabbage. The chortle led to a gasped out, "After trying to force sliced and boiled beets on a few cowboys, Amber has given up on that one."

Rory left the talkative man with the promise of a public meeting just as soon as it could be arranged.

Now, east into the rolling grasslands for the census or west into the hills. That was the question on Rory's mind as he stepped from the hotel into the bright sunshine of a grand summer day.

Completely unaware of his surroundings, for a few seconds, at least, with his mind on riding into the hills he had come to love, he stepped right into a situation that, at first, appeared to be totally out of his control.

The voice that stopped Rory in his tracks and drew the attention of the folks strolling the boardwalks was loud and gruff while, at the same time, managing to be a bit whiny. "Heard there was a two-gun kid sheriff down this way. Mak'n a name for himself. Never misses a shot, they're say'n. Put'n folks in jail. Put'n others into the cold, cold ground. That's what they're say'n. Judg'n by looks, that kid sharpshooter must be you. Heard about you up Montana way. Quite a story been mak'n the rounds of campfires and drinking establishments these past months. Heard some stories up in Cheyenne too. Thought I should come down this way to kind of sort it all out. Find out if it's all talk or if you're the real deal."

Rory stopped and turned a bit, putting his left side toward the talker. Taking a quick study of the man, he saw a black-hatted, rail-thin fella not much older than Rory was himself. The man wore a dirty, wrinkled shirt tucked into a pair of hard-worn canvas pants. His soft jaw and clean looks told Rory that he had either shaved that morning or, perhaps, grew little facial hair and shaved only seldomly. The man's hands hung loosely at his sides, his fingers twitching, as if in anticipation.

The Colt the challenger carried was hung low on his left side, with a rawhide lace looping the holster and tied around his thigh. It was a gunfighter's rig, set up for a left-handed man. The whole scene presented the sheriff with a situation he hadn't faced before. Gunfighters looking to gain a reputation were few and seldom seen. To Rory's knowledge, those that followed that path restricted themselves to the wilds of Texas and Arizona, with a few, like the killers that raided their gold camp, holding out in Montana. He certainly hadn't heard of any gun-handy visitors in Colorado.

Except for the one time in Montana, Rory had never depended on a fast draw, and he hadn't practiced since the Montana fight. Of course, he didn't actually draw that time up north. He left his .44 where it was holstered and simply tipped the leather and squeezed the trigger.

That he should be facing this situation now, totally unexpected, on such a beautiful morning shocked him. Knowing the man wasn't just going to turn and walk away, Rory said, "I don't know you, fella. Don't know what brought you down this way. I've nothing against you and nothing to prove. Why don't we walk together over to the dining room and have a talk over a cup of coffee?"

"You can't talk yourself out of this, kid. If you're a fake, you can unbuckle your hardware, let it drop into the dust, and walk away. I'll add your rig to my collection, and we'll all know you as a fake and a coward. Of course, if you think you're up to it, you can draw. Now!"

Two Colts banged so close together, it was difficult to tell which was first. The evidence though, showed a sagging challenger, slowly folding into the dust of the street. He was down, but he wasn't finished. Not quite finished, in any case. He squirmed into position on the filth of the road and slowly raised his weapon for a second try.

As it had been in Montana, Rory had not pulled his gun. He simply laid his hand on the butt, his finger into the trigger guard, tilted the left-pointing holster attached to the front of his belt, and fired. His lead went true. The challenger's lead dug dirt close to Rory's feet.

As the gunfighter lay on the road, his life slowly draining away, Rory said, "Don't try another shot. Lay the weapon down. There's a doc here that can probably put you back to rights. Now, give it up."

Not nearly as loud as he had spoken his challenge a bare few seconds before, the gunfighter said, "Can't give it up. Gotta keep try'n. To the end. That's the rules of this game."

"This is no game, and there are no real rules. You can

give it up, or you can die right there. But before you go, you'd best tell me your name."

"Sky. Sky Blue. Not the name I carried away from home, but I like it."

As if with his last strength, his gun started to lift. Rory waited as long as he could, and then lifted his right-hand weapon but held his fire. He could see the hand holding the gun was sagging, and finally, slowly, came to rest in the dirt of the road. Sky Blue would not be needing any more help.

The street had fallen to silence. But now, after a few seconds for the noise of the shots and for the burned powder smoke to clear, suddenly, there seemed to be voices from all sides. Rory reholstered his unfired weapon and turned from the crumpled form on the road, sick to his heart about the matter.

As he took several steps toward his horse, a hand fell on his shoulder. Grady Stiles walked along with Rory until they reached the horse before saying, "We all saw it. You had no choice. Stupid. Young fella like that. You gave him his option, and he made the decision. You had no choice left to you. I'm sorry about it all, but I'm eternally glad it's not you lying out there."

Rory's mind was abuzz with contradictory thoughts. *Sheriff. My job. Challenged. No choice. Took another life. No choice. Seeking a reputation. Left me no choice. Stupid. No choice.*

He put his foot into the stirrup and lifted to the saddle. He looked down at Grady. "I hate that part of the lawing job. Will you gather up his stuff and try to identify him? Maybe find his horse. We'll talk another time."

With that, he turned the gelding and rode from town.

20

RORY LEFT TOWN POINTING NORTH. ON THE SPUR OF THE moment, he had decided to ride to the extremity of the county, which would be the Wyoming border. But first, he would find a quiet, treed grove where he could take some alone time. He needed to get away. Be alone. Hear the silence. Pray. Seek God's comfort. Or was it forgiveness he needed?

Regardless of the mess the fight had made of the morning, he still had a job to do. That he would get to the job in good time was beyond doubt. But it could wait. It could wait a bit. First, the silence. The healing. He was not yet immune to the taking of life. He hoped he never would be.

He found what he was looking for a little north and west of the old fort, along a tumbling, churning, rock-strewn river. It wasn't silent, but the white water crashing from rock to rock as it sought release from its mountain canyon was still somehow pleasing and calming to his soul.

Three days later, after sleeping, contemplating, and

sorting out what he could of the life he had chosen, he put out his fire, stowed the coffeepot away, and saddled his animal. He needed to get to the task before him.

The census. He had at first thought of east or west, the flatlands or up into the hills, as being his choices. But the decision to ride north had been settled during the past days, and north it was. His somewhat fading recall of the long-ago ride back to the Double J, after the incident in Montana, told him this was barren, or near enough barren country. He didn't expect to gather many names, but the riding would be good for him, and he would be able to report that he had scoured the county to its end.

At a small trading post attached to a stage station near the border, he found a good meal laid before him by the station agent's wife. He enjoyed the meal and took advantage of the opportunity to resupply. He made his purchases, stowed them in his saddlebags, and stayed the night. He was ready to get on his way early the next morning after a breakfast of side meat and eggs. As he was drinking his last cup of coffee, he found himself reluctant to leave these friendly people. But he could hear his father saying, *You'll never finish if you don't get started.* His father probably hadn't really said all the things he attributed to the man, but Rory's memory kind of wrapped all the sayings together into a usable gathering, no matter who had actually said them. He pulled out the appropriate parts and used them when he needed encouragement or wisdom. If it wasn't exactly what his father had said, it at least did no harm and brought back fond memories.

He paid for the meals and stepped into the saddle. With a friendly, "Ride well, young man," the trader and his wife stood side by side, waving him on his way.

He rode south until the barren country began showing more signs of shortgrass and a scattering of pine trees on rolling hills. This was all high country. He suspected the hills he was looking at off to the west would top ten thousand feet, a few might be higher. Knowing both he and his gelding would need to take it slow and easy in the sparse air, he swung off the stage trail and moved toward the round-topped hills. In three days of riding, he found only one small shack. As he approached the yard, he was warned off by a stern voice coming from a small growth of stunted trees he had just passed.

"Hold tight, stranger. State your business. No, don't turn around. Just tell me who you are and what you want."

"Rory Jamison here. Deputy county sheriff. Gathering names for the county to hold a vote. No trouble offered or threat implied."

Rory listened as footsteps crunched the summer-dried grass. By sound, he figured the man was making a careful study of both horse and rider, wishing to see his visitor face on without exposing himself unnecessarily. He sat still, as directed, knowing anything that happened up there would stay there. No one would ever know if this loner were to shoot and bury him.

After a full minute studying Rory, the man said, "If'n you got coffee to spare, step down and bring 'er out."

"I've got coffee. We'll boil some up, and I'll leave you a pack for another day."

A half-hour later, Lige Bannister had temporarily satisfied his craving for coffee, and Rory had added his name to the slowly growing list of county settlers.

"Don't know as they'd let me vote. Come jest fer the summer, ye understand, young fella. Cain't no way abide the snow thet gathers in these high up hills. Fer as I know, no one stays fer the winter, sept'n thet bunch over ta the Red Feather Lakes area. Feller over there come in ta go to ranch'n. Appears he jest might be mak'n a go of 'er, too, but he's welcome to it. Too cold. Me? Why I head down fer the warmer country, down ta Santa Fe. There's trails through these hills'll take a man down there and no one the wiser. Don't cotton ta most folks. Would have run you off iff'n I hadn't heard stories 'bout some new sheriff last time I was ta town. Thought to meet ya. Now you want the names of that rancher family off ta the northwest, ye kin ride up there. Take ye maybe two days, less'n ye were ta meet a grizzly. Or an unhappy Indian or two. Was I you, I'd jest give 'er a pass, or maybe write down the fella's name as I give it to ya. Met him jest the once. He was haul'n wood down to the fort. Pine. Cut'n split. Firewood, don't ya know. Hard way ta make a livn', were ye ta ask me. I'd jest as soon set by. Let folks fetch their own wood."

~

RORY STAYED ONE NIGHT, shared his stash of coffee in the morning, and rode off with the name of the Red Feather Lakes rancher included in the list of voting-age settlers. He would confirm the name with Grady Stiles the next time he was at the fort.

Rory found a couple of those trails Lige had told him about, but for the most part, he lost them again almost as quickly as he found them. And he found no settlers. Coming to appreciate the ruggedness of the country, he decided there would be no one settling the land unless it was a logger or a miner. Deciding there was no one living up there, what he wanted most was a way out of this wilderness. He came, at last, to a steep canyon, one that offered little enough passage for a man on foot and none, or nearly none, for a man on horseback. He turned to the east, hoping that as he moved toward the open country, the canyon walls would be less formidable. Finally, on the second day, he saw what he thought would be a way down. Of course, it could just as easily be a trap for rider and horse. Riding down might be possible. Returning to his starting point could be close to impossible.

Carefully guiding the gelding on a zigzag course across the heavily treed hillside, always moving downward, he, at length, found himself on the rocky bank of a tumbling river that could easily be the one he had taken refuge on after the shooting at the fort.

The rocky ledge allowed for horse and rider to continue their trek to the east. Rory was looking for a way across the river, hoping for an opening to the south. He found it a half mile downstream. The rideable ledge came to an end, so he had no real choice. It was go back, attempt to climb the steep hillside again, or step into the roiling water. The horse shuddered in fright, but with a gentle rubbing of the arched neck, along with some kind words, and some slight encouragement with the seldom used spurs, they moved forward. The river was no more than one hundred feet wide. The first thirty or forty feet were rocky-bottomed and relatively shallow. The horse then stepped into deeper water. Rory leaned forward, talking encouragement to the animal while he held his feet up, hooking his toes on the saddlebags. With the stirrups cutting small channels in the water, they moved another dozen steps before the river bottom again rose to meet the southern bank. They climbed onto a rock and gravel shore and into the trees. Rory dropped his dry boots into the stirrups and again rubbed the gelding's neck, talking encouragement to the horse as they found their way through the lower forest. They came out of the river canyon almost right at the old fort. Rory thought, *well, that was an adventure. Don't know as how I'd like to do it again, though.*

Wishing to see no one at the fort except Grady Stiles, Rory waited until late evening to enter the town. He tied the gelding off and walked to the back door of the ranch supply store. Grady responded to his knock almost immediately.

"Still open, Rory. You could have come in the front."

"I know it. I prefer not to be seen or get into any discussions with anyone. I just want whatever information you have on that gunman. And I want to confirm a rancher's name I had given to me up in the hills."

Understanding the situation, Grady laid out the information on the shooter and confirmed the name of the wood-cutting, uphill rancher. Rory thanked him and left, taking his evening meal at the Mex's chili house, where he doubted anyone would recognize him.

He would bed down at the spot he had used after that foolish front street shooting. One night and then, to work. But before he left town, he would have to replenish his coffee supply. The old hermit had talked him out of most of what he'd been carrying.

21

RORY'S EVERY DESIRE WAS TO RETURN TO THE DOUBLE J, sleep for three or four days, and forget the census taking. But he had agreed to the job. He had given his word. And neither of those facts left room for reconsideration.

West. West from the fort. He doubted there was anyone up there until he rode miles further south. But he still had it to do. He would go west, hoping for no more deep canyons. It would be all new country until he got far enough south to visit the BL and the Half Anchor Ranches. And that was assuming he could find them.

East, of course, would eventually take him to the Gridley home, and Julia. Somewhat embarrassed at his own thoughts, he silently added, *and the borrow of the Williamson buggy.*

East would also mean he could outline the flow of the rivers, but he knew the army had already surveyed those, so he would only be adding his amateur guesswork to their much more professional mapping. He had found no map at the post, but eventually, he would locate one.

He pushed those thoughts to the back of his mind, to be brought forward again at a better time.

West. Up into the hills. Much of that area was unpopulated, so he could get through it quickly. To the east, the farms and ranches were becoming more plentiful. It would take time to work his way through all of that. So west first.

He was drawn by the beauty of the hills and the ever-present, ever-drifting, ever-changing clouds, as well as their seeming distance and the mystery of their holdings. Were they offering much-needed rain? Did they contain the makings of thunder and lightning? He had no way of knowing any of that, but contemplating on it had become a bit of a self-entertaining game.

If there were settlers, he would try to locate them. If the land was still untouched, he would wend his way through the hills, heading south. It would all take time. It was best he got started. With his coffee replenished, he had adequate supplies, so all he had to do was tighten the cinch, climb aboard, and turn his back to the post.

Hours later, after riding through some of the most beautiful country God ever laid on His earth, a country begging for attention, but so far, still devoid of people, he made camp under the sanctuary of a huge pine, sheltered from rain and sun. In all the long day, he had seen no settlers, nor had he heard any sound he hadn't made himself. The land, forested mountainsides and high valleys both, was still there for the taking, and probably would be there years into the future, waiting for the ever-expanding population to push adventurous folks that way. Holding his gelding to a stamina-preserving pace, alternating between a shambling walk and an occasional trot, Rory wound his way through park-like grass and pine hillsides and then along the edges of steep cliffs covered with aspen, and above, higher than he cared to ride, bristlecone pines. This was all high country, welcoming and nurturing trees suitable to severe winters and drying winds.

It was a scramble but Rory, after a couple of back-tracks, found the trail he was sure led to the hill above the BL Ranch. Thinking of the widow Lander, who preferred to be called Patsy, or Patricia, and her son Kenny, he wondered what had become of them. The last time he saw them, it appeared as if Patricia and Alexander Sperry of the Half Anchor spread were chummy. Patricia had only been a widow for a short time, but in this rugged, newly settling-up West, a woman with only a young son couldn't be expected to hold a wilderness cattle ranch together. Rory found himself wishing them well.

Late in the afternoon, after following the cutoff that Ivan had led him on, the one that ended on a death-defying slide down a narrow path that pointed to a steep moraine of gravel and broken slate, he sat looking down at the BL. He had vowed never again, after that first ride.

It took until almost dark, but he finally located an easier route to the ranch. Patricia saw him coming and watched to see who it was. Getting close to the house, he could see the shotgun leaning beside the door. He shouted a hello and an introduction. At his identifying himself, Kenny Lander, fourteen years old and currently the man in the house, stepped from behind a small outbuilding, tucking a Colt into the top of his trousers. Rory shouted a special hello to the young man and waved his hat. Patricia turned to the door and disappeared.

A single night in the loft, plus a generous feeding of Patricia's cooking, prepared Rory for another day's ride.

Somewhat bashfully, Patricia confided that she and Alexander were waiting for an opportunity to ride down the hill as two individuals and ride back up as a couple.

Rory smiled as he said, "So there's going to be two Mrs. Sperrys on our census records, is there?"

Patricia simply smiled, perhaps as girlish-looking as she had appeared in years.

One week of riding brought Rory into contact with far more ranching operations than he had known about. Most were small. It remained that way until he arrived at the GS Ranch. The way the daughters, Allie and Polly, greeted and questioned him about his cousins, he could be forgiven for feeling like a traveling newsman. Everett quietly inquired about Nancy, when the two men were alone. Rory came to where he was sure they would be seeing more of the GS Ranch folks visiting the Double J.

In that portion of the mind where humor dwells, he rode away from the GS, trying to picture Everett attempting to tame Nancy to the point where the two of them could be alone together with no threat to life or limb.

After returning from the hills, the survey of the eastern ranchers was a simple task requiring little besides long miles of riding. Rory and Julia Gridley didn't bother borrowing the buggy, opting instead for a lunch wrapped in brown paper, along with canteens of cold well water that they hung from their saddle horns. Julia had offered to guide their visitor around the ranch country. They made a long day of it, meeting neighbors and discovering new settlers. Judging by the smiles the young folks carried on their return, Julia's parents figured there was a good chance they would be seeing the sheriff again. Rory feared the parents might have noticed the slight whisker burn on their daughter's chin, although she did her best to cover it up with some butter, fingered from the one remaining sandwich and rubbing it into the tender area.

On his return ride to the Double J, Rory chose to visit the fort and Grady Stiles.

"The survey of folks settled in the area is done as far as I can do it. It will have to be up to the town leaders to get their records up-to-date. I'm done with it. I need to get back to my sheriff's job. I'll get the records down to the state people and then it's up to you folks to call an election. The sooner, the better, from my way of seeing it."

He carried the same message to Stevensville.

As MUCH AS he disliked the big city and the endurance demanded of the traveler to get there, whether by horseback, stage, or private wagon, he figured he might just as well get it done.

Continuing the private game he had started on his previous visits, he opened the door to the state offices and charged right past Bertha, saying a bright, "Good morning, Bertha. No, don't bother getting up, I'll go right on in."

Oscar Cator shook his head, smiling, and quietly said, "Don't know how you get away with it but good on ya."

Rory laid the tablet with the informal district census written in his bold hand on the desk.

"More folks in the country than I figured. I may have missed some up in the hills. There're some tricky corners up there that could be hiding small-time settlers. I've put a mark beside the names of folks that have claims to the east of the actual county boundary. I'm thinking it will be a long wait for those eastern counties to fill up to where they can afford, or need, any fixed organization. You might want to include them in the voting."

With that, he took a seat and waited. Oscar was leafing through the pages, silently counting the names.

After a quick lunch together, Oscar looked at his young law enforcement protégé and asked, "So what comes next?"

"I've been in the saddle for weeks. And none of it was for law work, which, you may remember, is what I signed on for. I'll take a bit of personal time back on the Double J and think about where I want to be next year at this time. The sheriff position holds some interest, but it also has its downsides. I've got some thinking to do. I'll keep in touch."

22

SETTLING BACK IN AT THE DOUBLE J, RORY WAS LOOKING
forward to a solid week of rest and good food. He wasn't
home but a couple of hours when it became clear that he
would get no real rest until he told the family about his
travels and, in turn, was informed about the happenings
on the ranch.

"One of my last stops out west was at the GS Ranch. I
got all their names down and properly spelled, including
the ranch hands, but that about ended their interest in
politics. I'm guessing the family would fall into that
group that would prefer to just be left alone. The way the
country is growing and filling up, that wish is not going
to be met, but I said nothing about that to them.

"The real interest from the Strombeck family came
from Allie and Polly, and a bit later, from Everett. It
would appear that the choice for life mates is a bit thin
on the ground up in the hills, both male and female. I'm
not sure they're quite at the point of desperation yet, but
it may be close."

He grinned at the others around the table as he

spoke.

"I'm thinking, George, that you and Eliza could lift a considerable burden of concern from your shoulders if the two ranches were to get together, so to speak. Everett was particularly interested in news of Nancy. I told him she was too young to be off the ranch yet, and anyway, there probably wasn't a bridle and bit ever made to fit. I suggested he forget about it and look for someone who showed more leaning toward civilized behavior. I'm no way sure he was listening."

Before Nancy could respond, he continued.

"And that makes me wonder where Henry and Thomas are. I'm surprised they missed out on this good dinner."

George leaned back in his chair and said, "We finally figured you were right. It was time to make a decision. We managed to get past our fears and indecision. The boys rode off near enough a week ago. They'll be at the Galen spread by now. If there are no animals there they like the looks of, they'll have moved on to greener pastures. There's lots for them to figure out, from choice of animals to hiring a crew for the return trip to making arrangements on the rails. I expect it may be a while before we hear anything.

"If they make a purchase, they plan to brand the bunch before heading home. That will take some time. Time and a crew.

"In the meantime, again, at your suggestion, we sold the current herd, cows and calves together, to the K Slash. Ambrose King is gathering a few neighbors for a drive. They should be here in the next couple of days. All we'll have left will be the yearlings and the bulls. We've staked the future of the Double J on that decision. We were all in agreement, so it seemed the thing to do."

~

A SHORT FOUR DAYS LATER, unable to rest, Rory rode down the single shopping street of Stevensville, tying his horse in front of the marshal's office. Ivan, sitting at his desk inside, watched him ride up.

"Morn'n, Sheriff. I haven't seen you in a while. How did the politicking go?"

"Didn't much care for it, Ivan, but we got it done. The list is safely delivered to the state folks, and it's out of my hands. I took a few days at the ranch, but I got restless. What's been happening in town?"

"Pretty quiet except that Doc's horse broke from that stuck-together corral out back of his house. Wandered through a dozen gardens and smashed down Gladys Rampart's roses before I could get a rope on him. Enjoyed his freedom, I guess. If it gets any quieter here in town, I'll find myself keeping track of whose cat had kittens, just to have something to do."

Rory grinned at his friend and said, "Well, I don't feel the need to get involved in any of that. Only thing is, Doc should hire some kid to ride that animal a few days a week. He'd be a better horse for that bit of work."

Ivan let that thought pass, saying instead, "What's next for you? I haven't heard of any law work need'n doing."

"I'm thinking of riding up to the old post. I kind of like it up there. Showing signs of becoming an up-and-at-'em town. More folks around there than right here in Stevensville. Mayor up there is claiming it for the county seat, although I don't know if that's official or not. I thought I might ride up to the I-5 and sort of filter through the forest for a ways, hoping to come out at the post or close enough."

23

RORY'S RIDE INTO THE HILLS WITH THE INTENT OF AGAIN visiting the fort started with a quick greeting to the Ivanov family. He had offered to escort Sonia, but she turned him down, offering no reason. The offer had been little more than a courtesy anyway, so Rory saddled up and thought no more about it. After the obligatory visit with the Ivanov family, he moved on into the forest, planning to stop first at the small holding settled by Kiril, Ivan's old-country friend.

Riding into the forest opening Kiril called home, he was met by the half-whine, half-bark of Kiril's dog. The pathetically thin creature slunk around the side of the house, took a long look at the approaching rider, and then crept back, whimpering, to lie at the feet of his master. Rory followed the animal around the cabin after shouting a greeting. There was no response.

When the front of the cabin came into view, Rory pulled his horse to a stop and looked with astonishment at the scene before him. He said nothing, just sat there while startled thoughts rattled through his mind.

He finally stepped out of the saddle, dropped the reins where he was, and strode slowly across the front of the cabin. The dog had been whining as if in despair. Now Rory knew why. Sitting in his usual worn-out chair in front of his cabin was Kiril. But he was clearly dead.

His head lay askew, resting on one sloping shoulder, and his arms hung loosely by his side. His rifle was across his lap. There was no sign of blood or violence. The dog lay at his feet, still whimpering. Rory, transferred immediately into sheriff mode, squatted before the dead man as if wondering what to do next.

As he looked the scene over, with several questions forming themselves up in his mind, the thought came, *This dog is starving.* He entered the cabin looking for something for the dog to eat. The small cold pantry held the last of a hind quarter of venison. Even stored as well as it had been, the temperature and the accumulation of days had turned the piece a bit ripe. It would be poor eating for a man but might suffice for the dog. He lifted it off the hook and took it outside. The poor animal could smell the meat. Leaping and crying, the dog grasped the meaty end of the bone and tugged. Rory let it go and smiled as the starving animal dragged it under the porch where he normally slept.

Turning to look at the corral, he saw that one horse was down, and the other could hardly hold his head up. There were dead chickens in the wire-strung yard. *This man has been dead for days, if not weeks.*

Into the following silence, Rory asked himself several questions, all wrapped into the single question of what to do next.

He turned his horse loose, knowing it would take advantage of the clear, running stream and the plentiful grass around the cabin. There was no chance of it wandering off as long as Rory was in sight. He walked to the corral, swung the gate open, and went to the standing horse. The animal was too weak to even toss his head in fright as Rory grasped the halter. He led the animal on a slow, painfully halting walk to the creek and, as with the gelding, left him there. There was water and grass. He could do no more for the beast than that.

Rory then went back to the corral and bent to the downed gelding. Sensing that there was still a bit of life in the starving animal, Rory boosted and prodded, trying to get him to his feet. Although the horse raised his head a few inches, he could do no more. There was a bucket upturned over the top of a corral post. He took it and walked to the creek, returning with a half-filled bucket of cool water.

He forced the horse's lips apart with one hand while he scooped water from the bucket with the other. As the first small taste of refreshment seeped through clenched teeth, the animal opened his eyes wide and his mouth just slightly. By the time Rory had scooped the rest of the water toward the now-opened mouth, thoroughly wetting the tongue, the horse was showing a bit more interest in living. With more nudging and slapping on the shoulder from Rory, the horse finally lifted his head and then partially rolled, as if to rise to his feet. Rory talked encouraging words while he pulled on the halter ring. The seriously weakened animal took two tries at standing, falling back each time. On the third attempt, again with Rory's encouraging words and the constant lifting on the halter, the gelding staggered to his feet. Rory let him stand, gathering strength and stability before very slowly leading him to the creek. It was all he could do. The rest was up to the horse himself.

Now he had to decide what to do with the old man. If

he had been able to ask, he was reasonably sure Kiril would say to bury him where he had lived. Seeing no other real option, Rory went to the barn and found a shovel. Two hours of sweat and hard digging in the rocky ground had Kiril covered over in his shallow grave.

GRIGOR AND PAVEL stood outside the barn watching as Rory rode back into their yard. The two weary horses followed on leads. The dog made a nuisance of himself running between the horse's feet, seemingly back to strength and happy to be with people again. With no preamble, he said, "Rode through Kiril's place. Dead. He died sitting in his chair outside the cabin. I buried him under some pines in the sideyard. That's his two horses and his yard dog trailing me. Like if you would take them under your care until I try to sort out the right thing to do. That's a good dog. If you can't find use for him, I'll take him down to the Double J.

"These animals have all been starving, but a few days of good rations will have them back to where they should be. Give me the rest of the day, and perhaps tomorrow, to do my own looking, and then, if you can spare the time, you might ride up to the cabin and look things over. There's more than likely stuff worth the saving. Anyway, I'd appreciate it if you could do that, for me, if not for Kiril. I know he was not your friend, but this family was all he had."

24

Rory turned and rode back up to Kiril's small holding. The place, and the dead bachelor, intrigued him. Seeing nothing that was obviously suspicious, he entered the cabin. It was surprisingly neat and tidy. The dishes had been washed and stacked on a sideboard to dry. The bed was made with care, as if the old bachelor might have a military background. There was a wide shelf of foodstuffs, all stowed in glass jars, a caution against flies and invading bugs. The cold pantry, in addition to the leg of venison he had already fed to the dog, held a bowl of eggs and a dried out half loaf of bread, along with a few potatoes, and enough carrots for a single meal.

There was a growing garden on the sunny side of the cabin, showing good promise for the picking when the season was ripe.

Rory walked outside and turned to study the cabin. He looked at the corner joints that had been cunningly mastered with a broad ax. The logs fit tightly, needing a bit of moss chinking only in a few spots. Somehow, glassed and framed windows had been hauled up from the village. The door swung on factory-built hinges. The door stoop and steps sat tight to the bottom log, firm and square, held together with three rounded wooden pegs.

Rory completed his study, both inside and outside, remembering again how many topics of conversation he and his father had explored during their gold mining time.

Any man who loves wood and knows how to use tools will leave a heritage to envy by lesser skilled men. Cattlemen, bankers, train engineers, they all have a valuable place in this world, Rory, but a builder leaves something for the future. The home that kept him and his family snug in the winter will keep his children and their children snug, as well. We do well to respect a man like that.

Rory found himself thinking that his father would have looked on Kiril's work with acceptance and pleasure.

I don't know what else you were, old man, but you were a builder, that's plain enough.

He walked to the barn and saw the same evidence of care. Everything of value, pitchforks, axes, shovels, all were standing neatly in a row, leaning against the inside of the feed room wall. Two saddles rested on saddle horses, while a gathering of harness was carefully hung on pegs in the tack room, although he saw no sign of a team.

There was a small stack of stored hay in the loft.

He didn't enter the chicken coop, knowing the birds were all dead and whatever eggs hadn't been collected would be best left where they were.

He wanted to look around more carefully, wondering what Kiril did for money. He again thought of the cantankerous old man, dying alone, as he had lived. *We leave it all behind eventually, don't we, old man. That you died sitting in your chair must have come as a surprise for you. I wonder. Well, it doesn't matter now. Too late anyway. But I wonder if, wherever you are, it's at all like you imagined it would be. But we all have to wait to know for sure, don't we? Rest easy, old man.*

The sun's position told the world that it was just past noon. It had been a busy morning, but Rory wasn't ready to quit yet. It was still early enough in the day, and he was curious. He was on no particular schedule, so if he stopped for a few hours of sheriff's work, there would be no harm to it. He led his horse to the barn and took advantage of the shade to give the animal some relief from the heat. He filled the manger with fresh hay and dumped a half gallon of oats into the wooden receptacle built into the end of the manger. He placed a pail of water where the animal could reach it and set out to explore the small holding.

First, he walked back to the cabin. He entered with the intent of examining every corner. Every joint in the wood. Every stone in the fireplace. He was prodded on, in his mind, by the remembrance of finding the loose board in the judge's office and the string tied to a nail, with a sack of gold coins pushed well back from the opening.

He started with the small stoop outside the door, with the three steps leading to the hard-packed ground. There were no loose boards and, seemingly, no space behind the stairs, except a spot where the dog had been curling up on a pad of old feed sacks. Rory stood, brushed off his knees, and walked slowly around the building again. This time he was looking for anything that might appear out of place. But he arrived back at the door no wiser than he had been when he started out.

The small work counter where Kiril had prepared his food was built over three shelves held together with vertical pine boards, neatly sawn. There was no opening there. The interior walls and the rocks of the fireplace showed no weaknesses. There was no ceiling, just the underside of the roof rafters and boards with hundreds of nails protruding from where the shingles had been nailed in place. Rory admitted defeat on the cabin and walked down to the barn. On the way he glanced at the chicken coop, but he was revulsed at the thought of dead and half-decomposed chickens and rotted eggs. He went through the barn as carefully as he had the cabin but found nothing suspicious or helpful.

No one, not even the cantankerous Kiril, could live without a bit of spending money. Where did he get it from, and where did he hide it? He could hunt for his meat and keep a coop of chickens, but that didn't supply his coffee, sugar, and other staples. And his chicken feed. What did he feed the chickens, and how did he get it up to this sidehill hideaway? Rory chastised himself for not asking Browning, at the mercantile, about Kiril.

Giving up on the inside of the log barn, Rory walked around the outside, avoiding the single mound of barn scrapings, drying in the heat of the day. There was nothing to catch his interest until he got to the back of the structure, where a heavy growth of young aspens grew close, leaving rub marks on the barn wall from where the wind had worried them, and blocking his easy path forward. Even then, he might have gone around or doubled back, but there were a couple of bootprints leading right into the aspen grove. That in itself was strange, as the small trees grew very close together. But a couple of stubs from broken branches indicated further human movement, as if the tree trunks had been pushed aside to allow passage. With curiosity, but considerable doubts in his mind, Rory reached in and parted the branches. There, carefully covered over with several handfuls of dried aspen leaves, was a narrow trail into the deeper woods. Rory thought, *well, what do you know? You sly old man.*

He eased the trees further apart and stepped onto the trail. Within a few feet, it widened, so he no longer had to place one foot in front of the other. Clearly, the old man thought no one would get this far, so he had relaxed his vigilance. Expecting to find a dug-out safe of some kind or a box nailed high onto a tree, Rory, instead, was led along the path for over one hundred yards and then, surprisingly, downhill, into a larger clearing. The path hadn't been steep, but the trail he found leading out of the clearing was very steep. Since it had plainly seen heavy enough traffic to leave permanent impressions, Rory determined to follow. The only way down was to slide, perhaps grasping a tree limb here and there. The trail led to more questions. Slide down, perhaps, but how did Kiril get back up?

That question was answered when Rory found a neatly coiled length of rope hanging, sheltered, under the limbs of a large pine. He lifted the rope down and then looked for some indication of where Kiril might have tied it off. He found some rub marks at the base of a solid aspen and accepted that as Kiril's oft-used anchor. With the rope tied securely, Rory turned his face to the trail and fed rope out as he backed down the slope. On steeper spots, he could see where Kiril had braced his foot against a tree, or where he had grasped a tough limb for support. In truth, these indications were more likely made on the return climb.

Flipping the last of the rope free from his tight grip,

Rory stepped down onto flatter, solid ground. He tied up the end of the rope so he would be able to find it again and moved onto the trail. There were two more slopes, but neither required the assistance of a rope. At the base of the incline was a lengthy path leading to the east. Rory pushed on and a quarter mile further along he broke his way through the last of the bush and found himself looking at the back of Tippet's livery barn. He laughed out loud and said, "You old scoundrel, Kiril. What other secrets are you holding?"

25

MAKING HIS WAY AROUND THE TREE-SHADED LIVERY BARN, Rory stepped into the sunlight, coming upon Tippet from behind. When he spoke, Tippet leaped out of his chair, turning so fast he came near to spinning out of control.

"What in all tarnation are you doing to me, Sheriff? Man could die of fright. And what are you up to behind my barn? Ain't nothing back there but bush and a few broken-handled shovels and such. Ain't no call to be prowling around, sneak'n up on a man."

"I'm not exactly sneaking around, my friend. Catch your breath and come with me. Got something to show you.

"But, on second thought, sit tight till I find Ivan."

Although there was no one to guard, Ivan was sharing the guarding duties with Andy Speth. The two of them were visiting in the marshal's office when Rory walked in.

"Got something to show you, Ivan."

Andy said, "I'm just taking a few minutes away from

the shoulder-bending pressures of high finance, fellas. It's time I got back. No telling what kind of crises may have arisen while I was away. You fellas go do what needs doing."

Rory could find no logical retort to the bank apprentice's grim portrayal of his duties, so he said nothing.

With thoughts and questions about Kiril running every which way in his mind, Rory led Ivan and Tippet around the back corner of the big barn and through the bush and rubble, for half the length of the building. When he stopped, he gestured at the dim trail leading out of the bush.

The two men stood silently for a long quarter minute. Tippet finally asked, "What's that about? I have no cause to ever be back here, but for sure, someone has been. What's going on, Rory?"

"I'm trying to figure that out. Have you ever seen anyone looking as if they're heading this way? Perhaps around your corral?"

"Never."

"Did you know the old man that lived up by the I-5? Kiril, by name?"

"Saw him time to time. Spoke maybe just two or three times. Always walking. No horse. I thought that strange but then, the old man was strange anyway, so I let it go. Man has the right to do as he pleases, walk, ride, jump. Fly should he be able to. It's no matter to me."

"Have you ever seen anyone else around here, recently or in the past?"

"Doc's wife. She likes the horses. Doesn't ride herself, just likes to be around them. She asked if it was alright if she brought some carrots from her garden. Feed them to the corralled stock. I couldn't see no harm in it, so I said to go ahead."

Rory was surprised to have the woman named, but he had to follow leads wherever they came from, or led. But he did volunteer, "Strange, when Doc has his own horse that could use some attention. She ever meet anyone here?"

"Not regular. But a couple of times. Thrasher, that phony judge, he liked the horses too. Went for walks regular. Said he did it for the exercise after hours sitting behind his desk. I never saw as how he had enough work in this little burg to hold him behind his desk, but it was none of my business. Always stopped to talk to the horses on his way back from his exercise walk. Saw him pass a few words with Doc's wife a time or two. Seemed innocent enough."

"Thank you, Tippet. We're going to stay here a while, do some looking around. I'll let you know if we find anything. But you both might just as well know. Kiril is dead. I found him this morning. Seems he just up and died sitting in his favorite chair. Sorry to dump that on you Ivan but there it is. There's no changing the facts."

Rory had no way of figuring Ivan's private thoughts but the startled look on the man's face said clearly that the news was an unwelcome addition to the day. Neither man spoke as they watched the liveryman make his way along the side of the building.

Ivan waited until Tippet was around the corner of the building and out of earshot before he said, "We can talk of Kiril another time. For now, I figure you found more than you've said."

"Move into the trees a bit."

Ivan walked through the dense trees and undergrowth until he came to a small clearing, kind of like a meeting place where two or three people could talk and be totally hidden from view. He and Rory stood side by side, studying the space. Finally, Ivan moved over to where there was denser growth. He had spotted something. Pulling branches aside, he looked into the exposed space, then turned to Rory with a grin. It was all the invitation the sheriff needed. With their heads close together, the two men looked at a coffee can nailed to a tree, about five feet from the ground and covered with a piece of canvas, near enough the color of the aspen bark to come close to hiding it from sight. Neither man spoke.

Rory bent and pulled a small tuft of cloth from a thorn bush that grew among the gathering of shrubs and undergrowth. He held it up and twisted it through his fingers. It was pink and soft, something from a woman's dress probably. He held it out for Ivan to see more closely. Ivan simply nodded and turned his eyes back to the coffee can.

Ivan finally reached and lifted the canvas, exposing the opening in the can. Inside was a badly weathered note and two worn and tarnished ten-dollar gold pieces. He passed the coins to Rory, who rubbed some dirt off them and held them out to the light.

"Look here, Ivan. These are old. Or at least they have the appearance of being old. You can see from the discoloring and the scratches and scars that they've been kicking around for at least a few years. The scratches and scars are because gold is soft and easily damaged. I learned that much up on the gold fields. These are still good, as far as value is concerned, but since pure gold doesn't take on a tarnish, there's a mystery here."

Ivan pulled the paper out of the can and looked at it. He then turned it to Rory. With just a glance, the sheriff asked, "What language is this?"

"That's our family's language. Kiril's native tongue. I don't read it so well. Speaking the language and reading in that alphabet are two different things. My father could read it."

"Is that a signature at the bottom?"

"I don't think so. Might be goodbye or something like that."

As Ivan held the note in his hands, he turned to Rory and asked, "Where does this trail go?"

"To the back of another barn."

As if suddenly understanding, Ivan said, with some emphasis, "Kiril, that cagy old man was up to something."

Rory nodded in agreement. "I came down that trail, but we won't try to go back up. It's steep in one place. Very steep. He had a rope coiled and ready that I had to use just to get down. Getting back up would be a chore that proved nothing. Can't imagine how Kiril even discovered the way down. Trail must be three or four miles long. Took some work.

"I'd like if we could take a ride up the hill together. We need to try to sort some of this out. It's late in the day, but you can stay with your folks, and I'll bunk down at Kiril's. My horse is in his barn anyway. I'll be wanting to care for him."

By late afternoon, with Rory riding a livery horse, the two men pulled up in front of the small ranch house. Ivan's father came out and told them dinner was on the table.

Ivan waited until after the meal to pull the note from his pocket. He passed it to his father and waited. He did not mention the gold pieces. Mr. Ivanov glanced immediately at the note and then, his eyes widening, asked, "Where did you get this?"

Rory explained as much as he knew.

"I was hoping you could read that for me."

"I can read it. It is our language. But who could have written this that you now have it?"

Mrs. Ivanov spoke up. "You know who spoke our language. You don't have to wonder."

"Kiril."

They sat in silence around the table. Even when it was obvious that there could be no other answer, Rory held his silence. Finally, lifting the note off the table, Mr. Ivanov read, "Nothing new. Lawman could be a problem. Miss talking with you, Emiliya. Two coins for you. Again soon."

Mrs. Ivanov, who would have kept her silence in the old country, asked, "And who is this? This Emiliya?"

Rory only understood the question when Ivan turned to him and said, "Mother is wondering who Emiliya is."

"And I'm wondering that myself."

~

Leaving Ivan at the home ranch, Rory rode back up to Kiril's for the night. He still had troubling thoughts about what the loner had been up to. And then, if he had two gold coins, there was every probability that he had others. It was unlikely that he would give away his last two unless he had another source of income. But where could his stash possibly be? Rory felt he had been over every crack and crevice of the place, every possible hiding spot.

As he rode into the yard, his eyes scanned the layout again. Cabin, barn, corral, kitchen garden, hen house. Hen house! The chicken coop. He had shied away after his first look but maybe. Perhaps...

He tied a cloth he found in the cabin over his mouth and nose and walked to the house of dead chickens, rotted eggs, flies, lice, and fleas. And stench. Reluctantly he pulled the gate open and stepped inside the little yard. He first looked over the exterior of the small building and, finding nothing of interest, reached for the door. Flies buzzed everywhere. Thousands of flies. The combined reek of the uncleaned floor and the carcasses rotting in the summer sun was as bad as anything Rory had ever faced. But with determination, knowing the need for doing a thorough job if he was to call himself a lawman, he stepped into the dull interior. There were eight nests in two layers, four per layer. That was provision for more eggs than one man could ever eat. He investigated each one and, with a short stick he had picked up on the ground outside, turned over the dried out hay and rotted eggs in each nest on the top layer. He prodded the first three nests on the lower layer and found nothing. The last nest, the one furthest from the door, had a small block of wood wedged halfway in, creating a shallower nesting space. With renewed hope, Rory reached in, found a finger hole, and pulled out the wood. No chickens had been near the space behind the wooden barrier. A small canvas sack with a drawstring at the top rested on the clean wooden bottom. As he picked it up, there was the clank of coins. Nervously, hardly believing what he had found, Rory lifted the sack out, cradling the bottom in his other hand in case the sack had rotted, and backed out of the dreadful coop. He left the door open in the hopes that the place would air out some after the summer sun had dried or desiccated the remaining carnage.

He walked quickly toward the cabin, flinging his cloth face mask away as he went, and set the sack on the back stoop. Most of the flies abandoned him before he reached the cabin, but not all. He itched, or, at least imagined he did, from the hordes of fleas and lice.

Loosening the drawstrings, he glanced inside the small sack. As he suspected, it contained coins. Gold coins. Perhaps twelve or fifteen in all. He would count them later. Right at the moment, he had to get out of his stench-infiltrated clothing and have a bath.

His livery horse, borrowed from Tippet, was grazing beside the creek. The borrowed saddle was still in place. He picketed the horse, wanting it to be there when he climbed out of the creek. It wouldn't do to lose one of Tippet's rental horses.

He would need the spare clothing stowed in his bedroll. After walking to the barn, where his own saddle and gear were stowed, he unrolled his bedroll and removed the clean clothing. He then walked to the back door stoop and stripped to his skin, dropping the dirty clothing into a heap.

With a bar of blistering-strong soap he found on Kiril's washstand, he walked to the small stream that wandered past the cabin and waded into the shallow water. The stream, an offshoot of the larger flow on the further edge of the property, was too narrow to sit in effectively. Frustrated, he stood, naked as the day he was born, and dripping the small bit of water he had managed to scoop over his head and shoulders, walked to the larger stream. Sitting waist-deep in the cold mountaintop meltwater, he soaked and soaped head to foot for a solid half hour. Even after enduring that self-punishment, he was still sure that he could smell the chicken coop. He finally decided that he was sensing his own breath and the foul air he had drawn into his nostrils. Scouring his teeth with his finger helped a bit. With the abundance of water flowing around him, he cleaned his nostrils and sniffed cold water into his sinuses. Each of his actions helped some. The rest would take time.

The bath wasn't perfect, but it would have to do.

Cleaned and redressed in the spare clothing, he made an evening cup of coffee from Kiril's fixings and sat in the old man's chair, contemplating. He would stay the one night and then ride down to the I-5, hoping for some breakfast before he headed back to town with Ivan.

～

RIDING SLOWLY BACK down the hill with Rory comfortably saddled on his own familiar mount retrieved from Kiril's barn, Ivan became talkative.

"That old man had some start-up money from somewhere. He couldn't build that place of his or have the iron stove and the modern weapons and such without some money. It's doubtful if he brought it from the old country. Most who came, landed on these shores broke and wanting. I hate to think it of him now that he's gone and all, but he may not have been quite as honest as I gave him credit for.

"You showing me those coins you found only adds more mystery to a man I called friend and was in the habit of listening to and heeding for advice. But, even after saying that, I have to admit, I never gave his honesty or the source of his money a thought."

That short speech was followed by a full minute of silence.

"I never placed any importance on it before, Rory, but Kiril wandered all over these hills. Sometimes on horseback but often on foot. Walked for miles. Him and that dog of his. He's maybe the walkingest man I ever knew.

He never talked about where he went, but there's a good chance he knew the locations of most of the ranches. May have even talked to some of the ranchers or cowboys. There's no telling what he might have been up to."

Rory mulled on that for a short while and then offered, "Something to think on, Ivan."

By agreement, the two lawmen said nothing about what they had discovered after they reached town. Rory returned Tippet's horse and got his promise to say nothing of the trail behind the barn. He then rode to the Double J for a rest and a fresh horse.

26

Rory walked into the Stevensville Bank and directly to Jesse Ambrewster's office. He had always found it helpful that the banker only closed his door when he was with a customer. If the door was open, Ambrewster was alone. Holding back the information about the sack of coins found in Kiril's chicken coop, without a word, he laid the two gold coins found behind the livery on the desk in front of the banker. Then he took a seat and waited. Jesse bent over the coins without touching them. Then, with one finger, he turned them so he could more easily read the inscription and the date. Taking just a quick glance at the sheriff, he slid the top drawer of his desk open and lifted out a small, brass eye-loupe. With care, he twisted the loupe from its enclosure and held it to his eye. Still not touching the coins, he bent over the desk and took a long look, first at one and then at the other.

With caution, he used his letter opener to flip the coins over, a caution Rory found excessive considering the coins had been liberally handled already. Jesse studied the other side of each coin as carefully as he had the first. With a deep sigh, he leaned back in his chair and said, "Well, young man, when you were assigned the sheriff's role, it seemed like something that might be better than nothing. Really though, not much was expected from the experiment. But you continue to surprise me. Me, and a lot of others, I might add. Care to tell me where you got these?"

Although there was clearly more behind the question than what was on the surface, Rory was prepared for it. He had come to depend on the banker for his knowledge as well as the banking services. Knowing the banker would be full of questions, he had asked himself if he could refuse the information without breaking an important link, and aid, in his sheriff's duties.

When Rory had first returned from the goldfields, he had developed serious doubts about the banker, with no real evidence to back up his concerns. After working his way past those doubts, he had no desire to offend his banking friend. But until he cleared up a couple of things, he needed to hold some confidences to himself.

He had, furthermore, decided it might implicate Jesse unfairly if he dragged him into the story before all was known. Still, who better to have seen coins like that or have some idea of their source than a banker? The thought was still fresh in his mind when he was already feeling guilty, fearing he could be accused of using the man rather than trusting and working with him.

"It might be best if you didn't know right at this time. Safer. Depending on what else I discover. I'm thinking those behind this might fall a little short of being the citizen of the year. But I'd appreciate it if you would find an envelope to place these in and hold them in your safe as evidence. Evidence of exactly what, I'm not too sure.

But perhaps you can answer a question for me. Have you seen others of this type pass through your bank?"

The two men studied each other for a short while, the older banker trying to see into the mind of the much younger sheriff. The banker was a plodding, studious man. The sheriff would be a counterpoint, as a more impulsive youth. Jesse didn't want to either stifle or encourage that impulsiveness. Holding steady was more his style. Both men accepted the silence between them, which offered no answer to the asked question, taking it all as a delay to another day, when they might be more open with each other.

Rory was remembering something. He should have thought of it earlier. He said nothing to Jesse. He simply stood, said thanks, and walked out, leaving his question unanswered. He was wishing he had shown only the one coin and kept the other for a sample, but it was too late to take one back without raising even more questions than he had already.

Pondering on the money recovered from the phony judge months earlier and trying to remember, he slowly walked across the street and entered the mercantile. He waited until Browning was free and then walked to the counter. The two men passed some idle chat for a few seconds, giving Rory a chance to sense the mood of the town councillor and store owner. He hated walking on pins and needles, but he couldn't afford to lose the confidence of even one villager. Small centers being what they are, a careless question asked here could become gossip fodder by lunchtime. He finally turned up his courage and spoke.

"Mr. Browning, I'm hoping you can help me refresh my memory. You will remember that sack of money recovered from under the floor in the judge's office. I remember there were some coins in it. But I was pretty new at this back then. I didn't make a note of what kinds of coins or what their values were. We simply added them to the others held at the bank. I'm trying to remember if there were any gold coins in the bunch."

Browning grinned. "Seemed strange at the time. All that silver and just the one gold piece. Different though. Not a standard gold piece such as I see almost every day. Old looking. Scratched a bit. As if it had been handled carelessly or hurriedly. Tarnished."

Rory could feel his heart rate going up.

"Have you ever seen another like it?"

"Saw one just a while ago. Pretty much an exact duplicate. Took it in to cover off a month-end bill for a customer. Kept it. I can't afford to be hanging on to spendable money, but I liked that piece for some reason. Got it right here in the cash drawer."

As he spoke, he was opening the drawer he kept the day's take in. Lifting out the top tray, he reached beneath, pushed a few pieces of paper aside, and came up with a gold coin, the exact duplicate of the ones Kiril had left in the coffee can. And the others Rory had found in the chicken coop.

Browning renewed his grin and passed the coin to Rory.

"Is that what you're looking for?"

Rory already knew. He didn't need a careful study. The match was all but exact.

"Do you remember who paid their bill with this?"

With that question, Browning's grin faded. He seemed a bit embarrassed as he said, "Sheriff, we're getting close to the cutting edge of gossip and circumstance here. Yes, of course, I remember. But I'm going to hold that until you do a bit more footwork. I have no reason at all to mistrust that customer and friend. And I certainly can't see any connection with the judge and all the misdeeds he and his partner laid on our community. You come up with some connection, and I'll sure enough be honest with you. But, just not yet, a while."

Rory was disappointed, but he somewhat saw the merchant's side of it. If he told of finding the other two coins, it might make a difference in the storekeeper's mind. Still, a misspoken word could ruin a good person's reputation. And in this new West, a ruined reputation was to come close to being a ruined man, or woman, either one. He would accept the bit of secrecy, adding it to the secrecy already agreed to with the banker.

"Thanks, Mr. Browning. You keep that coin safe."

"I'll do that, Rory. Good work, young man."

27

RORY WENT BACK TO THE DOUBLE J FOR THE NIGHT. Sitting around the big dinner table, the talk ranged from the shortage of rain and the condition of the grass to the empty grazing land now that the K Slash had moved the herd out. That led to wondering how the boys were doing in their search for a replacement herd.

Finally, someone asked how his lawing was going. Trusting his family to hold a simple secret, he said, "Going pretty well right now."

"So, what are you working on?"

The question from Nancy, spoken in a tone of respect, showed the young lady in a more mature light than the teasing and quip-filled talk of the past. It looked good on her. And it felt good to Rory, as if he might be earning his position in the family's eyes after what he considered a fumbling start. He outlined the situation, holding back whatever he felt was critical to confidentiality. But the fact of the death of the uphill recluse couldn't be avoided.

"Kiril's death and a bit of my looking into things left

me wondering who Emiliya might be. I don't know everyone in town or around the country, but the name is unusual. I think I'd remember if I'd ever heard it."

Nancy quickly asked, "Where did you hear that name?"

"Just doing my job. It came along with some evidence. Written in a note. Strange thing. The note was not in English. Some other writing. Mr. Ivanov read it for me."

Nancy spoke again, with considerable confidence. "Emily. It means Emily in English, or close enough. I'd bet on that. And the only Emily I know around here is the doctor's wife. Emily. Emily Bodner, she calls herself, although her English is just a bit broken, as if she learned another language first. Em, the doc calls her."

Rory shook his head just a bit and asked to be excused from the table. Without waiting for an answer, he opened the door and stopped, thinking. He turned back to the table and said, "Please, that conversation stays right here. It's very important." He then sauntered to his own cabin.

Em. Sure enough, he had heard the doctor address his wife that way. Emiliya, in another language. Emily or Em in English. It seemed simple enough. Perhaps too simple? And what was Mrs. Bodner's native tongue? How could he find out? Mulling on this for a moment, he began to grin. *That's the answer. That should work.*

Now if he could only sort out the matter of the gold coins. Thinking back to the mess the phony judge left in the community and the single gold coin that connected him to Kiril and what was currently happening, he thought of the trail of the rustled cattle. That trail had led to the Panhandle and a Texas rancher. Speaking half aloud as the thoughts tumbled through his mind, Rory said, "If the Texas rancher had paid for the smuggled cattle in gold coins, there should be a lot of those coins still in circulation in the district. In fact, the judge's deposit in the bank could easily have been made in gold coins. But Jesse Ambrewster would surely have mentioned that. Finding just a few tarnished coins rather than an abundance of them was a mystery. And for another mystery, how did Kiril come to have some of the coins? And to add to the mounting mysteries, how were Doc's wife and Kiril connected?"

Adding to the questions rattling around in the sheriff's mind, he let his voice trail to silence. *Are the coins truly the same or at least similar? Was there a connection between them, or was it all coincidence?*

There was no shortage of both gold and silver coins in normal circulation. What connected these he had that could be used as evidence?

IN TOWN THE NEXT MORNING, Rory rode directly to the marshal's office. The day was threatening to be blistering hot, so he tied the gelding in the shade at the side of the building. Ivan stepped out and said, "Coffee's hot and strong. Take a chair. I'll get us both some."

After casually passing a couple of minutes talking about nothing in particular, Rory said, "Got an idea. It's a bit devious, but I think it will work."

"I don't know this word 'devious.'"

"It means to sneak around. To hide the true meaning or to disguise the purpose of your actions."

"Ah! As a man might do who wanted to get away from his woman for an hour or two."

"I hadn't thought of it in quite those terms but, I

suppose, yes, it could be like that. But you surprise me, Ivan. I thought you believed that husbands didn't have to give account to their wives. It was the woman's place to keep the house and the children and not ask questions."

Ivan couldn't miss the grin on Rory's face as he was talking.

Ivan took a swallow of coffee and looked off into the distance, over the rooftops of the buildings across the road. Perhaps dreaming of a long-ago time he had heard about from Kiril, but had never really experienced.

"I don't know, maybe in the old country it was like that. But maybe not. Perhaps it never was like that. Maybe that was mostly in Kiril's mind. And perhaps it is that on the long trip across an ocean and a continent that people change. Men and women find that they need each other in this new land. And so, the affection grows. And the woman no longer holds her silence, like before. But Kiril never had a woman. He told me that. So, he couldn't have known these things."

Rory was surprised that Ivan had taken the ribbing so seriously, becoming almost philosophical.

"I think, Ivan, that you will enjoy having a woman at your side someday. A woman who you care about and one that will speak, and you will listen."

Ivan pulled his eyes away from the blue sky and studied the boardwalk at his feet for a moment before asking, "So what have you found with these gold coins, and what do you plan to do next?"

"Ah, Ivan, it is not what I plan to do next, it is what you will do next, if you agree with my idea."

"And what is it that I am going to do."

"You are going to get up right now and walk across this road. To the bakery. You are going to buy some donuts. And you are going to say good morning to the doctor's wife, who I just saw walk into the shop. You are going to say it quietly, just to her, in your native tongue. Her name is Emily. The doctor calls her Em. That is very much like Emiliya, is it not?"

Ivan grinned and stood.

"Sheriff, your mind is very devious. Is that the right meaning of that word that you say hides the true intent?"

"That's it exactly."

Rory entered the little office to refill his coffee cup as Ivan crossed the street. He was gone a bit longer than Rory thought he would be, but finally, the bakery shop door opened, and a very flustered Em Bodner stepped out. Gathering up her long skirt, she rushed toward home, nearly colliding with a neighbor lady as she hurried along. The woman spoke to her, but she didn't stop or respond.

Within a minute, Ivan came from the shop with a small, white paper bag in his hand. He waited for a passing wagon and then crossed to where Rory was sitting. Without a word, he passed the bag to Rory and went to refill his own coffee mug. When he returned, Rory was already eating his second donut. Ivan had purchased a half dozen. He took his seat and said, "I believe I have learned a new word this morning. And its meaning."

"Learning new things is always helpful, Ivan."

"Yes. Well, it didn't help Em Bodner much. She dropped her coin purse when I greeted her very quietly in my native tongue. I had to help her gather up her coins. When I asked about the well-being of her family, I thought she would faint. She rushed out so quickly, the baker and I just stood there saying nothing. There is no doubt that she speaks our tongue."

"You are very good at being devious, Ivan. Good work."

The two men finished up their coffee and donuts in silence.

~

RORY'S next stop was the bank. Jesse was busy, so Rory hung around talking to Andy Speth. As soon as the other customer left, Jesse called Rory in. Rory's quietly spoken message was received with a grin and answered with, "Set the time. I'll be there."

He then walked across the road to the mercantile, leaving the same message and receiving a similar answer.

A short walk to the bakery and another, back to the dining room to talk with Ma Gamble, and the meeting was confirmed. They would meet in the back storage room at the mercantile. When the agreed-upon time arrived, each council member, plus the banker, assembled behind the closed door. Nothing of the meeting was to be leaked out. Rory was the last to arrive.

Ma Gamble glanced at him and said, "Come join us, Rory. Tell us what you've been working on and how the census is going."

Rory eased up to a burlap sack of feed and sat down. He looked the gathering over and said, "You've asked about two things. First, the census is done and turned in to the state office. Now I am trying to sort some other things out.

"As to what I've been working on, I have a question for you. All those months ago, when we discovered the judge and the town marshal were working together to rustle cattle behind the protection of a questionable law, we hoped to wrap it up with all the mysteries sorted out.

That didn't happen. The judge is dead, and the marshal is in prison. But that left several questions unanswered. For example, we don't know for sure how the judge got his information on the ranches. We don't know what brought the judge here in the first place. We don't know for sure who bought the cattle, although I came home from the city with a name that we have never verified. We don't know for sure where the money came from. If it was from the rancher, where did he get it, and do we care?

"Now, I've found a couple of things that may answer at least some of that. But the point is, does anyone care anymore? The rustled ranchers are back in business, buying cattle with impounded money and doing fine, so far as I know. The information I found could upset the milk bucket for a couple of folks. I wouldn't want to do that without a good reason. What do we have to gain by sorting it all out?"

The councillors turned their eyes from Rory to glance among themselves. Jesse Ambrewster, ever the cautious and conservative banker, said, "And what, exactly, could 'upset the milk bucket,' as it was so poetically spoken in your question, Sheriff?"

Hip Dawson, taking time away from his bakery, restated the questions and then answered them himself.

"I'm not sure I can know the right or wrong of chasing the truth until I have a better understanding of what the full truth is."

Jesse took the floor again to add, "Although I, too, wonder what the whole story will divulge, as long as we're alone and agree to hold a confidence between us, I think we should proceed. We can always decide to pull our horns back in. I don't mind telling you what I know. Again, in strict confidence. And as far as that goes, if this turns in the direction I believe it points to, it could well become a federal matter."

Ma laughed and said, "Then you'd best lay it out, Jesse."

"Here's what I know. All information a nonbanker would probably not come across. Or be interested in. Several years ago, there was a holdup that's never been solved. Four or five bandits got word of a wagon coming west. A wagon loaded with stolen Confederate government funds that had disappeared early in the war. There were two small trunks. One carried silver coins. The other carried gold coins. The coins were from among the last batch struck in the New Orleans Mint before it closed at the start of the northern aggression. In the confusion of war and the vast distances in the west, there was never a trace found of the gang or the loot. What it came down to was, in effect, thieves stealing from thieves. But they did it most effectively and got away clean, leaving several bodies on the ground behind them.

None of the coins came into circulation. Not, that is, until a couple of years ago. Even then, the bankers handling the money only singled out the coins, from among the many they handled, by the almost uniform tarnishing on both gold and silver. I'm no metallurgic expert, but from the little I know, pure gold—that is, 24-karat gold—does not tarnish. But gold that is not pure, that has small amounts of other metals in their mix, will pick up a tarnish, as will silver. Every mint had their own formula, but the mint that diluted the gold the most, with other metals, was New Orleans. Hence, their gold coins tarnished more easily, and quickly, than the other mints.

"In terms of the metal itself, these were not old. Metal, after all, is virtually eternal. But the coins that troubled the most observant bankers looked old, older than the date stamped into their design. The tarnishing and careless storage could leave that appearance.

"Now, let me show you something."

He glanced at Rory as he lifted a small envelope from his jacket pocket and slid the two ten-dollar gold pieces onto the tabletop. They were the ones Rory had entrusted him with.

"Rory can tell you where these came from, all in due time. But for now, without touching them, take a careful look."

He then laid an untarnished coin beside the other two for comparison. The difference was stark.

"Now, see here," he said, pointing with his desk pen. "Look carefully. You will see from the design of the tarnish that these coins have been stacked together for a long time. Not neatly stacked, you understand, but more as if they had slipped a bit, perhaps as the trunk they were stored in slid onto its side and rested there for a long time. That would leave more metal exposed around the edges than in the centers. You can see the partial circle in the tarnish, where another coin rested."

Knowing it had all been set up beforehand, Rory wasn't surprised when Browning set the coin he had held in his money drawer onto the table, sliding it close to the other two. The match was uncanny.

Ma then reached into her pocket and laid down a coin. Surprise overtook the gathering, but when Rory emptied the sack found in Kiril's chicken coop and spread the coins around, the group was dumbfounded.

No one spoke, waiting for Jesse to continue. Before he spoke, he pulled out the small brass eye loupe he had used back at the bank earlier. With it, he studied Browning's coin and then leaned back in satisfaction.

"Take a look, Ma. Look carefully, right under the eagle. What do you see?"

"There's a small *o* stamped there."

"Now look at Browning's coin."

"The same thing."

"They are of the same vintage, all 1860. Their tarnish is almost an exact duplicate, and they are all from New Orleans. That's what that small *o* means. I'd bet my bank that these are all from that payroll theft, hidden away in their trunks for all these years, either lost and then found again, or they were stowed where it was too risky to go after them. And I would bet my bottom dollar they have been either underwater or subject to rain more than just the once. But finally, somehow, they're back in circulation. And it would seem an unusual number of them have shown up in our little town."

Ma Gamble said, "Now I'm wondering, Jesse, if these coins, struck in the South, are really valid money."

"They are. First, of course, they're gold. The gold is worth nearly as much as the face value of the coin. Second, New Orleans, although it was in the South, was producing federal government coins. So, these coins are, in fact, US coins and worth their full face value."

28

THE MEETING FELL TO SILENCE WHILE THE TOWN councilors looked at the display on the table and then scanned each other's faces, hoping for some enlightenment.

Rory felt he had to speak, to put the meeting back on track.

"I am left with two questions. Other than that, I'm not much interested in spending time on a years-old crime that happened in another state during wartime.

"The first question is, how did these coins come to be in Stevensville, and into Kiril's hands? The second is, as long as no evidence points to someone in the town or county committing a crime, do we really care about any of this?"

Ma, although most would consider her uneducated, had shown over the years to be a woman of unusual perception.

"I think we would have to know the answer to the first question before we can address the second."

Rory nodded and said, "Yes, but before we get into

that, I'm wondering about something I should have asked before. Jesse, how did the judge make the deposit to your bank? Was it bills, coins, or a mixture of the two?"

"It was neither. It was a bank draft transfer. Large deposits are almost always by wire or by internal transfer delivered by stagecoach carrying the mail. I never saw any real cash money. That practice could change after the steam cars are in service here, but for now, we deal mostly in paper. Paper and goodwill."

Rory nodded again, "Good. Now, as I remember, you paid the ranchers out of that deposit with internal transfers into their own accounts. You didn't sit and count out the money. Dealing in paper and goodwill, as you phrased it. No actual money changed hands. And, at the end, when the funds you held didn't divide evenly, I made up the few dollars difference with the cash found under the judge's floorboards. It was necessary to give cash to only one person. The rest received a bank deposit slip only. And in that bit of cash, there was one gold coin. I remember it but didn't put it together in my mind until just now. Ma, did you get that coin from either Lavinia Flint or Ambrose King?"

"Good guess, Sheriff. Lavinia used it that time she was in town for several days."

"I wasn't really guessing, Ma. I remember sliding that coin over to her to help balance the payout. But now that we've gone that far, Mr. Browning, did you get your coin from Mrs. Em Bodner?"

Everyone turned to see Browning, who had still been hoping to hold the name in confidence, nod his head in silence, his lips pursed tightly.

Rory, returning to his questions, said, "Kiril is dead. I've searched his place top to bottom. If there's more to find up there, I don't know where it would be. But that he was in possession of some of the suspect coins is beyond question. That includes these other coins that I found hidden in his chicken coop.

"Someday, over coffee, I'll tell you that story, but right now, it doesn't matter.

"How he came by the coins is a question that stumped me until we, collectively, started putting it all together. The link, I think, we've shown so far, is the judge, a thief and a con man, and the sale of the stolen herds. And I might not have found that link if it weren't for the coins found under the floorboards in the judge's office. And from there to the K Slash Ranch.

"Perhaps it's time I told you what I found behind Kiril's barn and behind Tippet's livery."

It took only a couple of minutes to describe the trail down the hill and the coffee can message box at the bottom. Laying the weathered note on the small desk and pointing out the name Emiliya brought several gasps of surprise. The confirmation that Em Bodner spoke the same language as Kiril was a total shock. The fact that Em spoke another language was well known. That, in itself, meant nothing. Many people had learned their English after arriving from another land. But tying it all together with the mysterious Kiril, the dishonest judge, and the trail of matching, and probably stolen, gold coins had to point to more than a coincidence.

When he was finished with the story, he said, "To wrap this thing up, I believe I have to talk openly with Mrs. Bodner. But, again, the question. In most ways, this is over for us. Do we care anymore?"

Jesse Ambrewster said, "I care. I don't wish to sound self-righteous, but government money was stolen. And yes, it was the Confederate government, but we are trying to bring the nations back together. That should mean that we are doing what we can to have an honest society. No one in this county will be in any danger of accusation. Everything our friends and neighbors have done is honest and justifiable. I can't see how they can be hurt."

The silent nods provided Rory with the go-ahead he had been seeking.

The meeting broke up with each one taking possession of the coins they had brought to the meeting and giving a pledge of silence.

ON THE WAY TO see Mrs. Bodner, Rory went past the marshal's office and invited Ivan to join him. The two men walked together to the little house where the Bodners lived, and where the doc had his small clinic. Rory tapped on the door, as was the usual procedure, and then stepped into the waiting room. Em Bodner opened the door to the living quarters and looked at her visitors. With a troubled expression on her face, she gasped lightly and lifted her hand to cover her mouth in a gesture of concern.

Rory had no desire to prolong her misery at their presence. He said, "Mrs. Bodner, I'd like to talk with you if you don't mind. Can the doctor join us?"

"Come in. We've just stopped for afternoon tea. Would you like some?"

"We won't bother with the tea, thank you, and we won't trouble you more than necessary either. I just have a bit of a mystery to clear up. Straightening that up, I'm sure, will help me clear up a larger mystery."

"Come in. Have a seat."

The two men stepped into the small parlor, greeted the doctor, and sat down, both placing their hats on their knees.

"Mrs. Bodner, please be assured that no one suspects you of doing anything wrong. But there's a mystery that needs clearing up, and you could be the key, to part of it anyway. The mystery surrounds certain gold coins that somehow found their way into our community. There are, of course, many coins in circulation, but these are quite distinctive, and they seem to have an unsavory history. I don't care about the history. It was long ago and far away, and I'll leave it for others to solve.

"You used one of those coins, Mrs. Bodner. Used it at Mr. Browning's mercantile. Although Browning wouldn't divulge the name of his customer, I've seen the coin. He set it aside because of its distinctive look. We found more of those coins, Mrs. Bodner. They were with a note addressed to you. I have it here."

Rory laid the note on the table, along with the two coins that he had brought with him. Mrs. Bodner's hands were shaking, and the doctor had a quizzical look on his face.

"The note is a bit faded and weathered. I take it that it had been there for a while.

"Of course, I couldn't read the note as it's in another language. But Ivan recognized some of the words. He doesn't know that alphabet well enough to read the whole note, although he speaks it well enough. So, we rode up the hill and had his father read it to us. Of course, the note was written by Kiril, the loner who lived up above the Ivanov Ranch. From what I've been able to piece together, Kiril and the Ivanov family are from the same country and district in old Europe. They weren't friends, except Ivan here, formed a sort of friendship with the old man. But you also kept a relationship of some sort with him, Mrs. Bodner. And you speak his language. I'd like if you would tell me about that, Mrs. Bodner."

Doc spoke for the first time, asking, "If you are so sure of all this, why don't you ask the old man yourself?"

"The simple and unhappy fact is that Kiril is dead."

Mrs. Bodner again gasped and placed her hands in front of her mouth. She started to shake in shock, and Rory thought she was going to cry. But she stifled the shock and settled for a couple of deep sobs.

Doc said, "What do you mean dead? Are you sure of that?"

"Found him dead, and buried him myself, Doc. He'd been dead for some time. All his chickens were starved, dead in the coop and yard. Not a speck of feed in sight. His dog was nearly starved, and his two horses would have been dead in another day or two."

"What happened? Could you tell? Any marks on him?"

"No marks that I could see. He was sitting on his favorite chair beside the cabin. I've seen him there a couple of times before. His rifle laid across his knee, again, just as I'd seen him before. It looked like perhaps his heart simply decided it was time. Anything at all, of course, is a guess.

"But back to the question, Mrs. Bodner. I did a thorough search of Kiril's place. Fed the dog and the horses. They're now at the Ivanov Ranch for safekeeping. Found a trail behind his barn. It wasn't easy, but I followed it. It comes out behind Tippet's livery. Very well disguised back there, where no one ever goes, except you from time to time, Mrs. Bodner."

Doc studied his wife with obvious questions in his mind, but he held his silence.

"Mrs. Bodner, we're dealing with the theft of government funds here. And we're dealing with cattle rustling. Again, let me say that I hold no suspicion pointing your way. But I really hope you will tell me what you know. To help me clear this all up."

Em Bodner's voice was so low all three men leaned a bit forward to get every word.

"Kiril was a cousin. A distant cousin, although we knew each other in childhood. The Ivanov family are not related. I didn't even know they were in the district until we had been here a year or more. The Ivanovs don't come to town often, and we had never crossed paths. Kiril somehow met Ivan's father, and although they didn't really get along, he decided to build up near them. Thinking of home and the old country, I guess. Kiril chose to come here because of me. Again, a connection with home. Through a letter from the old country, he had somehow tracked me down.

"That bush trail was his connection between us, and to ease his shopping trips, as well. He was a strange man. Hard and bitter in many respects and dismissive of most women, but we had been friendly in the old country when I was a child. Kiril was considerably older than me.

"When he built up in the woods, he promised not to be a nuisance. He only wanted to have some connection with home and family. And hear the old language from time to time. Even that was strange. He came from a hard family. His father was a tyrant. The children knew no, or little, family love. They were builders. Good at the trade and always working hard, but the kids saw none of their earnings. I have never been to Kiril's cabin, but I would imagine it is a credit to his father's training.

"He worked out that trail and discovered he could arrive behind the livery barn. I met him once when I was spending time with the livery horses. I often talked with them and fed them carrots and such. Kiril surprised me when he came from behind the barn. We visited. I still speak the old tongue fairly well.

"I came to America quite young with an older sister. We both went to work for wealthy New England families. The lady I worked for demanded that I learn English, and that I learn it well. She was a good teacher, and I learned. So, you see, I hadn't seen Kiril for several years. It was a shock to have him come from behind the livery right when I was feeding the horses. We talked. We remembered family from home, and we laughed about our childhood antics. He asked me about the happenings in the area. I guess we gossiped, but it seemed harmless. I told him the news, and he listened, seemed interested."

Rory interrupted with a question.

"Did you, perhaps, tell him that Mr. Flint, of the K Ranch, had died?"

"I'm sure I did. My husband is the doctor, and that information crosses our doorstep regularly. In any case, it was a well-known fact, and not a secret."

"Did you ever talk about the Double J?"

"He asked. Said he had heard some rumors of a partnership and that one of the partners had disappeared. I assured him that you and your father would be returning. Someday, even if not soon.

"We visited three or four more times, and then I found a note with a couple of coins in that coffee can you discovered. After that, I found two more notes. And each time, two coins. I have not spent them. I still have them. He said he was repaying a bit of the money my father had lent him toward his passage to America. I knew of no loan, but I had no one to ask, and it no longer seemed important. And I assure you, Sheriff, there was no involvement on my part in anything illegal or questionable."

"I never thought there was, but you have helped a great deal. Thank you. Now, did Kiril ever say where he got the coins?"

"He mentioned just once that he did the odd favor for the town marshal. It was easier for the marshal to ask Kiril what he had seen and heard in the backcountry than it was to ride all over the ranchcountry himself."

Ivan spoke for the first time.

"That seems a bit strange, considering that Mike Wasson was the town marshal only."

Rory stood and said, "Doc. Mrs. Bodner, thanks. You've helped immensely. I think we can make this thing go away completely, pretty quickly. And, Mrs. Bodner, if you still have those coins, I recommend that you take them to the bank. Speak with Jesse Ambrewster personally. Have him break them into smaller coins. That could save some talk around town when you go to spend the money. You can trust Jesse's discretion. Now, thanks for your time."

29

RORY DISMOUNTED FROM THE BODY-SHATTERING stagecoach in downtown Denver instead of at the county office. Each time he rode the bouncing, dusty, rattling contraption, his hatred for it grew. Now he needed a night's sleep and a good meal before he met with Oscar Cator. He had just a little shopping to do also. He checked into the hotel he had stayed at before, took a bath, and walked down the stairs for dinner. The item he had purchased was left in the room, ready for the next morning, when he hoped it would have the desired effect. He chuckled a bit to himself as he thought about it, wondering what would happen if his plot backfired.

Dinner was good, although the dining room was packed and noisy. A night's sleep would put all of that and the stage ride behind him.

The next morning, with his purchased gift in one hand and his satchel of evidence in the other, he entered the county office.

"Good morning, Bertha, I see you're minding the store in your usual efficiently cheerful manner. It's a comfort to know that our government has faithful workers caring for our interests. Here's a little something I found for you. I hope you like chocolate. Our friends over at the Cadbury company put these together just for people like you."

Tapping on Oscar Cator's door brought the response, "It's not locked." Rory thought he could sense a smile in the voice.

The two men shook hands, with Oscar holding back a laugh. As Rory took a seat and laid his hat on the second chair, Oscar studied the young man and shook his head.

"No one but you would even dare."

The office partitions stopped short of the ceiling, allowing the voices and other noises of the surrounding area to penetrate, or escape, each private enclosure. Oscar's words were so quietly spoken that Rory almost missed them. More loudly, Oscar asked, "So what have you got for me this time."

Rory opened the satchel and pulled out item after item, including a small sack of gold coins. When he set the coins down, he said, "I purchased these from their owners with money impounded from other cases. We can now consider them as county property. You can hold them as evidence if anything ever comes of what I'm going to tell you."

He then went on to explain the new findings on the judge's cattle rustling case. Oscar took notes as he listened. When Rory finished the story, he said, "Kiril was the pipeline, the story spreader. He walked the hills and brought information back to the phony marshal, who gave it over to the phony judge, who, in turn, found a way to get a liberal amount of money into Kiril's hands, all in gold coins.

"Mrs. Bodner—Em Bodner, the doctor's wife—inadvertently did the same with matters she knew about from the doctor's office. But since most of that was already common knowledge in the town, she didn't receive any pay, except what came back through Kiril, and we don't know if he was paying her for information or simply sharing for old times' sake. I doubt if it matters, anyway. That's it. That's all I have. If you're going to get more, I'm thinking you'll have to get it from Mike Wasson, wherever he's stored away.

"In any case, it has probably become a federal matter. It's certainly over my pay grade."

After a moment of reflection, Oscar said, "Mike Wasson is down at Canyon City. Good locks on their facility. I expect he's safe and sound."

Rory hoped to end the matter with, "You do as you wish, my friend. As far as I and the good folks of Stevensville are concerned, we've washed our hands of it.

"There is one other thing to consider, though. A suspicion only, and not one I'm prepared to chase. The question is, what caused the judge to choose Stevensville? It would seem that he had some of those coins well before he sold the rustled herds. Where did he get them, and what other districts had he been pulling that rustling thing in? What other cattle had been run down to Texas, and did the same rancher buy them all? That's at least a state matter in my mind. Perhaps even federal. In any case, it's not something a nineteen-year-old pretend sheriff with no training could possibly sort out.

"If the Federals want to chase that Texas rancher to track the trail and history of the stolen payroll, they can get right to it. But the feeling up at Stevensville is that it's no longer a town or county case. We've closed the book on it."

Oscar stared at the ceiling for so long Rory thought he had forgotten what they had been talking about. But finally, he dropped his view to look Rory directly in the eyes.

"Good work, Sheriff. I had kind of closed the book on that matter myself. I was not aware of any payroll theft, so I didn't think to pursue it. One rustler was dead, and the other in prison. That's usually enough. There is no doubt that strange things have taken place in ranching circles in Texas, where the longhorn reigned supreme for so many years. But that's a Texas matter and maybe best left alone. It's possible though, that the Rangers or the Federals will see it differently. I'll see this information gets to the right bodies, and they can take it from there. They can even go down to Canyon City and interview Mike Wasson if they wish.

"Now tell me what you've heard from the towns regarding the holding of an election."

30

RIDING THE STAGE BACK TOWARD STEVENSVILLE, IN HIS mind, comparing the jostling, dusty, slow punishment, to the cushioned and upholstered seats in the steam car on the trip home, after buying the upgraded bulls, Rory found himself wishing for a speedy arrival of both the rail lines and the telegraph. Money had been raised, and roadbed was being prepared both to the north and south of Denver. To the north, the rails would connect the fast-growing state to the transcontinental running through Cheyenne. South, he assumed, the target would be Santa Fe, although that was just a guess. Provided the route chosen came somewhere close to Stevensville, Rory would make his last stage trip sometime in the next year. *If my body holds together that long.*

At the one-night stopover on the long stage ride north, the big-bellied cook promised a buffalo steak dinner. Thinking back over the dinner the next morning, Rory had some doubts about the provenance of the meat. He found himself remembering the greasy taste he couldn't wash out of his mouth, more than he did the dinner itself. But the knowledge that Stevensville and the Double J were only a few hours further along raised his spirits, and his hopes of bodily survival.

When the whip, sitting high on his forward seat, with the shotgun guard hanging on to the bouncing seat beside him, hollered, "Whoa. Whoa up you horses." the four men in the passenger compartment sat up and took notice. Two of them, men of the frontier judging by dress and manner, picked up their rifles and held them at the ready. Rory opened his topcoat, freeing his access to the two belted Colts. The fourth man, a bit older, city-dressed and refined, held his briefcase on his lap, safely tucked under folded arms.

There was no logical reason to pull the stage to a halt at that point. They were between stage stops, and there was little settlement in the area. Still, stopping they were. Rory set his hat on the bench beside him and stuck his head out the side window, stretching to see what was ahead. He waited until the stage was nearly stopped, before the dust began dispersing and he got a clear view. Without pulling back, he spoke to those inside.

"Southbound stage is on its side on the road. One horse down, the rest in a tangle of leather. One saddled horse running loose. Two bodies on the road."

He sat back down and pulled his hat down tight. The two frontier men looked eager for a fight. Rory, thinking of the times he had exchanged lead, was hoping the situation was under control.

One of the frontier men sneered at the man with the briefcase.

"Maybe could be we'll see a little action. Best you run and hide behind the bushes, fella. Only real men needed here now. No city men nor cowards. Jest get in the way. Take this kid showing off his two-gun rig with you. Got no time for kids pretending to be men."

The city man grinned without taking his eyes off the speaker. Using touch only, still holding the sneering man's eyes, he snapped the briefcase open. Holding the case with his left hand and reaching in, still without moving his eyes or dropping his grin, he withdrew a stunningly crafted, long-barreled, elkhorn handled .45 Colt, a beautiful and deadly weapon. He deftly gripped the piece, thumbed the hammer back, and held it within a couple of inches of the speaker's nose. No words were returned, but the deep gulp of air taken by the arrogant frontiersman matched the grin on the face of the briefcase holder.

Rory was somewhat amused by the interplay but chose not to respond to the insult directed at him. He figured there was enough trouble in the world without him unnecessarily adding to it.

The stage ground to a halt, and Tate, the driver, climbed down. The silence was broken when he shouted, "What goes, boys?"

"Done got held up, as your eyes would clearly show you, if'n you wasn't too old to see clear. Course, a man might could figure it by his ownself if'n he was to half try. That horse and those two men ain't jest tak'n a siesta there in the road."

"I can plainly see that, you miserable old fool. Now tell me what happened, and who are those men lying there? And where are your passengers?"

"No passengers this trip. This was a special run. Holding bank money for the big dealers down to Denver. That's why the guards. The shotgun, that's him lying there beside one of the holdup men, he was killed right off. Shot from behind that brush. Never had a chance. The horse was next. One of the guards, him standing over there with his eyes open to the trail the holdup gang took, he leaped off the tipping over stage and shot that fella on the road. Shot him right out of his saddle.

"We had a bit more of a go-around, tossing lead here and there, but we were seriously outnumbered. We took the wise course. Dropped down into that little gully there. The holdup boys got the bank's money but no more of our blood. One dead was enough. Beats me how that gang knew this was a special run. No passengers, just the two small strongboxes. And the mail."

The two frontiersmen laid their weapons over their shoulders, as if they were going on parade. They looked disappointed when they heard there was to be no gun action. The city man had quietly slipped his long-barreled Colt back into the briefcase. He walked around the stage and the remaining horses, studying the marks in the road. He then climbed high enough to push his head into the interior of the tipped-over stage and looked all around. Easing himself onto the top of the conveyance, he lifted the door and dropped down inside. He was out in less than a matter of minutes, saying nothing, but Rory was sure he saw the man push something into his jacket pocket.

Rory walked away from the two stubborn, opinionated stage whips and knelt beside the dead men. It was not difficult to identify which one was the dead thief. He had a bright red, polka-dotted bandana still covering most of his face. Rory bent to the shotgun guard first, turning him so he could see the man's face. He didn't know him.

He then turned his attention to the dead gang

member. He didn't know him either. Rolling the man onto his back, Rory started going through his pockets. The stage driver hollered, "Hey you, leave that fella as he is. We'll not be stealing from a dead man. We'll wait for the sheriff. He'll not want anything touched."

Rory stood and said, "Has someone gone for the sheriff?"

The responding silence answered the question for him.

"Well, I expect he may be a while arriving if no one has gone to search him out."

He finished the exploration of the man's pockets before he stepped toward the gathered men and pulled the badge from his pocket.

"Rory Jamison, county deputy sheriff. I'm going to ask you men to get back in the stage and proceed on to Stevensville. Before you go, let's tip this rig back onto its feet. Unhitch those horses and pull the harness from that dead animal."

The two frontiersmen were giving Rory a long study, saying nothing.

When the horses were cleared away, the men gathered on the roof side of the stage and, with the whip saying when, began to lift. The unit was soon back on its wheels, although there had been some serious creaking and a couple of loud cracks when it fell back onto its rightful position. The company would have to take a careful look at it before putting it on another run.

The two frontiersmen, finally finding something to do that they would be able to turn into a story they could exchange for a free drink in many a small-town saloon, loaded the two dead men into the broken stage.

The whip was leading the three-horse team back

toward the now upright rig, and Tate was climbing onto the driver's seat of his rig. He hollered down, "Climb in, men, we got no more time to waste."

Rory walked slowly and cautiously toward one of the loose, saddled horses. The animal shied just a bit, backing away a few feet, but Rory soon had the dragging reins in his hands. Mounting, he caught up the second saddled horse. He rode back to the stage with a question.

"Where did this second horse come from?"

The stage driver spat an ugly wad onto the dusty road before speaking. "We downed another'n a' the gang. Not dead, you understand. Fella act'n like he was the leader said to get him up on his own horse, but they couldn't catch it. Spooked. Didn't know gunfire I'm guess'n. Or the smell of blood. Most likely stole. That's him you're riding. Finally threw the wounded man over the haunches of another animal, behind the saddle so's the rider could take a grip on him, and took off in a hurry. You can follow their tracks right over there if'n you got eyes to see."

"How many would you guess in the gang?"

"One down here on the road. One shot bad enough. Leaves, I'd say, seven. Maybe eight. Lot happen'n right at that time. Lotta dust. Everyone mov'n and runn'n 'round. Everyone shoot'n. Fella could a' got hisself hurt if'n he was to stick his head out jest to go to count'n. Could be six, could be nine. But I think eight is the better number. One doubl'n off with the wounded man, like I just said. Two mules runn'n on leads."

"Mules?"

"You don't appear to be deaf, young fella, so I don't understand why I'm hav'n to repeat everyth'n."

Rory loosened the rope from the saddle and dropped

a loop onto the road. Speaking to whoever would listen, he said, "Take a hitch on that dead horse."

The city man bent and grabbed the rope. With quick efficiency the man soon had the loop in place. "Pull away."

He followed as Rory dragged the animal off the road and loosed the rope when Rory allowed the tension to drop away. He then asked, "You going after that gang?"

"That's what I get forty a month for. Of course, that includes all the coffee I can boil over an open fire and the excitement of dodging lead from time to time. Easy money."

"I'll grab my gear and come with you."

"Now, why would you want to do that?"

"Grab your kit, and let's get going. The tracks are clear, and there's hours of daylight left. We'll talk as we ride."

"Your choice, but you know we're heading out with no bedrolls and no provisions. Could be a long, cold, hungry ride, with more excitement at the end than what's really good for us."

"Sounds like an adventure."

Rory rode over to the impatient Tate.

"Tate, I'd like if you would carry a message to Ivan, over at the marshal's office in Stevensville. Tell him what happened here and that he should load up a pack animal with bedrolls, camp supplies, and such. Enough for himself and two others. Tell him where the gang was headed. General direction, anyway. Looks like due east from here, but it will probably swing to the northeast before long. Tell him to get Key Wardle from the ranch supply store. Have him mind the marshal's office. The kid has been going crazy trapped in that store. Tell him to tell the kid not to shoot anyone, unless it's absolutely necessary. Tell Browning what's happened and have him send word out to the Double J."

Tate just nodded and put his rig into motion, with a holler and a crack of the whip that cleared the horses' backs by a good foot.

31

THERE WAS JUST RORY AND THE CITY FELLA, AS RORY HAD silently named him, still at the site of the holdup. Rory dismounted and flipped one stirrup onto the saddle seat. He looked over at his riding companion, who was fussing over the other captured horse, and said, "Must have been a long-legged fella that rode this bay. I can't hardly reach the stirrups."

"I'm doing a bit of adjusting here too. But we'll be better in the long run for having a comfortable seat."

As an automatic gesture, both men lifted the carbines in the saddle scabbards, checking them for loads and testing the action. Rory glanced at the other man with a small smile.

"Nice of these fellas to leave us their rifles. I don't know about this blanket roll though, looks to be pretty roughly used. We'll see about that come evening but right now, let's ride."

"We'll take just another couple of minutes. Stand down while I pull this suit off and get into my jeans."

With that, he opened a large carpetbag he had lifted

down from the roof of Tate's stage and unrolled a clean pair of jeans along with a checkered wool shirt. As he stripped his fancy suit and collared shirt off, showing no embarrassment in his stage of undress, Rory was surprised by the man's physique. Hidden under the carefully measured and cut city suit were broad shoulders and well-muscled arms. His full chest narrowed down to a rider's hips and waistline. Rory figured the man would be able to take care of himself.

When the shirt and jeans were comfortably adjusted, the man reached back into the carpetbag and removed a rolled-up gun belt with a single holster on the right side. The holster was empty until he snapped open the briefcase and took out the long-barreled Colt he had troubled the loudmouthed man on the stage with. The suit and shirt were carefully folded and placed into the carpet bag. He saw Rory watching.

"You look after your gear, young man, it will be there for you when you need it. Takes but a few seconds to do it properly. Now, let's step up and ride."

Would have enjoyed my father, Rory thought to himself.

They stepped the borrowed horses off the wagon road and, without the need for talk, fell in together, following the trail east. They rode a couple hundred yards before Rory pulled his animal to a halt and waited while his riding partner did the same, looking a question at Rory. He had thought to sort the situation out while they were still back at the holdup site but had somehow hesitated. When he found himself unwilling to ride further with serious questions in mind, he turned to look directly at his riding partner and, after hurriedly rummaging through several ways of starting the conversation, he withdrew from them all and simply said, "Have a need to know who I'm riding with. For all I know, you could be one of the gang, intent on either leading me astray or offering to put me in my grave. Best you speak up now, before we go any further together."

The man laughed and smiled at Rory. "No need to fuss, Sheriff. I know who you are. Knew it as soon as you stepped onto the stage. You match Oscar Cator's description exactly. You couldn't be anyone else. You might have noticed that I held back until I was sure you were taking that stage and not waiting over for some reason. For my purposes, we had to be on the same stage at the same time.

"Block Handly here. Deputy US marshal. New to this Colorado country. Been here just the once before, a few weeks ago. Been down in the panhandle of Texas the past couple of years. I'll tell you a story when we get time, but right now, I think we need to each earn that forty a month you mentioned."

Rory didn't move. Instead, he studied the man before him.

"Got any proof of that story?"

"Good man, Rory. I like a careful man. Especially in the law business. I see you don't wear your badge. Neither do I. The man who told me about you also told me about the pin holes in your shirt that almost got you into trouble. I was impressed that you could be so discerning and that you took the appropriate action. I pocket my badge for a different reason, but both reasons are valid.

"Now, don't get jumpy. I'm going to reach into my pocket and show you."

The marshal reached into a small pocket tucked neatly inside a leather vest he had drawn from the carpetbag, along with the jeans and shirt. It took a bit of fidgeting, but in a few seconds, he pulled out a badge and a printed document and passed them to Rory. The badge was easily seen and understood. Rory glanced at it and passed it back. It looked genuine enough. He then carefully read the document. The federal name and seal and the name filled in below, along with some statistics, describing height and weight and general build and looks, also looked genuine. Rory nodded and passed the document back.

"Let's ride. I'll have some questions after you tell me that story. But it can all wait. We have a gang to catch."

The marshal added, "And a couple of strongboxes to take back."

Rory responded, "Marshal, you'll have to understand. I don't much care about the bank money. I have no intention of putting my time or life on the line over someone else's money. My job is to catch the bad guys. Catch them before they do more harm or hurt someone else. That dead shotgun guard lying on the road back there was worth more than all the bank money in the world. It's just pretty pictures printed on paper as far as I'm concerned. If we find it, we'll return it. But right now, I'm concerned about the settlers out here that may be harmed or even killed by an escaping gang of thieves and murderers. Killed for a meal or a horse to aid the thieves in their escape. That's what keeps me riding. Not some banks' money."

Block Handly had no comment.

When Rory figured the horses had given about as much as they had to give, he pulled to a stop where a small half-circle of trees provided shade. There was a shallow draw through the grove that probably ran wet during the rainy season but was now dry. But he always carried a canteen, even on the stage. That, together with the canteens on both saddles, would be all the water they had. There would be enough for a small bit of refreshment for the two horses. The men could either take a swallow or wait for another opportunity, depending on their thirst.

"We'll pull up here, Marshal. Give these animals some rest. Never like to be found completely without some provisions. I've got a small bite in my kit bag. Just a bit of cheese and some dried meat. Might be a piece of hardtack left. Depending on how hungry you are, you can have some or let it go."

The two men stepped down and stretched their legs. The horses bent their heads to the grass. Rory waited while they had time to take several mouthfuls of grass before he took off his hat and poured a half canteen of water into it. Lifting his gelding's head with a grip on the bridle strap, he held the hat for him. The animal tossed its head once in question but soon caught the smell of water and eagerly ducked his head into the hat. Block was doing the same for his ride.

Surprising Rory with his willingness to take a small bite of cheese and meat peeled off with Rory's belt knife, Rory figured this man had seen some cold camps and perhaps some hungry days. With an hour's rest, they were back on the trail.

The marshal had held his silence throughout the ride, but after their rest, he asked, "What's out this way? I've traveled the West some but never been here before. Looks a bit like Kansas, but dryer and maybe a bit flatter."

"Don't know about flatter. I've never been to Kansas. But it's dry enough, for sure. Clouds seem to empty themselves over the mountains. Doesn't leave much for the grasslands. Still, the grass grows, and it's good feed for the cattle. Areas starting to fill up too. More ranches out this way than I first figured. Whether they'll be able to stick it in the long run is another matter. Might end up half-filling the country with dried-out, falling-over shacks, dry wells, and broken dreams. Mind you, north a bit there's a couple of rivers. They don't compare to the Colorado, or even the Snake, which I've seen up in Idaho, but they're wet, and they run the year around. More settlers up that way too. These tracks are angling to the north. If they stay that way, we'll soon enough be at the river."

Toward midafternoon, after following the northeast trail, the men pulled to a halt. They were at the river. While they stood down to rest the animals as they drank, Rory wandered over to a rocky ledge that appeared, from a distance at least, to have been disturbed. His father had warned him more than once to be careful with his curiosity. It could lead him right, or it could lead him into trouble. Rory pushed the concerns aside as he studied what looked like a new, man-made mound of rocks. He looked at it from every direction, measuring its length in his mind before bending to remove a couple of the top rocks.

He only had to remove three or four rocks before a piece of a man's shirt was exposed. Even with just that little bit of cloth in evidence, he could see it was saturated with dried blood.

One by one, he started removing the covering of the crude grave. When he glanced up, the federal deputy was standing there watching him. One more rock and both men could see the face of the dead man.

"Know him?"

"No, I don't Rory. Do you?"

"No."

Rory continued pulling rocks away until he could

reach into the man's pants pockets and lift his vest to check for anything stuffed away there. Nothing.

"Stripped clean, Block. I was hoping for some identification, but his pals obviously didn't want that to happen."

The two men worked together to lay the rocks back on the grave. Even though the man was a thief and, if he was the one that killed the shotgun guard, a murderer, Rory found himself feeling melancholy, troubled by the loss of even a misspent life. He replaced the last rock, leaned to stretch his back into shape again, and looked at his partner.

"I hope I never get used to this."

"If you ever get to where you don't care, Rory, that's the time to turn in your badge. Go back to that ranch of yours and make a better life for yourself."

Rory turned with some suspicion, studying the speaker.

"How do you know about my ranch? What's going on here? You're federal, but you somehow manage to be on the same stagecoach as me. I've never heard of you before, nor ever met a federal marshal. Don't know anything about the Federals. I'm just a temporary deputy, appointed by the state people. I'm not even elected. I'm of no importance anywhere beyond a day's ride from the Double J Ranch. But somehow, you not only get the same stage this morning, but now I find you know me and something, at least, about me. I say again, what's going on here?"

The marshal started walking back to where the horses were grazing. Rory walked along, waiting for an answer to his question.

When Block spoke, it was only to say, "I said I'd tell

you a story later. That promise still holds. Wait a while. Let's go catch us some bad guys."

"Not yet, Block. These horses are in serious need of rest. And I want to take time to go through these saddlebags. I expect the gang is getting to where they have need of some downtime, too, same as us. If they run their horses into the ground, we could catch them at a walk. I'm thinking they're smarter than that. We'll lay low right here until full dark. There's all the water and grass the horses need. We're not going to leave that until these animals have their full strength back."

Without a word, giving in to the much younger man, the federal deputy stripped the rigging off the horse he was riding. The animal had shown no desire to wander, but just to be sure, he rigged a hobble out of some strips of leather he found in the saddlebags. Rory stripped his animal also, but he had a couple of short lengths of line in his personal kit. For what reason, he couldn't have exactly explained. In any case, the animals were hobbled and free to eat and rest at their own desire.

Rory pulled some dirty clothing and one clean shirt from one saddlebag. He felt the need to wash his hands after handling the dirty clothes. In the other saddlebag were two letters, along with the man's personal stuff: razor, comb, bar of soap, a sewing kit, etc. Rory sat down on a rock, enjoying the last of the day's sun, and opened the letters.

"Nothing much here, Block. Just personal family material. He had a wife and kids waiting for his return. The man was a fool. Leave his family to traipse all over the country after easy money. Well, what he got was easy, I suppose, but it was lead, not gold. There's a name here, though. Lance Newley. Ever heard of him?"

The federal deputy's head snapped up. "You sure, Rory?"

"Sure, as I can read the English language."

"Lance Newley is the leader of a vicious gang of truly bad men. They've robbed and murdered all over the West. Always seem to know what's going on and somehow manage to stay one step in front of the law. He and his gang are on our wanted list and, most certainly, on the lists of the Texas Rangers. I didn't know what gang we were following, but I've been wondering how they happened along just when there was a special stage running to Denver with cash money on board. I'm betting the cash came in from some eastern mint, all fresh and ready to spread around.

"But the name Lance Newley explains a lot. As I just said, he always seemed to know. This is just an example of that."

Rory said, "You saw both dead men. Can you be sure one of them was this Lance Newley?"

"I can't be sure. I've never seen him, and it was always taken as a stated fact that he never allowed any of the gang to have their pictures taken. But if that letter has an address on it, this could be a help. The marshals have long wished to know where the man's family lived. He had a habit of lying low after each of his jobs. Sometimes for months. We could never find out where he hung his hat. But the word around was that his woman was just as tough as him. It would be good to find her. First opportunity, I'll send a wire. See if one of the boys can pick her up."

Rory pulled some papers from his pocket and spread them on his knees.

"What have you got there, Rory?"

"The stash from the dead thief back at the holdup

site. I'll look it over while you take a look in the other saddlebags."

Rory sorted out several pieces of scrap paper and one letter taken from the dead man's shirt pocket. The other shirt pocket had a half sack of tobacco, some papers, and a small metal tube of matches.

His vest pocket held only a much-abused pack of playing cards. There was nothing in his pants pockets to identify him, only a folding knife and a few coins. He opened the letter and, after reading for a few minutes, said aloud, "Treb Appleby. You know him too?"

Block laughed right out loud.

"Well, I should holler, I do. Know the name anyway. He and Newley were two of the worst. Good to have them gone. I take it that's his horse I'm riding. There's nothing of value in the saddlebag. Not valuable to me, I mean. Perhaps some of it was to him. These boys were traveling light, as if they didn't figure on going far, or had the help they would need at the other end. Anything of value must have been left at their hideout.

"Mind you, there's a dried-out half a chicken sand-wich in there. At least, I think it's chicken. I get much hungrier I may soak it in the river water to soften it, close my eyes, and eat it."

"I'd always heard how tough the Feds were. We've not been on the trail but for a few hours and you're danger-ously close to whining."

"The tough ones are the young ones, Rory. But I haven't worked in the field for a couple of years. At home in my own bed every night. Enjoying my wife's good cooking. Sit by the fire and read a book in the evenings. A man gets soft."

"So, what is your job? And while you're talking, I'd

like if you'd tell me what you found inside the coach that I saw you stuffing into your pocket."

"You've got a good eye, young man. You saw that, did you?"

"I just said I did."

"Yes. Well, it wasn't much actually. Just a torn and crumpled-up piece of telegraph paper with a name scribbled on it. A name, and also the name of a town back down the road. A town in Nebraska, if my memory hasn't failed me. I figure it's the name of the telegrapher and the town the message was sent from. Pretty sloppy writing. Hard to read. But I don't know what else it could be.

"The thing is though, that scrap of paper has the name of the railroad printed at the top. That name and the telegrapher's could lead us to the source of the gang's information. Always hoping the man remembers who sent the wire."

Rory contemplated on that while he studied the marshal. He finally asked, as if he had been waiting for the information, "So what's the wire say, or was the message torn off."

"No, the message is here, at least, I think, most of it. It says, 'Cheyenne. Stop. Denver. Stop. Twenty-third. Stop.' I figure it means something was happening between those two cities on the 23rd."

"Who is it addressed to, Block?"

"Just says LN."

"Not hard to figure out," commented Rory. "Lance Newley. Cheyenne on the 23rd. That was several days ago. It would take that many days to reach this far by stage. Lance Newley could figure it from there and pick his spot."

Rory had moved from the rock he was sitting on as

the sun shifted across the sky, putting him again at the mercy of the afternoon's heat. He had found a cool spot on the grass, leaning back against a tree. He got himself comfortable, looked over at his riding partner, who was just closing up the saddlebags again, and said, "We've got some time here. And I'm in the mood to listen to a story."

32

"I ADMITTED MY SOFTNESS ALREADY, SHERIFF," BLOCK said, laughing at himself. "Now, while I tell myself that I could quickly regain my rugged, youthful self, I also admit that the theory has never been put to the test. Now, totally unexpected, that situation may be turning itself around here on these Colorado grasslands. And all because a stagecoach carrying bank funds was robbed and the guard killed, in a time and place where you and I happened along.

"The truth is that I haven't been in a situation for a couple of years where I could honestly say I had earned my forty a month, as you so wisely detailed the job. I have years of that kind of service and somehow, in spite of myself, had earned a promotion. Of sorts. My job this past while has had two main points to it. One was the detailed examination of evidence. Detective is the term most recently being applied to such work. So, while the sheriff or marshal or city policeman is doing the dirty work, running down criminals and eating poorly cooked food over smoky fires, the detective is warm and comfortable in his office, examining letters, notes, half-torn telegrams, plus coins and bills with identifiable markings on them. Items that may lead to one or more important arrests and convictions. Detectives are only used on the more complicated cases, and where there's time. A lot of cases are brought to an end on some dusty village street or down a half-hidden canyon when a lawman corners his quarry, and lead and powder smoke seal the deal. In a case like that, it's a bit late to try to sort out the details. If a man steals a horse and is caught with it, the brand on the animal pretty much says it all. So, no detailed detective work is called for. But when there's something more sophisticated in the crime, or where there's a question of guilt or innocence, we go to work looking for evidence.

"The second portion of my job is to keep my eye out for potential recruits, men who will do both themselves and the nation proud.

"When I received a packet of information some time ago, from Oscar Cator, indicating that there could be a tie-in between some work being done up this way, and a certain rancher in the panhandle of Texas, a man named Webster Cunningham, Big C brand, I decided that some detective work was called for.

"I should probably tell you that Oscar gave you full credit for solving that case and gathering up the information that was forwarded to me. So, anyway, here I stand on the backside of nowhere, judging from all I can see around me, hoping to help put an end to one of the worst, and most successful gangs in the West, and knowing that Webster Cunningham isn't going anywhere. I can get back to him later."

Rory pulled the grass stem he had been chewing on

from his mouth and said, "Tell me a bit more about that Texas situation."

"This Cunningham man has a shaky background, although there was nothing on the surface that could be easily turned up. And remember, more than just a few men and women, both, have come west hoping their pasts were drowned in the Mississippi River along the way. We can't hope to look into all of them, and I've been at this long enough to have come to the place where I believe most should be left alone. It's only when their old habits and happenings become new again in this freshly opened West that we take notice.

"For Webster Cunningham, our attention was drawn, starting with the question of how his Big C brand was growing so quickly, with entire herds, burned with what looked like blotted brands, being delivered to his Big C holdings. That, and the fact that he had no history we could find that would justify his possession of so much cash. We decided to take a look. Next thing I knew, I was on the stage heading for Denver.

"As it turned out, I arrived just in time to have Oscar show me a mound of additional information he had received just this morning. Imagine my surprise when he said that one Rory Jamison, temporary appointed deputy sheriff, had solved the case and delivered all the evidence to Oscar. The same Rory Jamison that he had credited with the original solving of the case, or at least, the case as it stood at that time. He further surprised me by saying that if I hurried, I could probably get on the same stage as Deputy Jamison, heading north. That would be my best opportunity to meet you and gain firsthand information.

"Oscar wasn't eager about me recruiting you, which

he said would be his loss, but the federal government usually gets its way. So here we are."

Rory studied the older man until Deputy Handly started to grin and then laugh right out.

"You look as if you had just as soon I had missed that stage, Sheriff."

"Or that I had missed it. This is not anywhere close to my jurisdiction. And here I am with a man who, if nothing else, is a good storyteller, and I'm chasing a gang of thieves and killers. I don't even know if the state will back me up, working this far from my own county."

"I will guarantee your jurisdiction, Rory. I can even call you a temporary deputy marshal if that makes you feel more secure."

Rory brushed off that choice, fearing anything that would tie him to the federal marshals and pull him away from the Double J Ranch for more than a short few days at a time. He settled for saying, "We're here, and we have to justify our pay, so we'd best get at it."

33

As he struggled to his feet, Deputy Handly walked to the small trickle of water that had held the horses close by and picked up the reins.

"We can ride till dark, Rory, as long as we can still see the trail. After that, we'll have to make a decision."

Pushing aside the age and experience difference in the two men, Rory said, "No. That's not what's going to happen. What's going to happen is I'm going to follow this trail. Try to find these men and keep them in sight, or at least close by. There's no way I'm about to tackle eight desperate murderers. My forty a month doesn't go that far.

"While I'm doing that, you're going to run the shoes off that gelding, getting back to Denver just as soon as you possibly can. Then you're going to wire every town, city, and village that has the telegraph. Any place within a three-day ride of here. Cheyenne, Omaha, and any place between the two. Dodge, Pueblo, anywhere in New Mexico, perhaps Las Vegas, and, if there are any honest folks down in the panhandle, wire someone down there too. You said this was a gang you wanted. This is your chance.

"You send those wires. And you make them sound urgent. It has to be you, because I have no such authority, nor a name to be recognized.

"Whatever law keepers you can contact are to raise a posse and get on the trail immediately, pointing to a spot somewhere east of where we are right now. The posses have to be in the saddle and riding hard through the night. I'm hoping they will have enough intelligence to not shoot me, or each other.

"Find someone around Denver with a chuck wagon and have them on the road fully loaded to care for a crew later tonight or by earlymorning at the latest.

"We're going to catch these guys, and perhaps, the bank will get its money back. But the important thing is that no more stage guards will be lying in the dust of a remote trail after earning their poor pay with blood."

Block Handly stared at the much younger Rory but didn't move or make any motions to step into the saddle. The silent standoff lasted perhaps five seconds before Rory swung aboard the borrowed horse. Another five seconds passed before Rory, becoming frustrated with the federal man, finally said, "Best you pass me the extra cartridges from those saddlebags. You won't be needing them."

With that done, he kicked his animal into a walk and then a lope. Block Handly watched him ride away. When there was one hundred yards between them, the federal deputy stepped into the leather, turned his mount toward the road, and urged him into a run. It was a full hour back to the trail and another couple of hours, or more, to Denver. Then he would see what he could do. He tamped down his concerns about leaving the young sheriff alone and in pursuit of a gang not noted for mercy. The sheriff had laid out the plan, and all that was left was to get on with it.

~

BLOCK PULLED his worn-down gelding to a halt in front of the railway station in Denver. He took time to allow the animal a quick drink from the water trough close by and then rushed to the telegraph booth. He had been composing the telegram in his mind as he rode along. It would be longer than most. If it cost the federal government a few extra coins to send a longer message, so be it. The message had to be clear. And urgent.

He had created a mental list of the towns the message was to go to. Now all he had to do was get it onto the wire. But then he thought of another way and nodded in agreement with himself.

He had spared a minute from time to time along his ride to think of Rory. If he judged the nature of the young man correctly, and he believed he did, he could have confidence that he was on the trail and doing his part. Would he be cautious enough? Young men can be impulsive. He hoped, for his own sake, that Rory wouldn't try to do it all himself. That he would wait for help. But even as he thought that, he knew help was many hours away.

Block, not a particularly religious man, found himself praying that Rory would do nothing foolish. That he wouldn't misjudge the nature of the gang he was after.

The telegrapher didn't even look up when Block walked up to the wicket.

"Busy. You'll have to wait. Be a couple of minutes."

Block, normally a self-controlled and patient man,

took an immediate dislike to both the man and his attitude. He fingered his badge out of the pocket he secreted it in and dropped it on the desk in front of the impertinent telegrapher. He then knocked the fella's eyeshade off, ran his fingers into the greasy mass of black hair and twisted. With brutal force, he bent his neck downward until his nose was nearly touching the badge.

"Perhaps you could study on that badge for a second and understand that you're not busy at all. But you're going to be, so listen up. You need to clear the lines in every direction for an urgent message. And understand that if you don't send it right, I'll yank you out of there and send it myself. I'm willing to bet I handle a key better than you do."

When the line was cleared, Block said, "Send this. 'Urgent. Stop. All law enforcement within three-day ride Colorado, east of Denver. Stop. Lance Newley Gang. Stop. Stage robbery and murder. Stop. Believe heading for Dodge. Stop. Indian Nations. Stop. Panhandle. Stop. Cheyenne. Stop. Rail line. Stop. Posses to take all caution. Stop. Gang extremely dangerous. Stop. Time urgent. Stop. Move immediately. Stop.'

"Sign it Handly, Deputy US marshal."

There was an immediate flurry of responses confirming the receipt of the message, far more than Block would have received if he had tried to send it, one by one, to chosen locations. While the key was still chattering out its messages, he reached back into the cage and picked up his badge. He then scribbled out a chit for payment from the forms the telegrapher had on hand, leaving the line that said 'charges' for someone else to fill in, and left. He had been tempted to wipe his hand on the man's shirt but quickly thought better of it.

The telegrapher hadn't said a word since he had first

touched his key. He had met many lawmen, federal, and others. But this man frightened him like no other had ever done. Clearly, silence and obedience to the marshal's directions had been his safest position. When the outer door slammed closed, he stood and stretched, ran his fingers through his long, greasy hair trying to wipe the soreness away, and replaced his eyeshade. Still pretty shaken up, he stepped to the back door and walked outside, stuffing tobacco into his pipe. He would need a few minutes to settle down and gather up his thoughts.

Block reclaimed the borrowed horse and rode immediately to the local county office. He stormed right past Bertha as if she didn't exist, heading to Oscar's office. With no preamble, he said, "Holdup and murder on the southbound stage. Lance Newley Gang. Sheriff Jamison is in the field, keeping tabs on their movements. Heading east. I need you to get every man you've got saddled up and riding within a half hour. Try not to shoot Rory or other posse riders. I've called in help from everyone within a three-day ride. I want this gang, and I intend to have them. Don't just sit there, get moving."

With that, he was gone. That Oscar already knew about the stage holdup, the news having been brought in by a traveller, and that the local men were moving, preparing, wouldn't have made any difference to the federal man, so he let it go.

Block headed for his own federal office, where he mobilized the few men available.

Shouting to be heard by everyone in the office, he said, "I need a rancher with a chuck wagon. Give me a name and directions. And I need a fresh horse. And I need them both now."

One of the deputies said, "Come on, we'll get you a

horse at the livery where I keep my mount. And I'll go with you to a rancher I know."

When Block had left the office, someone said, "I've never seen him like that before."

"And you don't want to be here when it happens again, or if this deal goes sideways. You can take it from me that doing what he says is by far your best option. Now, grab your weapons, and let's move. Bring a jacket if you have one. Night is just a few hours away, and we'll most likely still be riding."

As LAYMEN and posse-men were saddling up and riding from many directions, Rory was on the trail.

34

RORY WAS FEELING THE FIRST STABBING PAINS OF HUNGER. He hadn't brought his much-used saddlebags on this trip to Denver, so he didn't even have his normal bit of hard-tack and the usual block of cheese. And the little bit he had in the evidence satchel was long gone, shared with the federal man. Water was not a problem so far, but looking in all directions from the heights of his mounted saddle and seeing nothing that would indicate any form of moisture, he knew he had to conserve the water that remained in the two canteens that hung from the saddle horn.

He had slowed his gelding to a trot and then a walk after running it for a couple of miles. The tracks of the group of horses and two mules could not possibly be hidden, so he was able to follow at a good speed. Along the way, he had noticed some scuff marks leading off the trail. He pulled up and studied them for a moment and then decided to take a look. Someone had tried to use the side of his boot to hide where the tracks of two horses and, judging by the smaller size of the other hoof marks, the two mules, had turned off to the south.

A quick look at the turned-up soil and the broken stems of bunchgrass that Rory thought was blue grama, marked their passage. He thought, *foolish waste of time.* But with the tracks leading into a small hollow surrounded with dried-out brush, he knew he had to take the time to turn that way, continuing to hold his carbine over his knee as he rode. He had been holding his carbine the entire time. He'd had his own on the stagecoach, and whoever had been riding the horse he now possessed left one in the scabbard. He had no idea how many times he had wiped the sweat from his hand that held the weapon, but it was more than just a few.

Pulling to a stop and glancing into the hollow, he could see that he needed to spend no time there. Thrown carelessly under some brush were the two bank trunks. Empty and lying on their sides, their lids flopped open.

Well, they were an awkward load anyway. The money will now be in canvas panniers. Makes more sense for mule loads. And it makes no difference at all in their escape plan, thought Rory. *Don't know why they even bothered trying to hide that trail or these boxes.*

Within a few minutes, he was back on the chase. His eyes were becoming blurry from sun, sand, and wind. He found himself squinting and rubbing first one eye and then the other. None of it helped. Regretting the loss of time and the use of even a small bit of water, he pulled the gelding to a halt. He loosened the bandana from around his neck and poured a bit of tepid water on it, enough to soak one corner of the cloth. Then, taking a careful look around in case he had missed something that could rise and cause him misery, he dabbed a bit of moisture into each eye. The small ministration helped some, but it needed to be done a second time. Another small splash of water and another gentle wipe, together with several drying squints, and he put the plug back into the canteen, brushing off his desire to take a sip.

Even with his improved eyesight, there was no sign of the robbers, except the continuing trail of hoof marks leading ever eastward. Coming to the top of a small rise, Rory stopped to scan the land in every direction. Nothing. Nothing more than the same horse and mule tracks he had been following. It was coming on to evening. He had hoped for a bit of smoke. Unless the thieves left a spotter behind them, someone Rory failed to notice, there would be little chance the gang knew anyone was following. They must have trail supplies. If they would stop to prepare a meal before darkness set in, he might see their smoke. But as the sky darkened, he reconciled himself to the fact that his hopes would go unrewarded. With no smoke showing in the night sky, he changed his wish to the possibility of seeing their firelight.

His concern was not in losing the trail. He didn't need either smoke or fire to know he was on their route. The passing horses and mules had left a trail a blind man could follow. He was more concerned with the possibility of catching up and stumbling onto them unaware, if they had stopped to rest the animals. Either smoke or firelight would reduce that risk considerably. About the last thing he wanted was to stumble into the camp of eight desperate fugitives while riding one of their lost horses. The chance of shooting his way out of that situation was close to zero.

While it was still light enough to see distant outlines of small hills in the rolling land, and little more, he stopped to give the horse a rest. His intention was to ride until he found the fugitives' camp, hopefully sighting it in time to take cover himself. Then he would see what could be done.

Without bothering to extract his father's pocket watch, he guessed sundown had been about eight o'clock. Full dark had come about an hour later. He further guessed he had been riding two hours after that time, riding the sun out of the sky and continuing into the darkness. And still, with the dim moonlight, he could make out the wide trail the multiple horses and mules left behind.

Riding slowly now, in the interest of self-preservation, he and his gelding were both showing serious fatigue when he was finally rewarded with a glint of firelight. It wasn't showing a large fire, but it was larger than men on the run would normally show. That action confirmed for Rory that the men didn't suspect any followers were on their trail. Since there had been no sign of ranches, other than a handful of wandering cattle, during the many hours of riding, the men would feel confident in their aloneness. In the privacy of his silent mind, Rory thought, *probably not much I can do by myself. Still...*

He rode very slowly toward the campsite. When he was within what he guessed to be a half mile, he dismounted and tied the gelding firmly to a sizable bush of some sort. And now he was going for a walk. He wanted the ride to still be there when he returned. If he lost the animal, he would be in serious trouble. As a last thought that supported his decision to walk, he recognized that riding any closer would risk his horse smelling the others, a group he was a part of until that morning. A returned nicker would surely set the camp into full defensive mode.

35

BLOCK HANDLY FOLLOWED HIS GUIDE, A DEPUTY NAMED Wander, into the yard of the CT Spread. Their pounding hoofbeats roused the crew from their spread-out position in front of the cookhouse. Dinner was over, and the evening was still warm. Time for a smoke and a last cup of coffee.

The quiet of the evening was further shattered when Wander hollered, "Casey. Casey Tasker. You anywhere about?"

"What's with all the noise and excitement? Of course, I'm here. Where would you expect me to be, and what's got you all in a dither, Wander?"

"Need some men for a posse. Need your chuck wagon to carry enough to feed a crew. Need it now. And I mean right now. This here fella with me is a deputy US marshal. Name's Block Handly.

"How about you detail off a couple of men to rig out the chuck wagon, load it up with enough grub for fifteen, twenty men, three or four days. Maybe longer. Might want to send your cook along."

Casey Tasker stood there with his hands on his hips, trying to take in and make sense of all the rapidly spoken words. Finally, he said, "Dismount and give those horses a breather. Then tell me plainly what's going on."

Wander and Block stood to the ground while a man stepped forward to lead the two heaving mounts to the water trough. Taking a longer look, Tasker could clearly see that the two hard-ridden horses weren't going to make it through the night.

He shouted, "Pull those rigs and put them on rested animals. Pick good ones. And get back here quick."

Turning back to the two deputies, he said, "Now, tell me clearly what's going on."

Block quickly explained the situation while the men, more than eager for a change from the tedious ranch work that faced them day after day, waited to hear their boss agree to the marshal's request and start hollering out orders. The wait was less than one minute.

With a flurry of activity, the team was caught up and led to the barn where they would be rigged out. The cook was summoned and given orders to gather up the necessary supplies. Tasker then hollered out, "I need three men to stay with the ranch. Any of the rest of you wishing to join up with the posse, gather your things and saddle up a fresh horse. Be out here in fifteen minutes."

He then called to the cook, who had just turned back to the kitchen. "Grubs, I'd like if you would go with these men. You can hold your wagon free of the action. Shouldn't be any risk to your already half-wore-out body. I'll not order you to go, but I'd like it if you would. These men and the others will need feeding."

Grubs held the screen door open while he whined, "My bones won't take a lot of rattling around on no wagon, Boss. And who's going to feed the bunch that stays behind?"

"Pshaw. You old fool. I was cooking for the crew long before you slunk onto the site. Now, I got me these two strapping, strong daughters to work along with me. Might be wisest if we was to send you packing down the road and take on the cooking job our own selves. Save us all your wages and the listening to your moaning. Now get yourself rigged out and on your way. And no more whining from you."

Grubs took a long look at the boss's wife who was standing there with her two teenage daughters beside her. The girls wouldn't normally be described as 'strapping,' being almost of a delicate nature, but he knew that what Mrs. Tasker said was the truth. The girls knew how to cook. Reluctantly he went to his kitchen and began sorting out supplies to take on the chuck wagon.

The CT crew didn't quite make the fifteen-minute limit imposed on them by their boss, but in less than one-half-hour, seven riders plus the two deputies and Tasker himself pounded out of the yard, followed by the wagon handled by the complaining Grubs.

~

FROM CHEYENNE, an eclectic bunch of lawmen and cowboys, led by the one US deputy stationed there, led out on a southeast trail. The only directions given by the marshal were, "Stay together, fellas. And when dark closes in y'all got to close in too. Don't get separated. We're no good to anyone scattered all over creation. Now, let's ride."

There was a similar pattern developing from Ogallala, Dodge City, and a few smaller centers that were blessed with the telegraph that connected them with the outside world. No matter their starting point, every man was focused on upper, eastern Colorado. After serious consideration by the county sheriff there, it was decided in Omaha that by the time anyone from that city reached the target zone, it would be all over. Reluctantly, the sheriff stood down, leaving instructions with the telegrapher to relay any news immediately, even if he had to wake people up.

From the south, men saddled up and rode from Pueblo, Las Vegas, and Santa Fe.

With few exceptions, settlers, small-town sheriffs, and nervous bankers dotted throughout the newly growing West had heard of the Lance Newley Gang. Their reputation and the deprivations they foisted onto the scattered towns and ranches struck fear, even in stalwart hearts. Everything from theft to murder and rape was ascribed to them.

For ordinary citizens, those folks who were working long, hard hours and days to build something for themselves, and in return, were building a nation, there were few who hadn't heard the name and stories of Lance Newley and his gang's degeneracies. That the gang was feared was beyond doubt. That the citizens were determined to take advantage of this once-in-a-lifetime opportunity to bring the terror to an end was also beyond doubt. No one ever knew for sure, but the best guess was that between one hundred and one hundred twenty-five men were in the saddle, determined to end the gang and open the door to a better day. That many were still on the trail when the situation was brought under control, did nothing to detract from their conscientiousness, bravery, or their willingness to step up to protect their country and their neighbors.

36

Rory carried his fully loaded carbine in both hands, ready for instant use, and, over his shoulder, a catch rope that had been left on the borrowed saddle. The carbine in the borrowed saddle scabbard was checked for loads and pushed back into place, a spare in case of need. With his pockets loaded with extra cartridges, and assured that he was armed as well as possible, he set out for the campsite. The crunching of the brittle bunchgrass under his feet made silence almost impossible.

Early explorers and travelers who came that way, demonstrating their lack of real vision, had misnamed the entire area as the Great American Desert. For some, that description was still in their minds. Others had named the West as essentially flat. Both descriptions were wrong. Far from being a desert, the grass underfoot was known to Rory for the nourishment it provided for stock on the hoof. Nor was the land anywhere near flat. There were flat areas, to be sure. But there were also rolling hills, small and large. In general, the land rose imperceptibly as it neared the Rocky Mountains. And nowhere was it less than several thousand feet in elevation. Underfoot, the thin layer of loam that fed the grass would one day grow great fields of grain, corn, and such. But that would have to wait for irrigation.

Here and there, across the land, were gullies, folds in the earth, and rocky outcrops that seemed to rise for no particular reason. It was one of those folds, backed by a rocky ridge that Lance Newley had chosen for their night's rest.

The confidence that they had escaped with the bank funds, with no possibility of anyone following for at least another day, put the men at ease. Newley, who was alive, contrary to the conclusion Block and Rory had come to, said, "Finish your cooking and put that fire out."

"Never seen your horse take on like that, back there at the wagon road, boss. Could be he's still running. Might have picked up a bit of lead across his flank. Sure enough, something scared him. Sorry to lose Pock, but he left a good animal for you to ride. Course Pock was never known for his good eating habits. Anything in his bundle fit to eat? I got a little extra here if you need it."

"Thanks. I'll make out. Now, everyone chow down and get some sleep. We're leaving out of here before first light."

RORY EASED BACK on his walk as he neared the slowly dimming fire. The crunching of the dry grass being stepped on sounded like thunder in his ears, making him wonder how far the sound would travel. To arouse the camp would turn out badly for him, he was sure of that. Perhaps the few rocks the men had settled down behind would stifle the noise of his walking. He could only hope, or retreat. And there didn't seem to be any retreat in his makeup. As he watched, the small shelter of rocks the thieves huddled behind went to darkness.

He stopped, studying the shadows he had thought were an extension of the rocks the men were behind. There were rocks enough alight. He had seen that from the reflection of the fire before it had been extinguished. But this was something different he was looking at. As he watched, trying to sort things out in the darkness of the night, something moved. Then into the almost total silence of the night he heard the tearing of grass. Horses. It had to be the gang's horses.

Folding himself to one knee, he stopped all his movements. The horses. The gang would need the horses in the morning. But what if the horses weren't there when they came for them? What if the thieves were set afoot? Or even if some of them were set afoot? It was unlikely he could spirit away all eight animals without arousing the camp, but what about one or two?

Rising to a low crouch, he moved toward the sounds of grazing. He slipped his feet between grass bunches as much as he could and very slowly approached the tethered animals. Was there a guard posted? If there was a shouted warning to the camp, would he try to shoot it out or turn and run, hoping the darkness would swallow him until he managed to get back to his own animal? He wasn't sure. He had never faced eight angry, healthy men. The possibility that he might get to do it only the once, troubled him. He calmed himself, searching his mind for some saying his father might have left with him. When nothing came, he stepped out again.

He took a few steps, then paused on one knee again, waiting. He looked carefully among the grazing horses for any sign of a watching man. If one was there, he was keeping himself well hidden. Wanting to be sure of what he was doing, he counted the horses. It seemed reasonable that they would all be held together to make handling easier in the morning, or during the night if something arose that meant an immediate breaking of the camp.

Five. Not eight. Five. Were three animals held closer to the night camp, or had the whip on the overturned stage been seeing men who weren't there? He couldn't be sure, so extreme care was called for.

So now Rory had to make a decision. Make a try for a couple of horses or turn in retreat. He had no intention of attacking the camp. *Got no death wish, even for forty a month.*

He would try for the horses, knowing he could always sprint for darkness if he was discovered.

As he neared the closest horse, the animal's head came sharply up, but the neighing noise Rory feared didn't materialize. To save the horses from tangling themselves, the picket pins were spread over a considerable area. The first one he felt through the darkness was soon pulled. Gripping the pin and giving a slight tug on the rope, he shuffled to the next nearest one, with the horse following. Two. He would settle for two horses and be thankful for even that. He repeated his actions with the second picket pin and slowly, carefully, watching in every direction, rose to his feet. Still moving slowly, he headed out, walking back to where he had tied his own mount. With fear rising in his mind and heart, he moved out, step by step, listening for any sound of warning or alarm from the camp. Thankfully, the night remained silent.

A slow, half-mile walk took him back to his own mount. He might have missed the spot altogether in the darkness if the horses he was leading hadn't smelled the other. As they called to each other, he hurried his steps. Even over a half mile, the sounds might find their way back to the camp in the hollow. Talking quietly to settle his own animal, he tightened the girth and reached for the slipknot holding the gelding to the bush. Then he hesitated. What was he going to do with the two captured animals? On his walk, he had visualized leading them miles away before he turned them loose. But in reality, they could easily cover that distance if they chose to return to their mates, the animals they were familiar with. If that happened, Rory's risky night's work would be wasted. But there was another choice.

A decision made, Rory pulled the slipknot and mounted his horse. He then gathered enough of the lead ropes from the other two animals to secure them to the saddle horn. Judging he had his direction right, he moved off, back the way he had come from the east. The led animals followed without any balking.

Counting off the time and by pure guess at their speed, he figured he was close to five miles away from the gang's night spot. Even if it was only four miles, he didn't believe the sound of a shot would carry that far. Again, he securely tied his own mount and walked the others away fifty steps. Turning, saying silently, "Sorry guys. You deserve better than this, but lives are at stake."

He drew one of his .44s and walked down one lead line until he got a firm grip on the halter. The darkness of night made for poor shooting, but with his hand gripping the halter under the animal's chin he had no real problem finding the forehead. Going by feel plus the little bit he could see, Rory placed the muzzle of his handgun just a small space above the horse's eye and slightly off center to clear the big bone at the front of the animal's skull. After hesitating for three or four breaths, he eased the gun a few inches away from the flesh of the horse and squeezed the trigger. The horse dropped like a stone, quivered a couple of times, and lay still. The second horse pulled back a bit at the noise but then relaxed again. These horses had heard gunfire before.

The second horse was put down quickly and reluctantly. Saddened at what he had to do, Rory gathered up the reins on his own ride and headed back to the gang's camp.

Repeating his motions almost exactly, Rory soon had two more horses' tether pins loosed and was just turning to walk away when a voice shouted, "Hey. Who goes there?"

In a flurry of activity and instant thoughts, Rory swung onto the bare back of one horse and pulled the lead rope tighter so it could be used with the halter as a hackamore of sorts. He then lifted his .44 and pegged a shot at the shouting man. He didn't hit him, but the man dove behind a rock outcropping, putting him out of the picture, for a while anyway. Before the other men could break out of the camp, Rory turned his gun on the horse he was leading and dropped him there. He then took aim at the last tethered gelding. Two weapons exploded into the night, but the shots were far from Rory and his jittery horse. Settling the horse and himself as best he could in the seconds available to him, he pumped off three shots at the other gelding, and then, as he watched the animal fall, he turned both his guns loose at the men cowering behind the shallow, dry swale. With the last horses alive now in his possession, he made a break for the safety of darkness. He hadn't ridden bareback enough to really have the hang of it, but his natural instinct was to tighten his legs against the horse's flanks and lean forward, to take a mane hold. He somehow made it back to his saddle animal.

His actions were almost becoming routine. Put down the last of the gang's horses. Pull the slipknot on his one horse. Mount quickly, giving thanks that he hadn't loosed the girth. Turn to the east and ride.

A man can walk a horse down when the conditions were right, but he couldn't catch a running horse. Or even one held at a steady trot. In any case, the gang wouldn't know which way to look, and with the crimes behind them, and fully understanding the result if they were captured, they would be more interested in escape than in catching Rory. And escape would mean walking or sharing the time on the two mules. But for Rory, it was enough for this one night. He rode away, still wondering if there had been other horses tethered in the camp. He wouldn't know until morning.

37

BEDLAM, FINGER-POINTING, AND BLAMING DOMINATED the Newley camp as the sun was poking its head up over Kansas and throwing a bit of light into the small rock enclosure. Exercising his authority, Newley finally got the men settled down, at least to where the threat of shooting each other was set aside.

"So, what are we going to do, Boss?

"We're going to have a quick breakfast and set out on foot. There can't be more than that one man following. If there had been more, they would have attacked the camp. We still have the mules to carry our packs and the money. There's got to be a ranch out here somewhere. Those cattle we saw yesterday belong to someone. With any luck at all, we'll find that ranch and have whatever horses they have on hand. Now see to your food, and let's get on with it."

"I sure do hate to leave my saddle behind," whined one of the outlaws. No one commented.

The gang had walked less than one mile when one of the gang members looked back.

"What the... Back there. Not more than a half mile. Someone riding Treb's horse. Following us."

The group stopped and turned, studying the sight in the semi-light of early morning.

"How do you know that's Treb's animal? Can't hardly see it clear in this poor light."

"If you had an eye for horses, as much as you have an eye for helpless ranch women, you wouldn't be asking that question."

Newley again had to stop the men from shooting each other. When the crew was settled down, Newley said, "Bring that mule over here." With that, he pulled his Sharps Big Fifty from the saddle scabbard and, as best he could, cleared it of accumulated dust. He had tied the fifty to the mule back at the campsite. The men were carrying their much lighter carbines, but the fifty would be a load to tote over the miles that stretched before them. Leaving their saddles and bedrolls behind when they set out walking was bad enough. They weren't about to give up their rifles.

Thumbing a load into the single-shot weapon he had at one time hunted buffalo with, he laid it over the tied-down pack on the mule. "Take a hold of that halter." The man holding the mule shortened his grip and laid one hand on the mule's neck in the hopes of comforting him, knowing the firing of the fifty was likely to throw the mule into a bucking frenzy or, perhaps, set off an earthquake.

Newley sighted the weapon, compensating a bit for distance and not really caring if he hit the rider or the horse. If he got the horse, they would soon have the man. If he got the man, they would have the horse.

Newley aimed carefully, whispered, "Now."

The man holding the halter bore down, giving Newley as solid a shooting platform as possible.

The gang leader squeezed off the shot. He may have taken out his intended target if the mule hadn't decided, at that very moment, that he had about enough of the flies bothering his eyes. He didn't move much, but it was enough. The deadly chunk of lead kicked up dirt and grass close enough to Rory's ride to startle both horse and rider.

With a gasp of surprise, Rory turned the horse and kicked it into a run, turning this way and then that, hoping to evade the next shot. Rory never considered himself any kind of an expert on firearms, but he knew the difference between a common carbine and a buffalo gun. And he understood the difference in the shooting range too. Distance. He needed to put more space between him and that shooter. He needn't have bothered with the zigzag, though. By the time Newley fished out another load and had it where it could do him harm, Rory was too far away and had dropped into a slight swale, hiding him completely. *Didn't know they had a buffalo gun, horse. We'll have to take that into serious consideration.*

The gang set out walking again, with Rory following over a mile behind. Even with the periodic swales and hills, there was no chance of losing the gang. His one concern was to watch for a man who may have dropped back, hiding in the questionable cover, hoping to shoot Rory and capture the horse. He lowered that risk by riding well around any abrupt changes in the terrain. And he still hadn't had a clear chance to count the men he was following. Were there eight or just the five whose horses he had eliminated?

His other two concerns were hunger and sleep. Only

a half canteen of water remained. He had repeatedly calculated distances and time during the long night, thinking that the crew from Denver should have caught up by that time. But there was no sign of any other riders. But off in the distance, he saw a trail of smoke rising into the dawn. Deciding it came from a source to the south of the gang's chosen route, Rory slanted his horse in that direction, still keeping the walking men within sight.

As he crossed over another of the small grades, he could see that the smoke was rising from a ranch house chimney, faintly seen, at least three miles to the southeast. To keep Newley from turning that way, he would have to get between them and the ranch. Asking more from the tired horse than he wanted to give, Rory kicked him into a trot. Still staying out of Big Fifty range, he placed himself where he could do the most good, hoping to protect the rancher and keep the gang from stealing horses. The buffalo gun bothered him, but it would only take a single thundering shot to awaken the ranch to their presence. There wasn't much else he could do without putting himself at serious risk.

～

THE GANG HAD TAKEN A SITTING-DOWN rest, so Rory decided he could do the same. The isolated ranch was now far behind them, and there was no other settlement in sight. A short quarter mile from where Rory had been riding, there was a rise in the land, a mixture of grass and jagged, broken rocks. Rory figured there might be a bit of shade for him. If there was enough to get the horse some relief, so much the better.

Squinting his eyes and assuring himself that his sight

was dependable, Rory counted only five men in the fugitive's camp. With that confidence, he swung to the side and approached the rocks. When he was within one hundred yards, a voice said, "Now don't you go to shooting, Sheriff. I'm too tired to die right now."

Startled, Rory held up, swung his carbine toward the source of the voice, and hollered, "Identify yourself."

An arm rose above the rocks, an arm holding a saddlebag. "Got some fixn's here, Sheriff. Big beef sandwich. Biscuit or two I ain't et yet."

Thinking he recognized the voice, although he couldn't figure how the man would be there so soon, he hollered, "That you, Ivan?"

Slowly the man stood to his feet, "Ain't no other, Sheriff. You hungry?"

"You know I am. But how did you get here so fast? I wasn't expecting you yet. You're a welcome addition to this little party, though."

"Got a good view of those others from up here. Bit of shade too. Come on in."

Rory swung his horse to the left to ride around the rocks and stepped to the ground in the welcoming shade. The two horses snuffled for a moment and then ignored each other. Rory took off his hat and wiped his forehead with his sleeve.

"Sett'n up to be a hot one."

"You got that right, old buddy. Here, take this pouch and dig in. Ma had a lunch put together and wrapped up before I got my horse saddled. Sonia threw in the apples and the biscuits."

Speaking around a bite of bread and roast beef, Rory said, "All that doesn't explain how you got here this quick."

"Tate, he near drove his stage animals into their

graves. Drove all night without stopping except to change teams just the once. Rolled into town just afer full light, hollering and making a fuss. Had half the town awake and wondering. Never seen him so excited. Or angry. He singled me out for instructions, sent by you. I saddled my horse while Ma put some things aside, like I just said.

"I was all set to ride out when Tippet comes from the livery with two horses on leads. He hollers me to a stop and says, "Swing your saddle onto one of these. Ride till he's got no more to give and turn him loose. He'll come home. Use the other the same. Hold your own off till the end. Now ride hard. Wish I was young enough to ride with you."

"I done what he said, and here I am. I was off track by a mile or more until I heard a single shot a while back. Sounded like death riding a thunderstorm."

"That was a Sharps Big Fifty, Ivan. Buffalo gun. I've only ever seen one up close. But there's no forgetting the sound. Once a fella's heard that black powder boom, he's not likely to forget. A miner I rode out of the Idaho hills with brought down a buck with his when we were running close to the end of our camp meat.

"I was sure some surprised when Newley up and let 'er bang after aiming it my way. Shoot a mile, some say. Sure can't go after it with just my carbine anyway. We'll have to hang back and simply follow these birds, keeping them in sight until more help arrives."

"You want to sleep some?"

"Nah. I go to sleep now it would take another shot from that fifty to waken me. We'll take our ease here for a bit and then see what that bunch are up to."

"They may not be up to much at all pretty soon, Sheriff. Turn around and take a look."

Rory twisted around, holding to his sitting position, not wanting to give up on the shade. Ivan was pointing off to the southwest. Perhaps two miles away, he saw a group of riders followed by a wagon. Seeing that the posse, if that's what it was, could ride right into trouble if Newley unloaded with the fifty again, Rory eased to his feet and reached for the saddle girth. He swung into the saddle and, without any word of instruction to his friend, rode into the open. A single shot from his skyward-pointing carbine brought the approaching riders to a halt. Every eye seemed to be turned Rory's way. He waved his hat and rode down the slight grade. The untrusting riders spread out in a defensive line and then slowly rode forward. Rory rested his carbine across his knees and raised both arms into the air, as a sign of peace, or at least to tell the men that he wasn't going to shoot again. He heard hoofbeats behind him and knew it would be Ivan.

It took ten minutes for Rory and the slow-riding group to close the distance. There was no run left in his mount, nor in Ivan's mount either. In any case, after all the hours these men had been in the saddle, riding through the night, a few more minutes would matter not at all.

Picking out the one man who would know him, Rory hollered, "Hello, Block."

Block Handly grinned, although he was too far away for Rory to see, and kicked his horse in the deputy's direction. The two men closed the distance and shook hands.

"Welcome to my little party, Marshal. Those boys are hidden in that small hollow of rocks up ahead. I stopped you because there's a Sharps Big Fifty in their camp.

Man using it knows how to shoot. Haven't yet figured a way around that."

Ivan, riding up beside the two lawmen, said, "We could just sit here and let them starve. Might not take so long either."

"Block, I'd like if you would say hello to my friend and sometimes deputy, Ivan. Good man on the trail and second to none in the mountains. Ivan, Block is a deputy US marshal. We're out here under his say-so. His jurisdiction, you might say."

In acknowledgment of the authority carried in the officers' badges, Ivan grinned and said, "So which of you do I ask what's next? For my part, I could use some grub and a night or two of sleep. Could be you fellas feel the same."

Block offered a weary grin in return. "Let's ride down to the wagon. We butchered out a CT steer a few miles back. Could be the first of his own beef Casey Tasker, he whose chuck wagon that is, has ever eaten. The boys will have a fire going, and the grub hustler will be greasing his pans right smartly. My bunch hasn't eaten or slept either."

A raft of introductions was made, and 'howdies' exchanged. It wasn't long before the odor of boiled coffee and hot grease filled the air.

Rancher Casey Tasker detailed off two of his men to return to the rock shelter Rory and Ivan had recently given up.

"You can see what you need to see up there, boys. Keep that Big Fifty in mind, and don't try to get brave. We'll deal with that bunch in good time. Won't hurt for them to sit where they are for a spell."

An hour later, the men were fed and full of coffee. Two new men were sent to the lookout. Everyone not needed at the moment lay their heads on their saddles and dropped off to sleep as if they hadn't slept for days. Rory closed his eyes for barely an hour before he was back on his feet and trying to figure a way out of the stalemate with the Gang. Ivan didn't sleep at all, pacing from one end of the small campsite to the other, mumbling about the situation.

The first indication of more help arriving came from the men at the lookout. A single handgun shot brought everyone's eyes that way. A man was standing waving. When he had the attention of Block Handly and Casey Tasker, he turned and pointed to the north. Whatever they saw was still out of sight for Block, but he assumed it might be more help.

Tucking his shirt in and adjusting his hat, Rory said, "I'll ride out there. See what's going on."

"Not alone, you won't." responded Ivan.

Within seconds the two friends were in the saddle and heading to where the lookout had pointed. Once past the rise in the land, they could see riders easing to the southeast. They kept their eyes peeled for any sign of aggression as they closed the distance. They were within easy pistol range, facing fifteen determined men, before one man, wearing a shiny badge, called the approaching riders to a halt. He pushed his horse ahead with a shouted, "Cheyenne Sheriff here. Who might you two be?"

"We're the ones that have been praying you'd make it before we fell asleep in the saddle. Denver bunch just arrived a couple of hours ago. Chuckwagon down there with grub and coffee. Be best if you'd stage your men's breakfasts off, maybe five at a time, with the rest of you staying here."

"You need say no more. It's been a long night. Two

men dropped out when their horses could go no further. The rest are ready for whatever is needed."

"Parcel the men out for that grub. Federal marshal down there. We'll find out what he plans."

"I take it those are our targets down in that hollow. Don't see any horses. Surprised they're not running for their freedom."

Rory answered, "Bit of a sad story there. Doesn't matter right now."

Having become cautious since his time in the gold camp, Rory waited until the others rode out. He didn't want them behind him. As the bunch were riding past the lookout with the two men still stationed there, one called out, pointing to the east, "Looky there."

Under a dust cloud rode a dozen or more men. The only place to the east Rory could think of was Dodge, but he had long admitted he didn't really know the geography as well as he should. Although he had never been there, he knew Dodge to be a talked-about place, and he knew it was more or less east.

After much arm waving from a Denver rider, the Dodge bunch stood down, finally understanding there was danger, from what, they couldn't yet know. Again, Rory took it upon himself to ride toward the Dodge City men. He closed the distance in just a few minutes of hard riding. After introductions and assurances that it was all coming together as Block and Rory had originally hoped, the Dodge men broke into two groups, with one bunch following the smoke and the odor of frying beef, as they made a wide circuit of the gang and their buffalo gun.

The reception at the chuck wagon was much like the one from the Cheyenne riders. They had all traveled a long way and were anxious to bring the arrests or shootings to a head, and with that action, to see the last of the Lance Newley Gang.

The gathered lawmen and posses staked out or hobbled their horses around the cooking fire. A couple of men pulled their picket pins and moved them further away after Grubs explained, with a wave of his double twelve gauge, that horses and camp kitchens were a poor mix. Finally having the space he demanded, he turned back to his grill and coffeepots. A man from Cheyenne took soap and a bit of water from the barrel strapped to the side of the wagon and washed his hands. He then took the butcher knife and started, with considerable skill, to cut more steaks from the hind quarter of CT beef. Casey Tasker seemed to wince with every cut, even though Block had promised him full payment for value when the bunch got back to Denver.

Grubs was all set to yell the Cheyenne helper out of his kitchen, but the good-natured butcher grinned, pointing the knife at the cook, saying, "Don't start, old man. I can do everything you can do, and better. Anyway, this bunch is too much for one man."

Grubs went back to his pans, and within one hour, everyone was fed, with the Cheyenne group and the Dodge bunch back together, holding their positions, partially surrounding the Newley Gang on the north and on the east. To the west and south were the Denver group, the larger of the posses.

259

38

THERE WAS NO ONE IN THE CROWD OF MEN WITH A weapon capable of neutralizing the threat of the Big Fifty. To Rory, it all seemed like a foolish standoff anyway. The five unhorsed men, hunkered down in their rocky hollow, couldn't have any hope of outrunning or standing off forty or fifty fed, partially rested, and determined men. Tiring of the whole matter himself, he decided to try appealing to common sense, hoping some such a thing existed in the gang of thieves.

Rory swung into the saddle and, signaling Ivan to follow him, headed for the northern edge of the circle of lawmen, the area now held by the Cheyenne posse. Several men watched them go, not knowing what was planned. He had simply said, "Be ready." to Block and rode away. They joined the two watchers stationed at the small hill and turned toward the gang.

Rory said, "Stand here, but just a few feet away, Ivan. Pouch your carbine, and don't make any threatening moves."

To the two watchers, he said, "You men stand down. No shouting and no shooting."

He then lifted his carbine into the air, pointed straight up, and fired off one shot. The attention from the five desperate men was immediate. Rory waved his gun in the air before slowly passing it to Ivan. Ivan lowered it to the side of his gelding, holding it wide so the gang could see. Rory then lifted the second carbine from his saddle scabbard and held it overhead for a moment before passing it also to Ivan. Ivan quietly said, "One of you men take these from me."

One of the watchers rose to his feet and gathered in the offered weapons.

As the five fugitives continued to watch, Rory slowly opened his jacket and lifted his hip-mounted Colt .44. He waved it in the air as he had done with the carbines, and passed it to Ivan, who tucked it behind his belt. Hoping the gang didn't know about his side-holstered Colt, Rory pulled his jacket closed, and then, holding both arms fully extended above his head, he kicked his horse into a slow walk. By now, every eye in the camp was on him. Praying no one would do anything stupid, he rode forward. Second by second, watching every move the five made, Temporary County Deputy Rory Jamison walked his horse toward the huddled gang.

It was a long, tedious walk at that slow speed. No one said anything or raised a weapon until, when he was more than halfway to the hollow, Lance Newley slowly raised the Big Fifty, taking aim at the approaching rider. Rory's heart seemed to rise into his throat, but he kept riding while still holding his arms extended. To run now was to invite bedlam from all points.

As Rory was wondering what Newley's intentions were, a haggard-looking man standing beside him reached over and, looking directly into the eyes of the gang leader, gently pushed the weapon down. It was clearly a plea for sanity. No matter what damage the fifty could inflict, it would be a totally temporary victory. Within seconds the five would be lying in the dust, and each of them had to realize that.

Rory rode to within easy talking distance and whoa'd the animal to a halt. Although they were getting tired and starting to feel as heavy as lead, he still held his arms in the air. For a few seconds, no one spoke. Then Newley asked, "You the one that run off our horses?"

Rory took the question as a break in the stalemate. He slowly lowered his arms.

"Couldn't chase you all into Kansas. Not by myself, I couldn't. No food. No rest. Five tough men. Had to do something."

"You shoot those animals?"

"Don't matter any now. What matters now is that you men have a decision to make. I'm trusting you to make the sensible choice. You see those men out there? Those are citizens. Lawmen. Husbands. Fathers. Settlers. They've ridden the hours through from Cheyenne, Dodge, and Denver. There's more on the way from Pueblo, Santa Fe, Las Vegas, and down in the panhandle. All called in with the telegraph. Those men are tired, and they're determined. They're here to protect their homes and families. Their towns and their country. And there's no quit or backing out in them.

"It has to be obvious that you're not going free this day. You can't outrun our horses, and you can't outfight forty men, with more on the way. I'm offering you safe passage to the protection of Deputy US Marshal Block Handly. He and the others will see to it that you're safe to Denver. Then we can all get some rest and go about our own business. There's coffee and beef at the chuck wagon. I'll guarantee your safety that far.

"You men lay down your weapons. All your weapons. No holdout guns kept behind. It's a bit of a walk to the camp, but you have it to do. Let's do it now."

With that, silence fell over the small hollow in the Colorado grassland as the gang members looked at one another and, finally turned to focus on their leader.

Finally, one man spoke. "You expect us to just walk out of here? You'll only hang us anyway."

Rory responded, "I won't hang you. And no one here today will harm you. Whatever a court of the land decides later is up to them. But we're only a posse. We don't pass judgment or sentence."

Rory was getting weary of the indecision confronting him. It moved him to say, "Beautiful morning, men. The sun is shining. We're all breathing God's good air. We're all enjoying the life within us. You come with me, you'll get to enjoy that life for today at least, and for however long it takes for the law to do its work. Even prison is better than the grave.

"Couple of years ago, fellas, I scratched out a hole in an Idaho forest. Buried my father. He'd have given all he had for just another day of life. Lonely place. No one coming by will ever know a good man lost his life and lies there. Lies there for all eternity. Not sure I could even find the spot again. Eternity is a long time, men. And if you remember the teaching of your childhood, you'll recall that only just the one man ever came out of his grave to live again. That's not good odds for you or me. On this earth, anyway.

"No, if I was you, I'd take what life I could still grab. Seems to me that lying dead in this grassy hollow, your body bleeding from the lead that tore through it, is a poor ending."

With that, he sat silently. It was about half a minute later that Newley himself, without looking around at his men, ever the singular leader, stepped forward. Instead of dropping the Big Fifty, he passed it up to Rory.

"You're a hard man to shake off a trail, Sheriff. You've won. For today anyway. Take care of this Sharps. It's an honest weapon. Made me an honest living, before all this."

Rory nodded at the man and lifted the Sharps to rest across his lap. Newley unfastened the buckle and dropped his belt holster and weapon.

With a shrug and a foolish grin emanating from a mind that might not be quite right, one man dropped his carbine and reached to unbuckle his gun belt. The holstered Colt and leather belt made a small thudding noise as it hit the turf. That started it. One by one, the men unbuckled. Lance Newley then led his men out of the hollow.

The entourage walked a bare hundred yards before they saw a couple of men leading saddled horses toward them. They stopped and watched them approach.

"Mount up, men. No need to walk."

Rory stopped where he was and watched the men ride away. He had a feeling he might never again see anything to match the ending of the Lance Newley Gang. He was desperately tired. His horse was worn down. His friend Ivan was tired. The hard traveling posses were done in. But every man had done his duty, and it was over.

Carrying the fifty, Rory rode over to where he had passed Ivan his weapons. Ivan was riding toward him. The two men met without a word, and Ivan passed over the guns. With the rifles wrapped in his left arm, their butts resting on his thigh, and his .44 back in its holster, together they rode to the chuck wagon. Rory wanted nothing more that day but to start home. Still sitting his horse, he sidled up beside Deputy Block. The deputy said nothing while he watched the cook lay out coffee and beef steak for the captured men, as he searched for words. He then turned to the young sheriff.

"That was a brave and crazy thing you did. I've never seen the like, Sheriff. Might never again."

"I've promised these men their safety in your name, Block. I'm trusting that was a good promise."

"It is. And I'll repeat it if necessary. Right now, with that CT beef filling their stomachs, I'm not sure they care."

"Someone will have to gather up their weapons and camp stuff. Saddles and such too, back there a few miles. Can't leave a mess like that lying about."

"We'll look after it all. What are your plans, son?"

Rory was a bit uncomfortable with the too-familiar title, but he responded, "We're going home."

"You going to take a night's rest first?"

"We can rest at home."

The gathered men stood silently, every man there understanding that this young deputy had saved them a shooting matter. They understood, too, that when the lead started flying, there was no true way to predict where it would stop or who might be standing in the way. Wise men men wished to avoid that.

Rory and Ivan rode from the camp, turning their mounts north, leading the packhorse with Ivan's extra gear and weapons.

A few silent minutes later, Ivan said, "I get powerful hungry time to time. But not to worry. I got a sack of biscuits and a couple of cans of peaches, few other things, from the wagon."

"I hope you plan on sharing that."

Ivan laughed and said, "I'll share. Let's ride."

A slow trot was all the weary animals had to give, but it would be alright, they were heading home.

ANOTHER MAN'S GOLD

A SNEAK PEEK AT BOOK THREE

True to history and full of action, award-winning author Reg Quest delivers book three in a series that shows the lengths a sheriff will go to for his county.

Sheriff Rory Jamison has finally settled into his position and been deemed a man who gets the task done. But when a cattleman from the remote Wyoming Hill country—who's been giving Rory problems for some time now—moves his family into new territory, Rory knows the rancher is sure to cause problems.

Meanwhile, an attempt to put an end to the tarnished gold coins problem is underway. When it becomes a federal matter, a U.S. marshal insists that Rory accompany him on a gold and cattle hunt into west Texas.

Wanting a peaceful county—with no one challenging the law—Rory is determined to do what he can to make that happen. But first, he must deal with complications in the West.

Full of deception, gun fights, and dealings with powerful men, Rory is on a steadfast mission to end a lingering problem...and protect the county he cares about so earnestly.

AVAILABLE NOW

NEWLY ELECTED COUNTY SHERIFF, RORY JAMISON, HAD been slowly riding, and then crawling, through the eastern Colorado grasslands, onto a rising edge of a swale, for what seemed like hours. In point of actual fact, he had been dodging prickly pear and beehive cholla for little more than a few minutes. His 44-40 Winchester, which he had hoped to balance across his arms as he crawled, had caught on the taller growth so often that he had finally taken it in his left hand, leaving his right hand free to grasp one of his belted .44's if the situation deteriorated to that point, although he had securely buttoned his canvas jacket, top to bottom, to protect his belted weapons. The move slowed his progress even more.

TWO DAYS BEFORE, about mid-morning, a frantic twelve-year-old boy had ridden a lathered and done-up bay gelding recklessly down the single main street of the old fort, pulling to a dust-gathering stop in front of the recently constructed county jail and sheriff's office. His actions startled a couple of slow-walking wagon teams and caused one buggy horse to break from its half-asleep stance and charge, in fright, down the street, drawing the buggy, and the farmer's daughter who was taking a rest in the shade of the fringed top, while she secretly admired a young cowboy busy with toting sacks of provisions from the general supply store to a buckboard tied off not far from her.

The girl didn't scream or bother crying for help. She simply plucked up the reins, brought the animal under control, and turned him towards where the boy had drawn to a stop, hollering for the sheriff. She was busy gathering up the words she would use on the kid when the sheriff stepped out of the door, asking what all the noise was about.

"Rustlers, sheriff. Pa sent me in, hoping for some help. He's alone on the place, with just Ma and me and a couple of kid sisters for help. If Pa goes after the rustlers, it would be just me and Ma on the place. The kid girls ain't no help. Likely never will be, being girls and all. We can't no way do the work that needs doing, and anyway, Pa's mighty cautious about leaving his family alone."

The girl in the buggy, who had pulled to a stop close by, said, "Where's your hired man, Jody?"

"Pa says it looks as if he's one of the rustlers. Anyway, he's gone, and all his stuff and truck gone with him."

Sheriff Rory said, "I take it your name's Jody, young fella. Where's your ranch at?"

"We're a bit north and maybe fifteen miles east."

The girl in the buggy, who seemed to have invited herself into the conversation said, "That would work out good for you, sheriff. The Trader's Triple T is right close to the Gridley spread. Not more than a few miles. You could probably get a dinner, and maybe a look-see with Julia. If you play your cards right, that is."

Rory turned to the girl with a grin on his face.

"And who exactly are you, young lady, and shouldn't you be in school?"

Jody spoke up. "That's Trish Hampton, Sheriff. I'm not so sure even the teacher would want her in class. That's suppos'n we ever get a school. Never stops talk'n. Thinks she knows everyth'n. She lives out our way too. Thankfully, not too close. With Jody, the more miles away, the better."

A man walking up behind the buggy said, "Unfortunately, there's some truth in all of that sheriff. I'm Buzz Hampton. Trish is my oldest. Oldest of four. She does talk some, and that's a fact. Doesn't appear to be any solution for it. None I've found yet anyhow."

Trish remained silent while the two men shook hands.

Perhaps giving some indication where Trish might have learned her habit of speaking out of turn, Buzz questioned Jody, taking over the sheriff's normal role, and asked, "What's this about rustlers, Jody?"

"As I just was telling the sheriff before Trish butted in with her two cents worth, Pa's missing about fifty head. Tracks are plain. East, about two days old."

The young girl couldn't seem to hold back her every thought and question. "How do you know they were rustled? They might just have grazed further away. There's no fences out that way. They could be anywhere."

Jody, with a disgusted look on his face, said, "A girl wouldn't be expected to know, but cattle on the loose don't bunch up and drive themselves off in one direction, walk'n a straight line like."

Rory's patience was being tested, but he found the whole matter somewhat humorous too. The boy was right in everything he said except, perhaps, in his opinion of girls. Rory figured that had a good chance of changing before long.

When all the talk had been done, and Rory had more exact information on the location of the Triple T ranch, he suggested Jody take his gelding to the stable and stall him in trade for a livery rental animal for the ride home. The bay gelding didn't have another fifteen miles left in him.

Finally Rory found himself standing alone, with Buzz Hampton climbing into the buggy while Trish tongue-clicked the horse into action.

~

RORY AND JODY rode side by side on the long trail to the Triple T. At the ranch, a discussion with Logan Trader had Rory convinced that a theft had indeed taken place, and that the guess of a two-day start might be accurate. Mrs. Trader cranked things up in the kitchen and put an early dinner on the table. Rory set out well before dark, following the wide trail the driven animals had left in their wake. Always admitting to himself that he knew too little about tracking, he couldn't tell if he was gaining on the herd, but there was a good chance he was. His big Double J Ranch, bred and raised blood red bay riding animal still had some travel left in him. A blind man could have followed the trail, allowing Rory to ride well into the late evening. He stopped to rest the gelding at the first trickle of water he came to. With a few hours of sleep, he was back in the saddle. He had never really enjoyed his own camp fare. After several long-distance rides in his job as sheriff he had developed the habit of riding early and making his coffee and the first meal of the day when the sun was noon high. That bit of self-discipline had become the pattern of his life on the trail.

His gelding had stepped right out, and now the signs of travel were much fresher, judging from the still sloppy, wet droppings, if nothing else. Then he saw dust on the far horizon. It was too far away to identify its source, but given the sparseness of the settlement in the area, it was a safe bet to lay the grey mass to the rustled cattle. That there were still substantial numbers of buffalo running on the plains entered his mind, but he pushed that concern aside in the belief that he would have time and space to retreat to sheltering distance, if needed. If the buffalo swept the cattle along with them the game would be over and the cattle probably lost. Thinking it through, Rory decided he could close the gap between the herd and himself considerably, with no fear of being seen. If it was the rustled herd bunched up under the dust, the riders would be pretty busy pushing for their destination, with little time for studying their back trail.

Rory urged his gelding into a slow lope, knowing the animal could hold that pace for mile after mile. He knew that he, too, would be raising a dust cloud, although it would be much smaller than the one he was narrowing in on. And, he rationalized, if the riders were enveloped in the dust up ahead, they would never see the small cloud on their backtrail.

As he closed in on the herd, the objects beneath the dust became identifiable. He was able to brush the concern about buffalo out of his mind. He could not yet distinguish cattle from horse and rider, but that would soon come. He pushed the gelding a bit, thinking to close the gap by another mile or so. Reaching that vantage point, he could see there was a single drag rider. It was enough to satisfy the questions running through his mind. A light pull on the reins brought the gelding to a stop. Proceeding at a walk after a ten-minute rest in a bit of shade would keep him in contact with the stolen cattle. He would stay with them until nightfall, assess his situation at that time, and form a plan.

First, while there was little chance of the rustlers seeing what he was doing, he scouted around until he found a bit of sitting water that had gathered in a hollow at the base of a couple of stunted cottonwoods. The shovel marks around the hollow suggested that the hole was man-made. He stepped to the ground and bent to the water, carefully checking for snakes. He truly hated snakes. Scooping with his hands, he managed to enlarge the hole, letting another small bit of water seep in. He then slipped the bridle from the gelding and dropped the saddle to the ground, knowing the well-trained horse wouldn't wander. The small bit of water available was less than what the animal really needed, but it would have to do. He had adequate for himself in the two canteens he habitually carried.

As the gelding pulled at the summer dry bunches of grass, Rory leaned against the cottonwood and tipped his hat down to shield his eyes from the glaring sun. He would catch a bit of rest while he trusted the horse to warn him of anyone approaching.

As evening slowly drifted over the land, Rory saddled the horse and made his way toward where he had last seen the dust cloud. The cattle couldn't have gone more than four or five miles in the time since he had last seen them. Wanting a look at the camp, if he could do it without exposing himself, he stepped the geldings pace up a bit, watching carefully for an outpost guard. But the land was so flat and so barren there was little chance of avoiding exposure for the rustlers or for himself. Rory heard the bawling of thirsty cattle before he saw them or the rustler's camp. Ahead, just a half mile, was a slight rise in the land, leaving a small swale behind it that Rory intended to try to use to his advantage. In a bushed or forested area, he would have tied the animal off and walked the last half mile. But in this open country, it was clearly best to hold his ride close. He had no other means of escape.

ABOUT THE AUTHOR

Reg Quist's pioneer heritage includes sod shacks, prairie fires, home births, and children's graves under the prairie sod, all working together in the lives of people creating their own space in a new land.

Out of that early generation came farmers, ranchers, business men and women, builders, military graves in faraway lands, Sunday Schools that grew to become churches, plus story tellers, musicians, and much more.

Hard work and self-reliance were the hallmark of those previous great generations, attributes that were absorbed by the following generation.

Quist's career choice took him into the construction world. From heavy industrial work, to construction camps in the remote northern bush, the author emulated his grandfathers, who were both builders, as well as pioneer farmers and ranchers.

It is with deep thankfulness that Quist says, "I am a part of the first generation to truly enjoy the benefits of the labors of the pioneers. My parents and their parents worked incredibly hard, and it is well for us to remember".